A TALE OF TWO COLORS

WHITE & BLACK

VOLUME I

A TALE OF TWO COLORS

WHITE & BLACK

VOLUME I

ANTHONY WOOD

TIREE
PRESS

an imprint of

THE OGHMA PRESS

OGHMA

CREATIVE MEDIA

Bentonville, Arkansas • Los Angeles, California
www.oghmacreative.com

Library of Congress Cataloging-in-Publication Data

Names: Wood, Anthony, author.
Title: White & Black/Anthony Wood | A Tale of Two Colors #1
Description: First Edition. | Bentonville: Tyree, 2020.
Identifiers: LCCN: 2021934724 | ISBN: 978-1-63373-666-5 (hardcover) |
ISBN: 978-1-63373-667-2 (trade paperback) | ISBN: 978-1-63373-668-9 (eBook)
Subjects: | BISAC: FICTION/Historical/Civil War Era |
FICTION/War and Military | FICTION/Action/Adventure |
LC record available at: https://lccn.loc.gov/2021934724

Tiree Press trade paperback edition May, 2021

Cover & Interior Design by Casey W. Cowan
Cover art by Winslow Homer (1836-1910)
The Woodcutter, 1891, Watercolor on canvas
Editing by Gordon Bonnet & Amy Cowan

This book is a work of historical fiction. Apart from the well-known actual people, events, and locales that figure in the narrative, all names, characters, places, and incidents are the product of the author's imagination or are used fictitiously. Any resemblance to current events or locales, or to living persons, is entirely coincidental.

Published by Tiree Press, an imprint of The Oghma Press, a subsidiary of The Oghma Book Group. Find out more at www.oghmacreative.com

For my wife Lisa, with love and admiration.

ACKNOWLEDGEMENTS

WRITING A FICTION novel series is like following a path that leads to a destination unknown until you arrive. Staying on path would have been impossible without the help of friends and family. I'm especially grateful that my mamaw shared stories of my ancestors with me as a child. The impetus for this historical fiction series came from those cherished moments leading me to wonder, *why would my ancestor switch sides during the Civil War?* For suffering through the first draft and offering helpful feedback, many thanks go to Steve Davis, Joan Davis, and Wes Wood. I am indebted to Linda McCulloch jump-starting me into genealogical research and reading manuscripts for all five books. Thanks goes to my Uncle Dwight and Aunt Judy Wood who housed and fed me well on numerous research trips to Mississippi and offering continuous encouragement to keep going. For helping me become a better writer, I thank the White County Creative Writer's group I meet with each month. A loud shout out goes to all the nameless librarians, museum curators, and archive specialists who showed great kindness and patience as I learned my way around historical research—you are the true heroes of historical fiction.

It was my mother-in-law Joan who remarked after reading the first manuscript, "I hope you really find a good editor." She only meant well but I knew I would need publisher who could take my scribblings and make them into readable novels. Her wish was realized when I stumbled upon my new writing family, Oghma Creative Media. A special thanks to Casey and Amy Cowan, Gordon Bonnet, Dennis Doty, Bob Giel, and the rest of the gang at Oghma for granting patience and love throughout the publishing process. You, my friends, are truly wonderful. And Paul Colt, thank you for the thoughtful cover blurb.

To my wife Lisa, who after listening to endless hours of storytelling, research discoveries, and development of new plots and characters, offered invaluable suggestions... there is no better friend.

PROLOGUE

SOME THINGS GET CHOSEN FOR YOU

MORNING, JULY 3, 1863

Some of the best words ever written are letters never received.

E ITHER I DIE today, or the world changes. There's no other possibility. So I write my last letter.

Vicksburg Miss July 3, 1863

Dearest wife Susannah, the sun's coming up and it's hot as the Devil's Hell in these rifle pits. I can hardly touch my musket. No matter. There's no powder and shot left anyway. I shook the sweat from my head. Some hair came with it. I shook the mud from my boots. None of it came off. Sweat burns my eyes and salt crystals itch my back. It's so hot hens are laying hard boiled eggs. That joke isn't funny anymore. My skin feels like leather. I'm a bag of bones so thin I can't find my own shadow. I'm surely not the same man you married back in Winn Parish. My own Ma wouldn't know me now. Would you? Being here sucks the life right out of a man. Being away from you is what's really killing me.

I've received no letter from you in months, and this one probably won't get to you. The Yanks have us hemmed in tight. It don't matter no how. I'll be gone soon. Word is the Yanks will set off a mine underneath us anytime. They blew up some of the 3rd Looseana boys not long ago. It was a mess, but when the Yanks attacked, we held. I'm just glad my brothers Jasper and James are still alive after that fight and here with me. We've made it this far. Maybe we'll make it out of here. I doubt it.

Who would've known I'd be stuck in this stinking mud hole waiting to die, and tomorrow is Independence Day? Independence? For who? The Yanks? Our great Southern Cause? I know I don't sound too good Susannah. It's been hard these past 46 days, but I'm not complaining. Just telling how things are. Probably the best independence for me is to get blown to high heaven just to get it over with. Heaven sure sounds like a good place to finally settle. I'm ready. The Lord knows who I am. He can send His angels to come get me about anytime He's a mind to.

Somehow I know you hear my prayers. I look forward to no more tears and no more partings. Do you hear me when I sing your song?

Your faithful and devoted husband,
Lummy Tullos

LUMMY TULLOS, THAT'S me. I come from a long line of fighting people always moving because somebody else pushed us—Romans, Saxons, the British, but lately it's been church men and rich landowners who believe they're God on earth. But the best reason for moving was the search for new land. Cloud Tullos came from Scotland in the 1600s with the promise of land in a new world. Grandpa Temple would boast, "We were Celts of the moving and settling kind." I guess we still are. What started in Virginia ended on our farm in Choctaw County, Mississippi. So far.

I wipe the sweat from my burning eyes. The stories handed down about Cloud and our people don't stir my soul much today. My mud-caked clothes and the dust swirling on the dry treeless battlefield in front of me hold little promise. The stench of death and the shadow of buzzards overhead make me think I'll be buried in this dirt shortly. I haven't given up, but I'm about give out. The handful of chalky dust I grab from the floor of this rifle pit sifts like flour through my fingers.

A cannon shell explodes just in front of the parapet. Dirt rains down all around me like a cloud burst. When will this stop? Heck, I don't even hear the scream of the dang cannon shells anymore. Three minie balls thud into the soft ground above my head. In my mind I can hear the *thud, thud, thud* of my hoe as I chopped cotton on our farm back home. What I'd give to be there now. Hard work, good food, my people, and the peace of the surrounding forest sounds good right about now. Soft singing drifts down the line.

A man whose dark hair turned grey since being in Vicksburg sings an old familiar hymn. "Rock of Ages, cleft for me, let me hide myself in Thee...." Old Lucille used to hum that tune when she popped corn for me in an old pot and put black pepper on it when she had it. Lucille was a slave who was forced on Pa when he left his father to buy new land after the Treaty of Dancing Rabbit Creek. His father had several, but Pa didn't want anything to do with slavery. Ma wanted to take Lucille so she could care for her in her last days. Pa didn't argue. It was the Christian thing to do.

Sarge stumbles over empty cartridge boxes and busted bombproofs checking on every man on the line. "Stay alert boys—trouble might be comin'!"

A minie ball splinters a log near his ear. He doesn't even duck.

"What the hell do you think we been havin', Sarge, a dance party?" He turns to jab his finger at me like a bayonet. Sarge has saved many a good man's life watching over us like a father. Sarge ain't my Pa, but sometimes it feels like it. His harshness takes me back to the anger and violence Pa poured on me and my brothers growing up. At least Sarge *does* smile.

Suddenly the silence is so loud I can hear it crouched in this rifle pit. I stand up to stretch. I look behind me to the town of Vicksburg, then peek through a sniper's peephole at the Yankees' earthworks. The great blue army spread across the hills reminds me of my favorite story about our other ancestors, the Picts. The people painted blue, carving symbols on stones and dancing naked around the fire at night, weren't so easy to push. A Roman legion left the safety of their wall to fight our people but simply disappeared. They're still looking for them. Maybe we should come out from behind our wall and make the Yanks disappear. There probably wouldn't be much trace of us left if we did.

Young Edrow smiles as he scratches his name in a log next to my bombproof. He grins with two front teeth lost in the last attack. "At least they'll know I was here." Many a good man left his name and his life in these earthworks.

The Bluebellies stretch before us as far as the eye can see. I feel pushed right now—to my limit. We didn't invite them here, and we can't make them leave. I don't want to push anybody and don't want to be pushed anymore. But I *did* sign up for this. I'll keep my word.

I've gone back to those old family stories countless times defending these earthworks. Keeping them alive in my heart helps me stay alive in this hell-hole of hopelessness. I try to make sense of this war between gray and blue, between men who kill each other for no other reason than we're ordered to by generals and politicians who never get bloodied themselves.

When I meditate and hear the voices from the other side of the thin veil between me and those gone on, sometimes I get answers, sometimes I don't. Truth is hard to find, and sometimes hard to hear. It's just not as easy as white and black. There ain't much I can do about it this morning. It's too much to think about when life could end any minute.

I've stood my ground and fought like a demon in this rifle pit these past forty-six days. I didn't have much choice when I left Winn Parish. Enlist or get conscripted. That was the call. I volunteered. Some decisions get made for a man, and the cost can be beyond what he can bear. Giving myself to this southern cause has certainly been costly. I wonder if I'll survive this siege.

J. A. hands me a cup of rancid water and half a moldy hardtack biscuit. The man's been a brother to me since we left Winn Parish for the war. I gulp it all down fast hoping I don't puke it back up. I thank him and wave him off. I don't want to talk. He's good with that. I just want to return to my thoughts. Sometimes the mind can escape when the body can't.

My elbow itches like a mosquito is gnawing on it. I pull a piece of peeling dry skin from my sunburned arm. It bleeds.

Skin. Just a covering God used to make us like the flowers—many colors and different shapes. I couldn't speak my mind about that back home going to church with folks who taught their children Negroes had no souls. I guess that made it easier for the sweet old ladies of the congregation to watch their husbands treat slaves worse than animals. Right or wrong, they had to make sense of it somehow to carry on as they did. It was dead wrong. If you make a human an animal, then you can treat him like one. It never made sense to me. Never will.

But the reason I couldn't speak against it at the Winn Parish was I had a secret. I had a girl—though not just any girl. My girl was the loveliest creature God ever put on this good Earth. Her name was Susannah. But I couldn't tell a soul in those days about Susannah because she was black—as a lump of coal.

A cannon shell bursts overhead, and I draw up tight into my bombproof dazed. I come back to my senses and stand up, musket in hand.

"I don't give a damn what those little ole ladies taught! Ain't nobody gonna tell me my wife Susannah ain't got no soul!"

J.A. jumps, startled from his nap standing next to me in the rifle pit. That boy could sleep through a tornado storm—standing up, too. "What, what? Who ain't got no what?"

I lie. "The damn Yanks over that hill wantin' to kill us. If the blue coats got souls, they ain't good ones." I try to play it off, but talking out loud when I don't realize it will get me in trouble one day.

I feel a burning, like someone's eyes are boring holes in the back of my head. Sarge is staring at me with his mouth half open. He draws his jaw back up, shrugs, checks his musket, and looks back up into the sky to watch the buzzards circle. He heard every word.

A small voice from the other side of the earthworks whispers. "I heard what you said, Reb. Sounds like you're fightin' on the wrong side." I hunker back down into my bombproof dug into the side of the rifle pit hoping no one heard the Yank. I doze, asking myself why the hell I'm here. People still haggle over the same ole problems in the same ole ways, never learning from the mistakes of the past. My eighth-grade teacher, Miss Stansbury, told us the reason people don't like history is because it'd make them change if they learned from it.

A musket shot rings out in the deep silence that blankets the killing ground in front of us. I'm jolted awake from my daydream. I cock my musket ready for anything blue that might charge into this rifle pit. Nothing stirs.

Some man somewhere in the trenches lies dead this morning. A sharpshoot-er probably got him.

J. A. has fallen sound asleep again. His musket slides down his body out of his hands. I gently kick his leg to wake him. He snorts and straightens up, pulling his piece back up into his arms. I roll over onto my side and half fold, half crumple the letter to Susannah in my hand. I don't want to turn it loose. Or her.

I look up from this stinking rifle pit at the sun breaking through the clouds. Is what my ancestors bore as costly as me wearing this rotting grey uniform, stuck in this battered earthwork, defending this great city of Vicksburg, Mississippi?

"Nothin's changed." Somebody said people don't change. Only their clothes do. I could've been wearing the blue suit just as easy as the gray. It just depends on where a man is born. I didn't have a choice about that any more than the men in blue just a few feet away.

My tattered uniform smells like a latrine. It's pretty bad when you can smell your own stink above all others in this place of sickness and death. I could use a bath in McCurtain Creek with a bar of lye soap thrown in. Tying a cloth over my mouth and nose doesn't ward off the stench. The cloth stinks worse than the air.

Scratching the lice in my hair, I look up at the buzzards flying low above the field between us and the Yankees. Surrounded by thousands of Yankees and expecting an attack or mine exploding underneath us any moment, I don't think I'll live long enough to get that bath. I miss skinny-dipping on hot days with Susannah in McCurtain Creek.

Those memories give me little hope.

The heat sours my stomach, and the stench in this rifle pit makes my gut queasy. I puke in a hole dug just for that purpose. I can hardly hold my head up I'm so weak. I'm nearly done in, stuck in this hellhole called the 27th Louisiana Lunette. I've guarded Graveyard Road in these hills just outside Vicksburg about long enough. I'd go rest in that field of graves right now if the Lord would just call.

Barely surviving two major Yankee assaults, starving and watching good men die in this siege, eating rats and drinking filthy water, I think I just saw what's left of my life fly by in the hot dusty wind. It's just the passing shadow of a buzzard catching the updrafts from the Mississippi River. It patiently waits for death to provide its next meal. My life is slipping away faster than good church lady gossip travels.

As weak as I am, my hands are balled up in tight fists. I can't give up, and there's only one thing that will see me through—anger. It's the same hated anger that welled up in me to ward off my Pa and brother Ben and Lester and the other bullies who tried my soul for too long. Yet it's kept me alive to face the Yanks, at least up until now. If they push hard over the hill, I don't know if I have the strength to fight them.

I don't want to think about this right now. But I have to. Fading memories of a life barely lived keep me hanging on. I stuff the letter to Susannah inside my shirt. I wipe the sweat from my face again.

"At least I've made it this far!" I peek through the sharpshooter's hole again. Blistering heat burns my face, but it's not from the sun. It's from within. Should I just look a little longer and invite a Yank to end it all?

I shake myself. "I ain't giving up! Not me. Not Columbus Nathan Tullos. And Devil? You can take the thoughts of me doing myself in back to Hell where you brought them from! I've got some kind of life waiting for me after this. Yassuh. I've traveled too far, crossed too many rivers, and braved too many snakes, of the slithering and the two-legged kind, not to live the best of what the Lord has in store for me! Nawsuh. I ain't givin' in, givin' out, givin' up, or givin' over, no matter how worthless General Grant thinks my life is."

J. A. grabs the back of my collar and yanks me off my feet. "Get down you ignert ass fool, and stop your preachin' before you get your head blowed off!"

I let him pull me back before a minie ball finds the peephole and takes my eyeball out. It'd surely be an easy way out of this place. I sip a little water. I'm hot, hungry, angry, dirty, sorrowful, and tired.

A Yank throws over a hardtack biscuit. "Hey Reb, why don't you just give up?" I say nothing. "Don't you want to go home to that pretty wife of yours?" J. A. pats me on the shoulder.

"Can't! Ain't done with you boys just yet." The blistering sun hovers silently in the windless heat.

The Yank won't leave it alone. "You might get some of us, but we'll get *all* of you!"

"Whatever else happens, I'm comin' for you."

"No harm intended, Reb. Just testin' you."

"None taken, Billy Yank, but no more testin' today."

Chuckles rise from the stinking trenches on both sides, but not for long. The silence grows louder.

I touch my letter to Susannah. I'd rather be touching her.

I whisper up through the rising dust up to the rain heavy clouds gathering in the west. "Lord, are you there?"

A TALE OF TWO COLORS

WHITE
& BLACK

VOLUME I

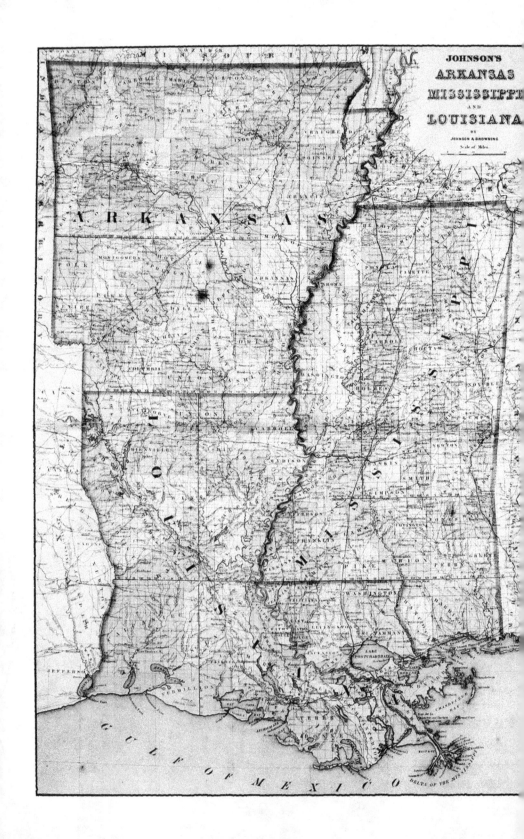

JOHNSON'S
ARKANSAS
MISSISSIPPI
AND
LOUISIANA
BY
JOHNSON & BROWNING
Scale of Miles

CHAPTER 1

TAKEN!

FEBRUARY 11, 1859

The big picture gets smaller when the person you love gets painted into it.

THE GREAT DEBATE is heating up and my anger with it. There's talk around the state capital that if an abolitionist president is elected, Mississippi will secede from the union. Some preachers are spouting God-given reasons why slavery is right while others want slaves free. Some sermonize on states' rights, while others call secession the Devil's work. Fistfights are common, especially in places like Bucksnort, where wine and spirits flow freely for a man with way too much cash to spend. I just keep my mouth shut. But Ma, she always talks, though often in hushed tones, about setting Negroes free.

"How will this country fare if all the men rush off to fight leavin' the crops in the fields to rot and the women defenseless, especially when most of us ain't had no slaves and ain't never gonna have any? Just because your Pappy Willoughby owned several doesn't mean you took to ownin' any yourself!" Ma shivers in anger like she does when she gathers eggs from the henhouse on a cold December morning.

"Heck, woman, you're the last person on God's good earth I believe is defenseless. And I know who my Pa was, mind you."

"Ain't fair, mind you, that we women and children won't fare well. Fight the Yanks with real power. Set the slaves free, now." She softly rails on and on. Pa patiently listens, knowing better than to argue with her. He knows she's right.

She's made it clear nearly every day that she wants to sign the papers to set old Lucille free. Ma can't read or write. If anything has to be signed, she makes her mark but always with a credible witness. Usually that's Pa. She just about has Pa convinced to free Lucille.

When asked why he didn't have any slaves, Pa always boasted, "Never needed no slave. I've got fine strong sons to work this farm!" It was the rare compliment Pa gave us on occasion at church or in town. Pa warned Ma many times to keep her thoughts quiet. He tried to convince her that Lucille was too old to free, and he only wanted to take care of her until she passed.

"Then at least let her die free, free as you and me. Give her the damn papers, and she can stay on with us until the Lord calls her home." Ma rarely cursed.

"The clerk at the government office in Greensborough will know, and he's a gossipin' bastard. It'd invite more trouble than it'd be worth." Lucille finally died when I was still a young boy, never getting her freedom papers. I'll always remember her.

When I'd help Ma with pecan gathering or berry picking, she'd whisper about the freedom God truly wants for all men and women. She's a strong believer in the Declaration of Independence, the rights her grandfather fought the British over in the Carolinas. She said all men are created equal and that the Lord set every person free when he died on the cross. But today, Ma doesn't hold back with Pa.

"Yeah, you remember your cousin Silas who joined up with Nixon's 13th Mississippi Militia, don't you? He named his first boy Columbus, too, just like you—except his middle name is different. Don't remember what the let-ter C stands for. Hmmm, Silas died five year ago down in Marion County, God rest his soul. Anyway, Pa you listenin'?"

Pa stops splitting kindling, draws up a knee, and gives Ma his full atten-tion. "Yeah, woman, you got both my ears pulled straight out. Can't miss a word you sayin', so spit it on out, and make sure you get it all out in one breath. I got things to do."

Ma squawks like a jaybird, "You're just tryin' to get your chores done so you can sneak a sip of moonshine before supper. Look, I'll have my say, Archy. I ain't like them fine and fancy ladies that follow behind a man who gives them everything they want makin' 'em lazier than a hound dog under the porch. I've cleared fields, planted 'em, toted a gun, and walked many a mile gettin' here. I'll be danged if we gonna lose it all for somebody else's fight."

Ma stands up with her hands on her hips. "Anyway, your brother Silas barely made it back home to Marion County. Runnin' around chasin' Creek Indians on that Escambia River down around Perdider—Perdida, or some damn ole place at the Gulf. I know it was hard on them folks at Fort Mims gettin' massacred and all, but it's all foolishness, just foolishness runnin' all over creation killin' folks for Andy Jackson for only eight dollars a month. If that wasn't enough, the great almighty Lord Andy Jackson had them rush down to Nawlins to fight the British, too. Couldn't even go home to check on their families before they went south.

"Them boys had nothin', no clothes, shoes couldn't be found, and no medicenes neither, and there wasn't nothin' but river mud for them to eat! And if they made it home they got no more thanks than the sand in their shoes for their trouble but left a trail of heartache for all them widows home with hungry children. I won't be havin' none of it, you hear?" Ma's madder than a nest of stirred-up red wasps.

"Don't make no sense, none at all. You boys need to figure out how to get along rather than havin' to see who's the toughest. No amount of yellin' at the top of your lungs in a fight is ever gonna get your enemy to back down. Them Yanks ain't gonna back down, and you know it. Just plain ole stupid, if you ask me. Folks ought to let other people live as they see fit. I ain't seen a baby born yet with chains and shackles attached nor with a bill a sale as a record of birth."

Pa is always the sweetest to Ma in these moments. He likes her fire. "Now Ma, you know a man's gotta do what he thinks is right under heaven."

"Yeah, Archy, and the women gotta take up the slack when the men don't come home. I don't care what the problem is. Most of what this fight'll be about has nothin' to do with what's goin' on right here on our farm. Hear me out. I don't want my boys goin' off fightin' in somebody else's fuss."

Pa nods.

Ma calms herself and resumes the point of her tirade. "Archy, I don't mean to throw a coniption fit, but just how can good Missip folks vote to declare independence to keep the South free when in the same stankin' breath deny another man his freedom?"

"That's not always easy when some men aren't thought of as men, you understand?" A tear falls. I didn't know she had such strong feelings about such things. But I agree. All I have to do is gaze at Susannah for a moment and know Ma's question ain't got to look very far to find a truthful answer.

Someone comes running down the road to our house. It's my best friend, Poole. He signals me to the side of the barn out of my brother's hearing. He's beside himself. I give him a drink of water.

"He took her, Lummy! He took Susannah!" was all he could get out.

"Who took her, how?"

"A gambler from Looseana, the one dressed all fancy in church last Sunday. Won her in a card game in Bucksnort from old man Mabus. Won her fair and square, but they're gone."

My Susannah has been taken away by a no good gambling slaver. I can't let that happen.

I won't!

CHAPTER 2

THE LONG WALK

FEBRUARY 12, 1859

A long walk makes short work of a cluttered soul.

"WHEN DID THEY leave?"

Poole catches his breath. "Yesterday by carriage to Carrollton to catch a hack down to Greenwood. You might still catch 'em if you hurry." I don't know what to do. A gambler has taken Susannah away, and I have to go get her back. All I know to do is start walking now, or the trail will grow cold. I pack quickly, tell Ma I'm leaving, and sprint to Null Road and turn east to Carrollton.

I'm in the middle of the national fuss now for sure. The big picture gets smaller when the one you love gets painted into it. I need the time to cool off and think straight about Susannah being taken away. I don't know which way this Louisiana gambler whose name I don't even know went with his old Negro servant and the three slaves, including Susannah.

How can a fine upstanding Baptist church-going Christian find his way into that Devil's den of sin to gamble away the love of my life? Just goes to show you he ain't learned that he really doesn't own another human being. He ain't the child of God he thinks he is. An observation, not a judgment. God takes care of that. I'm keeping my eye on the road before me, wherever it leads.

The gambler could take one of two ways, so I have to do a little gambling myself in choosing my path. I could head down the Old Trace to Jackson City which would be quicker, but I could lose the trail. Since the gambler is returning to Louisiana, he'll have to cross the Mississippi River at Vicksburg and go from there. I take Poole's advice and gamble to head west for Carrollton instead of southwest down the Trace.

I keep up the pace, my gait is smooth and my footsteps light, making little to no sound. I distance myself from my troubles as fast as a body's legs can go. I want to make Carrollton in less than three days if I can. It is unseasonably warm for this time of year, and I break a good sweat. At least it ain't warm enough for the skeeters to be out already.

My best friend, Thomas Poole—who I just call Poole—always complained that everywhere I go I walk like I'm headed to a fire. I travel light, carrying only the necessaries—a small tarp, extra shirt, my old flintlock squirrel gun, powder and ball, flint and steel for fire making, the hunting knife Pa made me years ago, food Ma packed without asking where I was going, and the little Bible my young cousin, Mary, gave me.

Tom Poole has been my best friend since I can remember. He grew up about a mile west of us close to the New Zion Baptist Church. He and I had a running competition started by our fathers. They took friendly bets of a jug of moonshine to see which of us grew the most at the end of the year. It was a seesaw contest, Poole winning one year, me the next, but finally Poole stopped short at six foot four, and me at six foot six. Neither one of us cared.

We've been like two peas in a pod growing up hunting, trapping, fishing, and getting into occasional mischief together. We even looked a bit alike, often being mistaken for brothers both having dark complexion, dark hair, and nearly the same colored eyes. School girls called us "Lanky and Stanky" until they started thinking about potential husbands. Neither of us were very happy when his folks moved their family to Greensborough two years ago.

Poole caught me by Bowie Creek near our farm and gave me a small hand-carved cedar cross. As kids, we carved cedar with our razor-sharp knives to see how long the shaving could be as it curled up. A trusted friend like Poole is like fresh-cut cedar. I'll miss his company. I pull the cedar cross out of my shirt and breathe in its fragrance.

I've never been out of the hills much before. Never was a need, except now I have to. Oh, we took a trip a couple of times to the Delta to hunt ducks, and such, but that was a few years ago. I've never really been out of Choctaw County come to think of it. I did wagon ride to Kosciusko once when Pa needed new crosscut saw blades for the timber we planned to cut for the new church and our lumber contracts. He also wanted to see the courthouse that burned. Rumor has it that the pro-secessionists fired it believing Attala County might vote against leaving the union. Me? I just want to leave all that behind. But, go to Louisiana to do it? Ha! And after a girl? Crazy-headed. Deep in my heart? Absolutely.

I kick a root, and my mind comes back to my path. I need to think about what I'm doing. If I catch a hack out of Carrollton down Big Sand Creek to the Yalobusha River, I can float to Greenwood by way of the Yazoo River. Then I could board the steamer Dime there on Saturday morning which will take me to Vicksburg in a week's time. If I need to go farther, I'll just bite the bullet and get a ticket good for Greenwood to New Orleans on the Commanche.

I looked at the boat schedules posted on the town billboard in Bankston before. I'm sure that's the way a wealthy man might travel with slaves stowed below in the hold of a steamer. A rich plantation owner won't walk or ride a wagon that far.

There are lots of plantations along the River, north and south, and many more deep into Louisiana where they can end up. Even if I make it to Carrollton on time, I still will have already missed the Dime out of Greenwood. But leaving out every Saturday, at eight o'clock sharp, I know I'll have a few days to spare for the next run. Anyway, I don't have enough money to buy a ticket all the way to New Orleans if I need it and eat too. The best I can do is to get to Carrollton, then on to Greenwood, and hire myself out for a few days along the way to fatten my purse and find out which way Susannah went.

As I head north to Greensborough I pray, "Lord guide me." I turn west, hoping not to meet anyone on the road, especially since I'm traveling at night. Never know who a soul might run into or what he might have on his mind. I trot along at a slow lope most of the night holding tight my old squirrel gun so as to not let the powder blow out.

I walk all day without running into anyone. As the sun goes down, I round a bend in the road to see a high-antlered six-point white tailed buck standing not thirty yards away. He doesn't know what to do. Neither do I. So I freeze. I'm not interested in taking him, though the meat would be good right about now. I need to save my few musket loads for any trouble I might run into, and I don't want to waste any meat I can't carry. The buck doesn't move. I watch him.

In a flash, he stands up on his hind legs, dashing to my left, then to my right before he hops into a thicket. His white tail flickers through the bushes in the fading light. I take a couple of steps, thinking he'll slip away, but the buck bounds into the middle of the road again still as a statue. Again, he leaps almost straight up with his front legs high in the air, turning completely around in a waltz like fashion, twirling as he sets both front feet on the ground.

This buck is dancing, moving to the rhythm of the breeze in the trees, to the sounds of the crickets, whipping this way and that. The buck dances in perfect time, always keeping a watchful eye on me. I watch, open-jawed, wondering why this majestic creature of the woods performs just for me. Then, off in a flash, he's gone, running through the tall sage grass fast as lightning. I believe it to be a sign from the Good Lord I'm on the right trail. It brings peace.

I wonder, enjoying the peace of the buck dance, can I walk this anger out of my heart? It follows my every move and gets me into trouble I never want. Can I leave it behind one of these hills I climb? I want to just start running, peeling it off as I race, never looking back. So I run, wild like a crazy man. Crazy. The meaning of that word depends on the person. I've felt for some time that one man's craziness is another's sanity. I'll choose my own meaning.

I run at least a half mile when I trip over a tree root and sprawl out like a bear ready to be skinned. My gun flies into the bushes and I hurt my knee. There's a little blood, but the cut isn't bad. I pull myself up slowly to feel a sharp pain in my side. That root somehow scraped my rib cage pretty good. At least there's no blood there. The only thing really hurt is my pride.

"Where you headed, deer dancin' crazy boy?" I freeze, slowly reaching for my squirrel gun. "You ain't gonna need that. I saw you dancin' with that deer I'd been sneakin' up on for an hour. I'd had him if you hadn't inter-ferred. Been in these woods all my life, and I ain't never seen nothin' like it. You touched in the head or somethin'?"

I can't see him, but I know what to say. "I been talkin' with the birds, runnin' with the rabbits, and climbin' trees with the squirrels since I could walk, so, I guess it's no big surprise that I'd dance with a deer. I talk to them. I believe they understand me."

The big Indian eases out of the shadows with a toothy grin. "I've been talkin' with them too for a very long time. Share a fire tonight, Deer Danc-er?" I nod. "Come on, then, I got a good place hidden off the road a piece."

I figure I can trust him.

We follow a deer trail into the brush. The big Indian glides over logs like creek water on smooth rocks and through thickets like wind breezing a fragrant honeysuckle vine. It's as if he's not a passerby but a part of all that surrounds him.

Once we get to his camp, the big Indian is a bit chattier than I've expe-rienced with others, but it's good conversation. He pulls out a piece of fat pine to start the fire and tells how he hid out as a boy in the woods when the Choctaws were forced to go to the Indian Territory. He refused to go, and after a while, they just quit hunting him.

He shivers just a little.

"I live like I always did, but the winters seem colder and the summers hotter. At fifty-two, I believe I'm slowin' down a bit." He looks me up and down as we settle beside the fire. "Son, you sure is a long tall man workin' on a long hard walk. How'd you get so tall?" I'm a head taller than him, and he's not a short Indian like most I've seen.

"Dunno, maybe from my Uncle Silas. He was tall, and I favor him a bit. I guess I got it all because my brothers are about your height." I stick out my hand, "Lummy Tullos, thanks for sharin' the fire."

The Choctaw thrusts out his hand and squeezes tightly. "I'm glad to know you. I'm Dan Creekwater."

He pulls out some hard bread, and I get out a couple slices of hoop cheese. The Choctaw bows his head and prays, thanking the Lord for our food and chance meeting. Then he takes to his food like a pig eating corn. I eat slowly knowing I have to make my meager supplies stretch. We sit without a word spoken between us. It's good to meet someone who makes for good company in silence.

After eating, I throw a couple of small sticks on the dying fire and ask how he learned to speak English so well.

"A preacher who worked with our people before they got taken away taught some of us to read and write. He was a real man of God. Now that he's gone to heaven, his son gets me supplies when times are lean so I can stay away from the towns." Dan rubs his forehead. "I believe in Jesus, you know. He's everywhere out here, all around us. I feel him. I see him, because I know he holds all of this together. Never could understand why white people try to put a God bigger than the sky in a box small as a cabin and tell us that's the onliest place he can be worshipped. I ain't got no reason to be in the white man's box with a cross on top, because Jesus is easy to find out here in my home."

He stretches out his hands, lifting them up to the sky and breathes in deeply. "I can even smell my Lord in the wind and the rain."

I lie still soaking up the cool breeze under an old oak as Dan stirs the fire, thinking about that buck, and hoping it won't rain. The tree frogs start to call which gets me thinking I better get out the small tarp I brought. Then she hoots. A barn owl. She seems lonely.

Dan cups his hands over his ears. "Mother owl wants her children to come be with her for the night." I wonder if my Ma wants me to come back home.

"Okay, crazy deer dancin' boy, can you talk with mother owl?"

I mimick her call. I want my forest mother to know at least this child is all right tonight.

It's not long until four owls swoop up into high limbs within twenty paces of my oak. One lights in the tree above me. It's like they're having a contest or something, as children will do, to see which one can make the screechiest, loudest scream to win a prize. It's an awful sound to some, but for me? It's music of the night woods. Each finally flew off after a mouse or something but opens the door for the next chorus. The barking of a red fox keeps me listening for any movement in the trees, but nothing ever comes. That's why I nestle near this big oak. Big, but with low enough branches in case I need to get up off the ground quickly.

It isn't long before the big Indian softly snores in rhythm with the wind blowing in the trees. Soft rain falling lulls me to sleep, and when the sun flickers through the bushes on my face to wake me, Dan's gone.

I jump up looking around to check my stuff. It's all here. He took nothing. Something good smolders on the coals. Dan left half a rabbit roasting on the fire. I'm ashamed I even thought he might steal from me.

CHAPTER 3

RUFFIANS

FEBRUARY 12, 1859

A man too hard on himself will be hard on another.

I'M GLAD THE first person I chanced on the road is a decent man. I pray for Dan Creekwater. I pray for his good soul that moves through life without much notice, except by the One Who Matters Most.

He said, "I want to walk though life not hearing my own footseps." It's good to spend a little time with a man who knows who he is and doesn't need others to affirm him. I'll think on that for awhile. I ask forgiveness for thinking ill of him this morning. I've had plenty of bad characters forced on me. Ruffians you can call them. Dan Creekwater ain't one of them.

Ruffians ahead of me and ruffians behind me. Will I ever be rid of them? I know one I have to face. The gambler who stole Susannah. I don't know what kind of man he is, but anyone gambling for slaves means there can't be much good in him. I'll find out soon enough. I want to twist his damn head off, but I need to think about something else. I need to keep my eyes open for the bad men on this road. I need to let my soul heal from the bad men I leave behind though still in my memory. Old wounds take time to heal. Sometimes they don't and are easily reopened.

Wherever this road goes I want something different and know it'll be found somewhere else than Choctaw County. How far will I have to go to get away? To put it behind me? To get it out of my soul? The anger, I mean. There's a part of me that's been angry all my life. I've been angry for so long and lived it so hard that not only does it seem like ruffians find me when I'm not looking for them, but I also create them when there really aren't any. That's what I want to unlearn, as they say. It's hard to not think people are out to hurt you when you can't remember a time when somebody wasn't hurting you.

All I want is peace. I just want to be left alone. At least I have time to get my head on straight walking to Carrollton.

There are plenty of ruffians back home, especially that bastard Lester. I don't like that word, but it best describes him. Pa said bastard has two meanings. One is a person who doesn't have a father as a child, which isn't his fault. But the other has a father to raise him right but doesn't act like it. Anyway, Lester ain't the real problem. It was more in the house where I grew up.

Pa was pretty tough on us, whipping us with anything he could get his hands on—plough lines, hoe and axe handles, cotton stalks, willow limbs, even a blackberry vine with the thorns still on it. It'd take a while for our backs and butts to heal. Wonder what you call a man who doesn't act right towards his children? What went through Ma's mind when she washed the blood stain out of our drawers after the beatings?

I thought it strange the way Pa'd get so mad, just mad all over, then get over it, but expect us just to be all right, all right immediately. I remember sitting in church trying to act right, like a ten year old kid can't, in a service going well over two hours suffering Pastor Dobbs's boring sermon. Poole and I sat on the second bench from the front with Ma and Pa behind us. Poole had stayed out all night chasing racoons, and his head was bobbing like a cork over a bream bed in late spring.

Pastor Dobbs pounded loudly on the pulpit, "If every good Christian could spend just fi-i-ive minutes in Hell, he'd straighten up right now." Poole jerked awake from his sleepy stupor.

"Get up, boy! He called on you to say the closin' benediction. Stand up and start prayin'!"

Poole jumped up and started in praying loudly about the goodness of the Lord, asking for good weather and good crops, forgiveness for sins, and safety from sickness. Pastor Dobbs stopped preaching. He just stared at Poole, hands gripping the pulpit, until he finished praying.

When Poole figured out what had happened, he didn't know what to do, so he quickly said, "Amen!" and sat down. He kept his eyes down because all eyes were on him.

Poole elbowed me. "I'll get your ass, Lummy Tullos." We nearly burst out laughing knowing he'd have done the same to me if he'd had the chance. I just beat him to it. Pastor Dobbs grinned at the opportunity to call someone down during service.

"Young brother Poole, I ain't never interferred when the Lord calls him to pray, and I done come to appreciate you practicin' your prayin' with the coons and possums of our fine county on up into all hours of the night. But you can be rest assured, young Poole, they'll be ready to meet their Maker at the proper time. What about you?"

I laughed so hard, though quietly, that my shoulders were bouncing up and down. In that nearly uncontrollable moment I let out a series of farts that bounced off the hard oak pew like a woodpecker on an old dead hollow post oak. The whole church wanted to burst out in laughter, but you just didn't do that at the New Zion Baptist Church. The kids giggled, and old Uncle Rube jolted awake from his light snoring.

"Don't think I've ever heard anythin' quite like that in church before. I thought the blessed Holy Ghost done come down amongst us all." He stood up and looked around.

"Now where'd them tongues of fire run off to? I've always wanted to see them!" The entire church fell apart in laughter. Pastor Dobbs gave Uncle Rube an evil eye only the Devil himself could conjure.

I couldn't help it, but then I felt what I thought was wire pliers grabbing the little hairs on the back of my neck, I thought the back of my head was on fire. Pa pinched those tender shoots like pulling ticks off a dog. He leaned up as he pulled me back.

"You best be givin' your heart to Jesus this mawnin', because when you get home, your ass is mine." It wasn't funny then.

Poole snickered, "I'll have to get in line to beat your ass this afternoon."

Pa tapped Poole's shoulder, "I'm sure your Pa'll have your hide later on today too, Thomas." Poole dropped his head and knew my Pa would ensure we both would get what was coming.

Pa is a good man at heart. He just didn't show it sometimes. He rarely drank, and he was faithful to Ma. In fact, he was the church going-est man I ever knew. Even still, everybody had such a high opinion of him.

Everywhere I went, I heard, "So you're Archy's boy. He's the best man I know" or, "I hope you grow up to be half the man he is. He's a good man!"

He was a good man, all right. But he was beating the hell out of us at home. I almost talked to a preacher about it once, but his son, the same age as me, said his daddy beat him, too.

Sundays for me were mostly good times. I liked Sunday school, but if the sermon was boring, I sneaked looks at the pretty girls all dressed up in their Sunday best. I liked the music and especially the singing. I liked hearing the old people sing the shape notes do re mi, do, re, re, fa, fa and so on. Most of all, I looked forward to the fried chicken dinner unless the preacher came home with us. Ma always gave him the best pieces. That meant we'd only get the bony parts, the backs and necks. I ain't complaining. It was still good.

Church was over that day, and I took my punishment pretty well. Pa meted out ten licks with his leather razor strop and two weeks shoveling manure out of the barn, all by myself. It was tough on a ten year old but worth it. I learned not to cry, because Pa would keep whipping us until we stopped. It was like he was chopping wood with his mind somewhere else. Either he wouldn't or couldn't stop until Ma cried out loud enough that he heard her. But there was that one day not long after I turned sixteen, when things really started to change. For the worse.

Pa left the New Zion Church in 1849 and still carried hard feelings about it. We attended Bethlehem Baptist with Ma the morning of the "event," as I call it. It was a good service, but I could tell Pa was hacked about something.

At the end of preaching he ordered us, "Let's go, now!"

I thought he was mad at something the preacher said. Pa drove the wagon with my sisters, and I followed alongside on our red mule, Sally. Pa started up about about one of his missing tools. Then he turned on me like a rabid dog saying I was responsible, and he'd have my hide when we got home. It just seemed to come out of nowhere, and he was mad all over.

These things always seemed to happen after church. Pa was way too hard on himself. But some of those good church going "brothers" acted like they were the Almighty himself when it came to telling us what the Bible said do. They were hard asses, and Pa was trying harder to please those men than doing what he knew was right in his heart. He left New Zion Church, but even that made him hard. Hard on us. I guess it goes without saying that a man who's hard on himself will be hard on another. And damn, he was hard that day.

I eased my mule away from the wagon, but he shot his words straight at me, like a bullet from a musket. "You busted the handle out of my axe again, and I'm tired of fixin' the damn thing!"

I didn't say anything. I didn't do it but knew little brother Jasper had, trying to kill a copperhead out behind the barn. Jasper swung at the snake and missed. He hit a pile of rocks, and the iron axe head lay on the ground with the busted handle left in his hand. I wasn't going tell on Jasper because I knew he'd get it. I quietly said that I didn't do it, but Pa just wouldn't let it go.

Pa yanked the brake hard as he rolled the wagon up into the yard, almost throwing Ma and the girls out of their seats. I tied Sally off to a porch post. I slowly walked up the steps as Ma and the girls rushed up the steps to get inside. I knew this wasn't going be good. Here he came, screaming loudly, right down on the back of my neck.

"You're dumb as a damn doornail! I can't trust you with nothin' I got!" He started recalling all the bad things I'd ever done like I'd done them yesterday. His hot heavy breath laid heavy on the back of my shirt. He was madder than a mule chewing on bumblebees.

I stopped, turned slowly, and looked him the eye, "You will no longer blame me for somethin' I didn't do." I said it carefully as I said it respectfully. I was sixteen then, no longer a boy. A couple months before, I'd been counted in the 1850 Census. They wrote down in the big ledger my occupation as farmer. I was so proud to be called a man, even if my Pa refused to acknowledge it.

"I'll knock you into the middle of next week lookin' both ways for Sunday, little boy!" His eyes turned blood red, and then he slapped me. Front hand, backhand, and then again, my head snapping left and right. I didn't move a muscle except for my head back and forth. I made no sound. I just took it. He stopped at seven slaps, that number Pastor Dobbs says is perfect. Well, this scene was just perfect. It was time I spoke up about this nonsense.

"How long you figurin' on doin' this? 'Cause I can go all day." I didn't feel the sting of the slaps in the moment, but I still have jaw troubles to this day because of them. I did feel a great emptiness in my soul. A part of me died that day.

Pa just stared at me, strangely, in surprised disbelief. Ma just stood watching. I could tell she went somewhere else in her mind when her eyes glassed over, blocking out what she'd witnessed. Later she said it never happened. Having experienced that kind of meanness myself firsthand, I know the mind can block things that seem to be beyond reality, even though it happened right in front of me. I understand how she wouldn't remember it. Or couldn't.

We just stood there, too. Finally, Pa walked away, shoulders drooping. No sixteen year old ought to ever have to go through something like that. He realized that, and wasn't too happy with himself. I guess he figured I was more of a man than he realized. Not only did I take the licks, I didn't defend myself or strike back. Raising a hand to my father never crossed my mind. Ever.

I've come to see my Pa like a picture puzzle you can buy in a store in Bankston. Nice picture but with several pieces missing. Important pieces. I love my Pa. Just not the scars he gave me.

I didn't feel much of anything inside for days after that, except for the pain in my jaw. I didn't really know how to deal with what happened. I can't say it surprised me that it did happen. My heart was sick and my soul a bit lifeless. I knew that something had changed inside me. What I did feel was a pain driven deep down into the soul of a sprouting young man turning to anger for relief. I just didn't know what to do with it.

That happened not long after Pa left New Zion Baptist Church in '49. I hated leaving my friends, especially Poole, but Pa never seemed happy there. He was trying to live somebody else's standard, and we paid the price for it. Violence at home always increased when things went worse at church. He said we left because he didn't like the way they treated Negroes, but it was

more than that. At New Zion he wanted to look good and righteous in front
of the good church people. Why that was so important to him, I don't know.
All I know is he couldn't do it so he took it out on us.

I often asked Poole to stay over Saturday nights in those days so he and I
could go fishing after church, but mostly because Pa had to act better if there
was somebody else around who'd witness his behavior.

The other time I felt the worst of it was a few years before the slapping
event when my older brother Ben was fourteen years old. Ben had a bit of a
wanderin' foot, too. His got him into a different kind of trouble. One night
he'd sneaked off to a saloon in Bucksnort reported to be a place of ill repute.
The proprietors didn't give a lick how old you were if you had a few bits to
spend on a drink or a whore. Long story short, Ben came home with the
liquor on his breath.

He almost made it to our room when our sister, Saleta, without under-
standing the consequences said, "Momma, Ben don't look right. He smells
funny, like that stinky elixir the doctor gave Elihu last winter for his chest
cough. He's wobblin' around."

Pa jumped up from sharpening his skinning knives, dropped them, and
grabbed Ben by the collar before he made it through the bedroom door.

"Drunk as a damn skunk in my house? You always have been a hard dawg
to keep on the porch!" He pushed Ben into the room, slammed the door, and
went to screaming.

There was banging around, more yelling, then Ben shouted, "No, Pa!"

I got nervous as a cat pacing around in a room full of rocking chairs.
Teary eyed, I turned, "Momma?" She was bawling, though without any
sound. I guess she learned to do that through years. The other children
gathered in the corner near the fire huddling close together. Rebecca held
Momma while Elihu and George quietly went outside, having experienced
this themselves.

I shook, not from fear, but from anger rising up in me like the devil himself when someone was being bullied. And my Pa was the bully that night. I
couldn't stand it. It went all over me, from head to toe, down into the deepest
part of my bones. Rage surged in me like an artesian well about to overflow.

I hated what was happening, and I couldn't let it go. I burst into the room to find Pa beating my brother down on the floor with his fists.

Pa barked out, "Who saw you? Everybody in Bankston will be talkin' about my drunk ass son!" Then Pa raised his right leg and stomped down hard. His boot landed squarely on Ben's head but glanced off when Ben pushed it away to cover his face. Pa went back to beating him with his clenched fists. Ben tried to anticipate the next strikes but couldn't fend off the blows.

I screamed at the top of my lungs, "Stop it!"

Pa stopped, turned to me slowly like a red-eyed mad dog with his ears pinned back, "If you don't get out of this room right now, I'm gonna kill you!"

At ten years old, you believe that the man who calls himself your father, and who is much bigger than you, can kill you. My young mind believed him. That night my mind went somewhere else in that moment seeing Pa beat Ben. I couldn't make sense of it. It didn't seem real. It couldn't be. I didn't want it to be. How could it be? He was our father. But that night, he was the devil himself. The world changed for me that evening.

In the days that followed Granny Thankful watched me from afar telling Ma, "That Lummy boy, he ain't been quite right after that, has he?" Ma could only tear up but held in her thoughts and her tongue.

So, I leave ruffians behind, family and not, but ready for any ahead. I believe the Lord prepared me well for any encounter, and I'm sure as hell not afraid of them. Fear? Heck, Pa beat that out of us.

Anyway, enough of that. I have my old squirrel gun for anyone who tries to rob me and the knife Pa made for me. Sharp as a razor. I make Carrollton near midnight.

I whisper, "I'll get some kind of work tomorrow and find out what I can about Susannah."

I slip into an old barn at the edge of town, and cover up with my tarp. I doze dreaming about the river. I always wanted to see Big Muddy. I will, and it'll take me to Susannah.

CHAPTER 4

THERE'S SOMETHIN' IN A NAME

EVENING, FEBRUARY 14, 1859

Don't forget whose name you wear!

I'M DOG TIRED, but I can't sleep. This move is a bit sudden, but its a good time to let God lead me on this journey. And when I arrive, wherever that is, I trust I'll be where I'm supposed to be. It ain't fate. I believe there's a destiny for anyone who listens to the Creator's voice and follows as best he can. Not long before Grandpa Temple passed back in '44, he pulled me close.

"Lummy boy, been watchin' you, and your Granny is right. You got the wanderin' foot, ain't no doubt about it. Just remember, you can become anybody you choose to be when you get where you're goin'. But do this one thing for me if you will."

"Sure Grandpa, anythin' you ask."

"Don't forget whose name you wear. Do the name Tullos proud wherever you go."

Columbus Nathan Tullos, a name that may strike people odd, maybe some as funny, others as different. But it's always meant a lot to me. We Tullos folks come from a long of line interesting first names—Claudius, Willoughby, Temple, Emaline, Elihu, Tapley, Mahaley, Burrell, Amariah, Saleta, Melvina, Archibald, and even George Washington and Benjamin Franklin—good names sealed off with Tullos like paraffin on the jam jar. Meaningful names. Names that sometimes have to be explained and sometimes defended. We Tullos boys never minded defending our names.

Columbus. It fits for the wandering foot I have, for the explorer who discovered America, at least the teachers say. I've wondered how he claimed to discover this New World when there were already people here. I've seen the big Indian mounds in the Delta. It wasn't mindless animals that came up with the idea to build those mounds. I've found too many of their tools that show they were skilled people, and the Choctaws I've met, well, they're as smart as anyone else. Probably smarter. They simply possessed the innocence of trust and lost their land in the process.

The bully, Lester, always made fun of them when they'd come around town. Some Choctaws, like Dan Creekwater, hid in the deep woods when the government made the tribes move to the Indian Territory. The remaining Choctaws didn't come to town but every once in a while for badly needed necessities. Lester picked on them for being weak and unable to keep their land, calling them a bunch of dumb critters. He did that to justify his wrongs against the other kids, taking their candy and pennies when their folks weren't looking. Must've made him feel like a big man, I guess. I don't like bullies.

As I listened to Lester rail on about the "savages," it hit me that wherever white people go, they seem to always have to take what others have possessed for a long time. And then claim God led them to do it. I scratch my head when I read the Ten Commandments which says Thou shalt not steal or even covet what another person has. Pa said that a man who covets bears a sickness of heart that makes him want things he never needed or were intended for him in the first place. From what I've seen, if white folks want it, then white folks take it. Manifest destiny, some call it. A destiny manifested in the minds and hearts of souless greedy men, I say.

And Nathan, well, that's been a troubling part of my name. Pa said he named me Nathan after his older brother who was born in North Carolina whose wanderin' foot finally led him to Texas. I don't want to go that far to find Susannah. But I will if I have to.

Ma said she agreed to the name Nathan because of the fire for the Lord she saw in my eyes when I was born. Ma let Pa have his way because it re-minded her of the prophet who confronted King David about taking another man's wife, having him killed, and lying about it in the process. I guess the boy who killed the giant bully Goliath let the power given him swell up his head. The bully slayer became the bully.

"You're like ole Nathan in the Good Book, not able to go along with what others say just 'cause they think they're in charge."

Ma believed the Good Lord gave me a good soul and out of it should pour truth, not as I see it, but as God reveals it. In other words, say what needs to be said, at the right time. I've had to be a bit careful about that. I've always been a mite fiery about religious subjects, mostly when one man claims he has the right to tell another what to believe about how a person can know God. In these hills, you can get into a fist fight over it. Imagine that, fighting over God's good truth. Men have been doing it for centuries.

Our people are good Baptists, but it amazes me how the tent revival reverends in the brush arbors try to out preach each other so they can get more converts to come their way. They sound like a bunch of screech owls run out of old Uncle Rube's broken down barn.

It's interesting to me that the very teachings each group claims to make them distinctive are really the things that divide them from each other. And they're proud of it. I've read Jesus's prayer in the Gospel of John. Not the one about leading us not into temptation and asking for our daily bread. That one was a prayer Jesus used to teach us how to pray.

No, I'm thinking on the one where Jesus hoped that all who call on His name would be one, that is, be united. Men dream up their own ways uniting people and for not all the best reasons. And while they're fussing about who's right, they all forget they nearly had to draw blood to break away from the Catholic Church or the Church of England to get where they are. Now, they're doing the same thing with each other. They make laws expecting everyone to keep that which they can't themselves. And then, they condemn other people who can't or won't obey their teachings. Foolishness.

Jesus once said that a house divided against itself won't stand. A fella from Illinois running for President says that same thing in his speeches about our nation. It's hard to argue with Scripture when you don't put the human interpretation on it. Funny thing though, Jesus was talking about Satan and his kingdom, not God's church there in the Book of Mark. Satan's got ahold of this country, and it's dividing, and both sides claim God is on their side. I wonder, how many sides can God be on?

Most are good people with good intentions, I suppose, but I resonate more with great grandma's Quaker roots Grandpa Temple told me about. She was part of our folks who moved with Richard Tullos from Virginia into the Ohio country. I guess you could say they're Yankees now. The Quakers seem more peaceful, probably because they find God in the quiet of their own souls more than they do in the outside fanfare and hoorah of a brush arbor meeting or in the strictness of a Sunday service.

Grandpa Temple said she spoke of Jesus's teaching that the kingdom of God is within a person. I agree. It seems to me that if we're looking for God on the inside, what's the big fuss about what it looks like on the outside, as long as it's right and good? If we find him on the inside, the outside will be right and good. And who, if he's seeking the kingdom within, has time to tell another how to read scripture and know God?

Many talk about the rights of the individual. So why can't that be true in how a man finds his way to God? Too many want to control what another man's walk with God must look like and where a person has to worship. They believe they have the goods on God. And, if a soul doesn't agree with them, it's to Hell with you. They mean it, literally. I've heard them say it.

It's about believing in Jesus and being who he created me to be. I try to listen to him to know what that is and live that to the best of my ability. After that, the rest is pretty much up for grabs. The disagreements have always been about how you do the "what's up for grabs" part. He did it on purpose so no one can claim they have the goods on him. But they still say they do.

Imagine that, one group of faithful, loving, merciful Christians preaching that another will go to Hell just because they use a pedal pushing pipe organ in Sunday church worship. It's those same people who forget that judging another person will get you sent to Hell even quicker. Still, it makes no sense to me that God would give sweet old Miss Bessie the gift of making beautiful sounds from a pipe organ and then some church leader tell her she can't worship him with it. Who gave her the gift in the first place? Man didn't give it to her, so I guess man can't tell her what to do with it. Where does that kind of misguided authority come from anyway, and why?

I guess some who claim the Bible to be the inspired word of God also tend to claim their interpretations are too. And most people, including many preachers, don't read the Book for themselves. They just parrot what they been told by somebody else. When somebody tries to make me obey what they only got from somebody else and has never read it for themselves?

"Don't piss down my back and tell me it's rainin'. I just ain't that stupid." Yeah, I said it. And out loud, too.

Jesus didn't come to bind us up only to put us in a cage full of laws. In fact, the people he was hardest on were the finely dressed, church going people called Pharisees who thought they had the goods on God. So I'm walking free with him and have for a long time in my soul. Going to Hell for missing a church service just because some man said so? Nonsense. Assembling with the saints in the name of the Lord never was meant to be a command but rather about being together with him and other believers.

It amazes me how all those preachers, reading the same Bible come up with so many different ways to get to heaven. There are as many ideas now about how to walk with God as there were languages when God got done with those Tower of Babel folks. It's about control. If a man can get control, he can instill fear. If he's got you by the throat in fear, then he can make you do just about anything and claim God told him to teach it. Fear is powerful when used for the wrong reasons. Using fear to get people to accept your Bible beliefs? That's the darkest sort of evil.

I'm glad I'm a reader, not only of the Scriptures but also of what surrounds me. It's not hard. There's a lot more scripture than just what's bound up in a book. You can't keep the God of this big universe locked up in paper and ink tied together in cow leather. For me? God's good creation is an equally "Good Book." And besides, even the old Apostle John said that if everything Jesus did got written down, all the books in the world couldn't hold it. So, I take it to mean we shouldn't try to lock him up in it.

I got in serious trouble with Pastor Dobbs one Sunday for saying there was more to God than just the Bible. He came down on me hard about it. And, it didn't really help when I asked him why we needed him anyway when I quoted right back at him the Apostle John's words that we really don't need a teacher because we have the anointing from God to teach us all things.

That day Pa smiled and whispered to Ma, "I like it when our son puts Columbus aside and lets Nathan talk. That boy says too well what I know true deep down in my heart."

So, I get it honest. Hickory nut didn't fall far from that old tree, and I'm glad. And I like that old Apostle John, too. He was the one who leaned on Jesus's chest at the Last Supper and heard the heartbeat of God. I hear God's heartbeat much better in the quiet of the deep woods than I ever have in the four walls of a prayer meeting house with some preacher railing on for the fiftieth time why I should stop lying and stealing. But that's just me.

I roll over on my back and give those thoughts a rest. The scent of sweet-smelling pines drifts into the barn where my eyes become heavier. The faces of Grandpa Temple and Granny Thankful form in my mind, and I'm reminded of the importance of my name.

When I'd leave the house to go to town or courting, Pa'd always say, "Don't forget whose name you wear!" Grandpa Temple must've told him that more than once. I need to wear my name well. Columbus for my wandering spirit, Nathan for my continual seeking of God. And Tullos, well, that's for the wildness of being one with nature and one of the people painted blue dancing naked around a woodland fire.

It's the Columbus part of my name that's got my feet moving to Louisiana with no fear about how I'll get there or what I'll find. And it's the same with the Nathan part of me, trusting the one who'll get me there. Columbus is the risk taker willing to go wherever the feet may step. Nathan is the seer who can envision what it can look like. And the Tullos part? That just means I'm not afraid and the wilder the better. So, give me a good reason, and I'm ready to go. Pretty much been that way most of my life.

When we were young boys, I was the one who couldn't resist seeing what was around the next creek bend or the other side of the far ridge. It's like I couldn't stop until I saw it, even if it meant getting home after dark and in trouble for being late for supper. I felt in those days like I was Columbus sailing his three little ships not knowing where he'd land. But he had to find the New World and was willing to risk it all to get there, no matter what. That's what this journey is for me, searching for a new world. I'm risking everything. I'll find it, wherever Susannah is. That's good enough reason to go.

"And I ain't looking back like Lot's wife did. A man can get turned into a pillar of salt staring too long at what the Lord leads him away from." It's cooling off, so I pull my coat tighter.

I wake to a rooster crow and the owner of the barn feeding his chickens. He speaks to them like little children. I grab my stuff, slick my hair down, straighten up my clothes, knock the dust off my boots, and sneak around the back of the barn to the owner's house to ask for work.

He has none but points me in the direction of a few town folk needing minor repairs done to their houses.

CHAPTER 5

CLOSE CALL ON BIG SAND CREEK

FEBRUARY 17, 1859

A song in the heart keeps the soul going in the right direction.

CARROLLTON, MISSISSIPPI IS much to look at with several big churches, more stores than in all of Choctaw County, some very fine houses and lots of folks moving about town. I marvel at the fine architecture and neatly trimmed yards. There's a peace about this place I like.

Carrollton is more refined than my hometown of Bankston, which is mostly a working man's town with the cloth, flour, and wool mills along with a tanning operation and shoe factory. Bankston is quite the bustling town stuck out in the middle nowhere but good for the folks who have jobs there. Bankston does have a couple hotels and several stores to choose from, but nothing like this. And, Mr. Wesson who owns the mills runs a tight ship. He won't allow any alcohol to be sold within two miles in any direction from Bankston. He made his thoughts known once when he visited Mount Pisgah Baptist Church.

"Alcohol and the Lord's good work just don't mix! The Devil's brew should be outlawed in the great State of Mississippi for good so we can make her the greatest in the Union!" After at church that day, Pa sat in his rocking chair sipping home brewed shine from a cool tin cup.

"Yep, this Devil's brew is terrible stuff. Two fingers of this nectar a day could make a man go blind. I guess then a man wouldn't have to look at that big-eared, hawk-nosed, shifty-eyed ole buzzard Wesson with all his money. And that stank from the tannin'? Wind shifts and a man can smell it for miles. Ole heavy stanky smell so thick you have to wipe off your teeth! Worse than a damn outhouse in the summertime!" Uncle Burrell, who worked at that very tannery, didn't appreciate Pa's words.

"Yeah, Archy boy, to some folks that smells like cash dollars. Ain't no worse than them hawgs you got down by the barn, brother." Pa turned away knowing he had stepped on the wrong set of toes talking bad about Uncle Burrell's livelihood. Uncle Burrell, Aunt Sarah, and the girls had come over to celebrate Ma's birthday and stayed the night. The pies Ma made were sweet and the company better, but Pa's disposition was sour as a pickle.

Uncle Burrell tanned leather and made boots in the shoe factory. It's interesting that he made his living in the same trade as Great Grandpa Cloud when he indentured himself back in the 1600's. Having a trade is certainly the settled part of our people. But Uncle Burrell did get the wandering foot again in '55. He, Aunt Sarah, and their three daughters left for Arkansas in a wagon, but Uncle Burrell died on the way. Aunt Sarah brought Emaline, Mary, and Mahaley back to Choctaw County. But Aunt Sarah soon after died, too.

Ma and Pa decided to take them in. With Saleta gone and Rebecca married, Ma liked having girls back in the house. Pa must've wanted a second chance to do better by children in the house. I liked having them around, though their constant giggling did get on my nerves a bit.

The town of Carrollton offers plenty of work for a man looking for it. It's a rich town compared to ours with many older folks having means to hire on a man for odd jobs mending and painting fences, removing brush, and replacing rotting boards and roof shingles.

My best chances will be working for the sweet old ladies. Not only do they pay fairly, one gives me room and board free for the three days. It slows my progress, but the jingle in my pocket will help me get down the road faster in the long run. I need enough to get steamer passage and ferry fare. As nice as the people are here, I'm ready to move on. Finally getting enough money, I walk to the landing where I hope to find a hack on Big Sand Creek.

"Say what you want to about Missip' folks, most are good people. But they do a very dark stain on their pretty white Sunday go to meetin' clothes." The stain of slavery is darker than Susannah's soft velvety skin. I look around to see if anyone's listening.

I take the few dollars I've made hoping the boat ride won't cost too much. I have to eat too. Lucky for me I meet a tall thin wiry man named Dale who owns a hack down by Big Sand Creek landing. His boat hand is down with a fever and can't make the trip. Dale offers me the ride free with food if I'll be his boat hand all the way to Greenwood.

"Works for me, suh, thanks. When can I start?" Dale grins toothless, eyeing me up and down.

"Well first of all, don't call me suh. That'd be my daddy, and he's in the cemetery up the street there. And second, don't jump too quick before you know what your gettin' into. There'll be lots of rowin' and snakes big around as your arm, sometimes longer. You good for it?" I nod. I'm not afraid of hard work, and I ain't scared of snakes. But I do have a healthy respect for them.

"What's your name, son?"

"Columbus Nathan Tullos," I say proudly.

"That's quite the handle you carryin' there! Dang, your name is about long as you is tall! You got anythin' shorter?"

"Folks back home just call me, Lummy." I catch and roll a hogshead full of local whiskey Dale rolls towards the hack.

"Works for me, Lummy. You can start now." The work is easy as is getting to know Dale.

"Dale, I ain't trying to be nosey or nothun', but did anybody else make the trip on your boat in the past week or so? Maybe a rich planter and a few slaves."

He rubs his chin whiskers, then scratches the back of his neck. "Well, you know, there was this one feller who asked me about passage to Greenwood. Yeah, now I remember, a rich man, his old servant, and three slaves. I remember because the planter was a talker but with good manners. He handled his slaves better'n anybody I've ever seen, like they was family." My heart leaps like a bullfrog poked at by a big blue crane. I hold in a big sigh of relief to not let on anything.

"The master kept singin' a song, oh yeah, that O Susanna song everybody likes. That man could really howl! Bu-u-ut, he decided not to take the ride.

Said he was in a bit of a hurry, so he caught a coach to Greenwood to board the steamer Dime. He wanted to get to Vicksburg and catch the ferry over to Desoto in Looseaner, but from there, I don't remember."

Dale pitches me another sack, and I let out my sigh like a cough. I stay my excitement about this news of Susannah and the song. I ask if he remembers the gambling man's name.

"Gilmut, Gillet, naw, oh, yeah, now I remember, it was Gilmore, yep, that's it, Gilmore. Why you askin'?"

I wasn't ready for that question. I play it off. "Nothin' really. He passed by our way not long ago. He's a card shark and can really roll them bones."

Dale shrug his shoulders, "Best keep your distance from them damn river boat gamblers. You ain't got no money now? Hell, they'll take your greenbacks and jingle your pocket change and smile whilst they slit your throat. Then, just for fun they'll chunk you off the steamer, and you'll find yourself supper for the catfishes and turtles. You remember that!"

"Sure thing, Dale." He sounds a little like Pa, but he's right.

We take off before daylight the next day. Mostly my job is taking a turn at rowing and pushing back low hanging branches and clearing the way of logs that might damage the boat or its cargo. Big Sand Creek isn't a deep creek, but it has a discernable channel if you know what you're doing.

When it's Dale's turn to row I also have to watch for sand bars and shallows we could get stuck on. And there's the endless job of keeping an eye open for snakes. With it being so unseasonably warm this early in February, the cottonmouths and water snakes have already come out of their winter dens to sun on logs and tree limbs.

The banks of Big Sand Creek have pretty tight turns in places. That's where the deeper water always seems to be. Those are pretty easy to navigate, but being new to this, it's not long before I get us stuck on a sand bar in a long straight shallower stretch I didn't see under the water's surface. They don't call it Big Sand Creek for nothing. Dale sighs but is patient.

"You'll get the hang of it soon enough. Watch the ripples in the water, and where there ain't but a few or none, that's where your current'll be. The more ripples, the shallower the water. Just listen to me when it comes your rowin' time, too. You've done some plowin' in your time by the looks of your hands, ain't you? Well, the man up front guides the man rowin' usin' the same gee haw as with a mule, you understand?" I nod.

It isn't long before I can read the water and with his rowing commands, I can "gee haw" to avoid nearly all the sand bars and hidden logs. The sharp creek bends, dog leg or hairpin, it doesn't seem to matter, always have log jams. That's where the snakes congregate.

Around a bend to find several logs jamming our way. I clear away all but a big one floating just under the surface with the long pole I use to push the hack along.

"Okay, Lummy, here's where you earn your pay." I know what that means. I've got to get out of the boat and either push the waterlogged tree out of the way or stand on it holding it down until the hack floats over it. I'm not afraid of the water, having waded and swam many a creek just like this one setting traps for raccoons and for fish in summers.

I'd already quit counting at thirty-five snakes of various kinds by this time, and it's only a little after noon. By ten o'clock they had slithered out of their dens and crawled up into fallen and overhanging trees to stretch out on the limbs to catch the sun's rays. Occasionally they slide off into the water as we pass with a wicked sounding splash, and every time I'd look around to see if any are trying to get aboard.

Just before noon, off to my left a rather large and long moccasin quickly slides over a log out of a backwater aiming right for us like he was coming out to challenge us. His head is up out of the water part of the time as he swims our way. I'm ready to strike when he slips under the water less than ten feet from our boat. I look back at Dale who's casually smoking his pipe. He shrugs his shoulders and looks up into the sky at the clouds.

I steadily poll the hack for only a few minutes when, dang it, if that same cottonmouth swims right alongside the hack just under the water two feet out. He's swimming at the same speed as the boat. He wants to catch a ride. I poke him hard with my pole. He disappears, but I keep watch.

Now here we are, can't go around the half sunken log and can't go over it. I carefully scan the logs and branches hanging low a moccasin would love to climb to sun himself. I put my leg over to get into the water when a three foot cottonmouth with a head as big as the bottom of a tin cup and thicker than the big part of my forearm catches my eye. He emerges out of the dark water like a demon from Hell sliding slowly onto the exposed end of the very log I'm about to wrestle.

Dale snickers, "Looks to be your friend from a bend or two back!"

It isn't funny, but he was just trying to keep me from making too much of it. The snake curls up in the sunshine sneaking through the willows, and it's clear that he has no concerns about me. He's letting me know that this is his territory, and he aims to defend it. I slowly pull my leg back in the hack not six feet from the snake.

"I believe I got another idea, if you're open to it!"

"I'm always lookin' for a new way to get one over on these damn water logged timbers and get around them needle teethed slithery bastards too! What you got in mind?"

First thing I do is to try and give that big snake a big rap on the head with my pole. He's not too disturbed at me when I miss, which surprises me, but it does strike at the pole just before he sinks out of sight into the dark waters. I tell Dale to back the hack up about thirty yards, get a good head of steam, and crank up his speed polling as best he can and watch me.

"Okay, Lummy, here goes, and this better work or you'll be swimmin' out ahead towin' this boat with a rope! Maybe you can get that cottonmouth to help you!"

I shudder as I lean over the left side of the small boat. "Go!"

Dale puts the muscle to it and the hack takes off. We move pretty good, picking up speed faster than I believe we could when a slightly submerged log a few yards ahead blocks our way. Just as we start over the log, I lean over bracing my feet against the side of the boat.

"Pour it on!" The boat rocks, but I dig my feet in hard against the rail. Dale's strong!

As we begin to pass over the ancient cypress log I push down as hard as I can with both of my hands, my head and shoulders going underneath the water. The weight of the water-soaked trunk carries the log much further down than I can shove allowing the hack to glide safely over. I pull myself back up and flop over on my back, breathing hard.

"Jumpin' Jehosaphat! Dang it, boy, but it worked!" I gasp for air.

"I wasn't sure it would, Dale, but it was worth a try, especially with that big snake nearby."

Dale waits until I catch my breath, and as I squeeze out my shirt, he sheepishly rubs the back of his neck. "Yeah, well, about that big ole snake. When you pushed that log down and the part of you that went down un- der the water, well, that cottonmouth slid right across your back just pretty as you please. If you'd come up any quicker, he'd either bit you or fell into the hack when you came back up in the boat as fast as you did. Either way, he would'a gotcha!"

I shudder again as cold chills run up and down my spine. I need to get that off my mind, so I take my turn rowing and let him watch the logs and snakes for a while.

"Dale, the song that Gilmore gentleman was singin', how's it go?"

"I thought you'd never ask. I learnt it in the tavern back up off the road you come in on. Goes somethin' like this." He clears his throat and takes a pose like a professional singer.

> *I come from Alabama with my banjo on my knee,*
> *I'm going to Louisiana, my true love for to see.*

He sang another verse and kept humming the tune. I can't believe my ears. Except for being from Mississippi, it fits me just perfect, from the top of my head right down to the soles of my boots. Don't think I'll be going to New Orleans, but who knows what the Good Lord has planned? So, I claim the song as my own. I change Alabama to Mississippi and go with it. Dale's not the wiser. We sing and sing it, then sing it again. It makes the journey easier. I row in time with the tune. It puts hope in my heart. The Lord must've sent that song to me.

About two hours before the sun sets, we camp on a sandy bank, out in the open, keeping an eye open for varmints, human and non-human. There's plenty of firewood in jams near where we pitch our tarps for the night. We stop a little early to try out one of his favorite fishing holes. I don't do so good, catching three small bream, but he pulls out a couple of nice bass and three catfish that makes for a fine supper with the fried potatoes he adds. Not a bad cook, that Dale. But how can you mess up frying fish and taters as long as you watch them.

We laze near the fire after our fine meal. The cool drifting off the water sends a chill through my damp clothes, so I huddle closer to the flames. Dale lies back against a log, smoking his pipe. He takes it out of his mouth, looks it over like it's the first time he's ever seen it.

"Yep, my ole Pap carved this here pipe made of ivory. He traded somethin' for it, I don't remember what, but I like the horse head he whittled into it." He just stares at it.

"Pap never paid for nothin' he could trade for. Yep, tighter'n bark on a tree, that one. But, I 'spose it's why I got this here boat and the decent livin' I make. He managed this hack since I was only knee-high to a grasshopper, and when he got down sick, well, I was still only a saplin', but I carried my weight. Just before he died, he gave me this here pipe, and I been smokin' it ever since. Ain't much else I got for as vices go, though. I jes don't have such appetites."

Dale stares at his pipe. "Wonder why Pa carved a horse's head instead of a snake's head or somethin'? He never did like bein' around horses much. Don't matter, it smokes good. I surely do sure miss him, though."

We get up early the next morning to catch fish for the next day or so. Dale puts out the leftover fish and potatoes and offers hot coffee with sugar in it.

"Dang, it's so foggy the birds are walkin'!"

I pick up a cane pole and head to the fishing hole. "Then maybe my luck'll change for the better fishin', since they won't see me comin'!"

About ten minutes into it, my luck comes through, and I catch two fair-sized buffalo and a catfish a foot and a half long. We load up our gear.

"What about the fish we caught, Dale? How we gonna keep them fresh?"

Dale pulls out a basket made from switch cane and willow limbs. "Put 'em in this. Even keeps out the snakes. And sometimes you can put out a line because other fish will come swim along side. What about that, Columbus Nathan Tullos?" We laugh.

The trip down Big Sand Creek takes us a couple more uneventful days. When we reach the Yalobusha, we hardly have to row in the stronger current that's easier to navigate. With more boats traveling this water highway, the boatmen keep the stream relatively clear of log jams. From here where the Yalobusha and Tallahatchie meet, the Yazoo River begins. It's just a short jaunt down the Yazoo to Greenwood where the steamer will be waiting. And, hopefully, Susannah.

CHAPTER 6

GREENWOOD ON THE YAZOO

FEBRUARY 24, 1859

A good man ain't hard to find, if you're tryin' to be one yourself.

WE ENTER THE Yazoo River at noon just in time for the Greenwood cotton gins and compresses to blow their whistles near the loading dock, signaling dinner break.

"You know what Yazoo means in Choctaw, don't you?" I shake my head. "River of Death. Don't know why, but it's kept me on my toes navigatin' her all these years." I shudder again at my close call with that thick black stumptail moccasin that crossed my shoulder.

Unloading the cargo at Greenwood takes no time. I help Dale reload the hack with the eastbound mail, catalog orders, and a traveler who wants to remain nameless. Now Dale is stout as a mule, but even a small man can get over on a big one if the conditions are right. And a man's got to sleep sometime.

"You sure about him? He's looks rougher'n cob, and he's got them shifty eyes, like he's hidin' somethin'."

Dale digs into his pants pocket. "I appreciate it, son, but I'm hidin' a little somethin', too." He pulls a silver plated pepper box pistol hidden in his belt under his shirt. "This 'river of death' thing ain't got nothin' on me. I've made this trip many a time and found two kinds of snakes out here—some slitherin' and some walkin'. This pistol will take care of them both!"

He spits tobacco and points to an Arkansas toothpick hidden in his boot. "Anyway, I'll have him scared as a sinner in a tornader when I get him up close to a couple cottonmouths. He'll think twice about laying me under with the fishes if he knows I'm the only one who can keep him alive if he accidently gets bit."

He rolls a shiny five dollar gold piece up in my palm and holds it there. "I know you're headin' somewhere fast and hope it ain't about no trouble. But if it is, just don't go off half-cocked. You're a good kid, and I don't want you hurt. I know somethin's goin' on about that Gilmore fella you asked about. Don't know, and don't have to, but I did hear you talkin' in your sleep about some gal called Susannah. I took notice too, that you like that song better than I do, and you sing it with a lot a feelin'.'"

Dale leans up closer. "That Mistuh Gilmore called that pretty black girl Susannah. Got no problem with it, Lummy. Had me a Choctaw wife once myself. Pox got her and my two little boys. I loved that gal and still carry a lot of grief over it. But hell, a man's got to do what's in his own heart. You go do your thing, just don't do it around these parts, and you know well what I mean. And by the way, you're welcome on my hack and by my fire anytime. But could you work on your fishin' skills a bit? A man can starve to death waitin' on your cane pole for supper!"

A tear forms in my eye. Can't help it, the man treats me like a son, better than my own Pa did at times. And I hate to think that way, but I do believe the Good Lord provides, and he's providing me with other fathers. Dale's gentle but firm ways are like a cool breeze on a hot August afternoon. He has the spirit of God in him.

Having some distance and time away from Pa will make me appreciate him more. I just wish it wasn't this way. He wasn't all bad, not by a long shot. But, I still have quite a ways to go on this road to lose the pain I carry. We Tullos children didn't grow up like everybody else and often the worst of our raising shows up.

"Dark cloud's comin' up in the west! Best be gettin' on my way, Columbus Nathan Tullos. See you when I see you, my good friend!" I walk slowly up from the landing towards town. I look back, wave, but Dale yells something. I can't hear over the sound of the cotton gins and presses starting up again so I cup my ears.

"Winn Parish!" I step closer.

"What?"

"I just remembered! That gambler said they was headin' to Winn Parish, Looseaner." I wave. He slides the boat into the Yazoo and heads upriver. His back muscles ripple as he strokes with the long pole. Just before Dale rounds the bend, he throws me a quick wave. My good friend.

I sit on an empty hog's head for a moment and take in the view of Greenwood. A peaceful name. Sounds like a place where a man can disappear and live in the cool shadows for a long time. But I have to keep moving. I chance upon an old timer chewing his tobacco like there's no tomorrow. He spits a stream of juice ten feet into the dust. I ask him to tell me about Greenwood.

"We-e-ell, it started out as William's Landing, named for the feller who settled her first and started up the cotton trade. Planters started bringin' in their crop to be shipped down the Yazoo and on to New Orleans. The Choctaw Chief Greenwood Leflore brought his cotton here too until he discovered that Williams left his cotton unprotected from the weather, and they got into a pretty big fuss."

"For spite, LeFlore built his own warehouse and landing three miles north and called it Point Leflore, but it didn't work out as the old chief had planned. By '44, William's Landing had grown into a nice little village. Now we gots a town hall, post office, three saloons, a passel of mercantiles and grog shops. We're comin' up in this world, don't you see? Funny thing is the place got named for Greenwood not long after Williams went under the dirt."

I thank the old timer and start up the bank from the river landing. Greenwood Leflore, the Choctaw chief who sold tribal land out from underneath his own people. The few Choctaws I know don't like how it all happened. They say that he wasn't even a true full-blooded Choctaw, born to some French Canadian trader named Lefleur and a Choctaw Indian princess. I guess being half European made it easier for him to sell off the richest cotton land in the world.

Being chief and all, he did what he thought was right for his people. The move was unavoidable with the swell of white faces headed west, but it's interesting that he made a way to stay here himself. Pa told me about the mansion Leflore built called Malmaison. Dale told me all about the fine china, the big columns, and fancy furniture Leflore had sent over from France. Wonder where he got the money? Dumb question.

Anyway, the Choctaws never kicked up too much of a fuss about it. Probably didn't know they could with so many soldiers around to "help" them on their way to their new Promised Land. A man doesn't ask too many questions when a bayonet is pointed in his direction. I wonder how they've taken to the new lands out West.

I wonder if Greenwood sent money to build them mansions, too? I'd like to ask him that question myself.

Dale said many Choctaws died and he helped bury them. As a young man during the removal, he worked for Hall's Ferry line in Vicksburg to make extra money when the government took them across the Mississippi.

"It was blood money. With my pretty young wife dyin', I came back to work with my Pa. Never thought much about women after that."

The town of Greenwood is the biggest in Mississippi I've ever seen except for Jackson City. Dang, I've never seen so much cotton. Rows and rows of the stuff pressed and wrapped in burlap from the previous season and stored here until they can get the best price, I figure. Worth a pretty penny, I bet. I just to take it all in.

My Uncle Rube grew cotton, so I'm not a complete stranger to it. He had the best cotton growing bottomland in Choctaw County. Come picking time, Pa took us boys to those rich bottoms not far from Aaron Wood's Spring to help him get it out of the field and to the gin. Then we'd send the bales off in wagons, but it was nothing like this. Uncle Rube always gave us a fair day's wage for a fair day's work. And cotton picking is hard work.

Pa picked cotton faster than lightning. The older boys were expected to keep up, picking both sides as they moved down the rows. Until I was twelve, I only had to pick one side.

One morning, Ben wasn't feeling too well, so he just sat down and quit picking. I don't think it was anything physical. He was just sick in his soul from the years of Pa's abuse.

Pa yelled at him, "You best quit piddlin' around, Ben!" Ben didn't move.

"If you ain't down here when I get to the end of this row, it ain't gonna go good for you, boy."

Ben shrugged, "He expects too much from us, like we're a bunch a damn animals, or even worse, like a bunch of damned slaves." I didn't like what he said. I just kept picking.

Ben didn't do as Pa commanded. It scared the living daylights out of me when Pa came at Ben like a man headed to a fight. He yanked up a big cotton stalk and pulled his knife from his belt, trimming off the branches as he strode towards Ben. Ben was snakebit and knew it. knew it. He just stood up, knowing there wasn't any sense in running, but he did, anyway.

Pa chased him around the field, Ben ducking and dodging, but Pa landed a few hard licks across Ben's bare back. Finally, Ben made it to the cut near the creek ditch and shimmied up an old catalpa tree like a young cat squirrel.

All Pa said as he threw down the cotton stalk, "Tha-a-a-t's all right! Be dumber'n dirt, boy! You're gonna get hungry sometime. So when you do, just bring this cotton stalk with you when you come, you hear?" Ben didn't say a word, perched like a buzzard waiting for something to die. That something, he knew, would be his backside when he finally decided to come home.

Ben came down and Pa beat him across his back until spots of blood appeared. Ma cried, Elihu gritted his teeth, and the rest of us sat still.

Rebecca leaned over to Ma. "Ain't never gonna do that to my child, and my husband ain't gonna do it, neither!"

Even at my young age I thought, *There's just somethin' really wrong with this picture.*

Pa was as mean as he was stubborn never realizing that the way he treated us was how he was raising us to be—mean and stubborn. I don't mind being stubborn, but I don't want to live my life being mean. I'm glad I spent a good bit of time with Uncle Rube in those days. He was stubborn, but he wasn't mean. He'd shake his head and wander back up to his house calling Pa an "ornery bastard" when he beat us the way he did Ben that day. Uncle Rube tried to take the edge off when we worked his cotton. The sad part was that we always had to go home.

Stubborn as a mule, Uncle Rube would argue with a fencepost. He had his ways, but he knew how to make money. He made good on cotton on his 500 acre farm out from Wood Mountain in the early '50's and was sitting pretty well. In the crash of 1857, Uncle Rube refused to sell his cotton when prices dropped to nothing. So, he lined up all his bales on his wrap around porch.

"I ain't sellin' my God-given hand-picked finest cotton in this part of the country to no Yankee for jack nothin' a pound. I'll burn the damn stuff first! For now I'll just let it block the wind come winter. I suwannee, it'll make a man lose his damn religion! And I ain't got much!"

Uncle Rube, an old confirmed bachelor, had plenty of money. He didn't believe in putting money in banks, having lost a small fortune as a young man when the one he put his money in Greensborough failed. So he buried his money, silver and some gold, in Mason jars hidden around his property. Once when I visited him alone, he showed me where he stashed it.

"Now don't come get this before I leave to walk the street of gold, but when I do, this'll help you at a time when you might need it the most. Don't tell no one and live by this rule I followed all my life—I don't mind spendin' money but hate wastin' it." I couldn't believe my ears.

"Uncle Rube, when in tarnation did you ever spend money?" He snickered and waved his arm out over his land, and I knew. He was telling me to spend my money on the important things. Still, he was tighter than a bull's ass on fly day, and I guess for good reason. He always felt like people were out to cheat him because he was good at making money. In his later years, he'd sit on his porch with his double-barrel shotgun watching for anyone who might come looking to steal from him. He couldn't stand a thief or a liar about as much as he hated to spend money.

Uncle Rube was so tight he could squeeze a quarter so hard he'd make the eagle scream and the pretty lady sitting on the other side jump up and run. He was a simple man requiring little. He loved canned sardines and ate the salty crackers that came free with them. During the scare of '57, Mr. Wesson, who owned the best store in Bankston, had to start selling the crackers for a nickel to go with the ten cent can of sardines. Uncle Rube fussed every time he darkened the store door about Mr. Wesson cheating his customers.

Mr. Wesson, who never hurt for money whined, "Time's are hard, Rube. I don't like it either." Uncle Rube spat on the plank floor missing the spittoon on purpose and didn't buy the crackers. He'd go home to sit on his porch eating his sardines without crackers.

"Can't give a man a few crackers to go with his sardines! Old skinflint's sittin' on a gold mine with his factories in Bankston. Damn him anyways. Ain't nary a soul fell off the turnip wagon on this here porch. Heck, that Wesson is about worthless as hen shit on a pump handle!"

Of course, nobody said anything to Uncle Rube about the fact that he had enough money stashed away build his own cracker factory five times over.

When Uncle Rube's brick chimney fell in after a tornado came through, he didn't want to pay anyone to fix it. So he did his own bit of construction. He sealed up the front door and used the hole in the fire place to go in and out of his house. Crawling in and out of one of the nicest houses in the county like a rat, and with all that money buried around his house. What a stubborn man. Runs in the family, I guess.

The whistle blows signaling dinner break is over. Two slaves struggle to push a small wagon filed with huge cotton bales down the hill toward a steamer.

"Where's all this cotton headed?"

The biggest of the two stops the cart and wipes the sweat from his forehead. "They takin' dis here white gold down to Nawlin's by way of Vicksburg." They joke about something I can't understand and go back to humming some sweet tune I've never heard before. It sure has a good sound to it. The sun warms my back as I think about what to do next.

How can these men be so peaceful in their spirits worked so inhumanly? I know they must have more God-given talents and smarts than to be just doing meaningless work. For the majority of white folks, meaningless mindless work is all these Negroes are good for. Mr. Wesson back over in Bankston didn't believe it.

The Semple engine that powers Wesson's factory, brought all the way from Providence, Rhode Island and admired by all who visit, is run by of all people, a Negro engineer. Mr. Wesson called the man Chat, who'd never seen or laid hands on any kind of engine before. He simply but taught himself and became the expert. There wasn't a white man in the county who could run it. Funny thing, Mr. Wesson bragged on his marvel of engineering but never said a word about his Negro engineer. I like Chat and on occasion stopped by to see the engine and visit with him when Pa sent me to get the mail or supplies in Bankston.

Chat and I fished together a few times, and finally he told me his real name. "I likes my name Josiah, Lummy. It reminds me I always need to be a'searchin' for the Lord's way of walkin' on dis earth."

He said Mr. Wesson gave him the name Chat, short for chattel. Josiah said that chattel is the Bible name for property, like cattle. Mr. Wesson wanted to make sure he remembered he was "still just a niggah so you don't let your new job give you the big head. Niggah's gotta know his place, Chat." I hung my head when Chat told me that. I want that part of my world to change. I start by walking from the landing into town.

With my belly full with catfish, Dale took from the basket earlier this morning, I'm ready to find work. As I stride into the small but bustling town, slave owners yell at the black men and women struggling under heavy loads. I pass an alley where two white men have a small sheepish black girl on her knees. I look away from her pain-filled eyes. I have to because what I want to do to those two men right now will surely get me put in jail and possibly hanged.

I speed up.

I'd probably lose my mind if I saw Susannah being treated that way. Rage would rise up in me like a dragon hurling fire, and somebody would be dead in the process. I have to keep my mind set on what I'm doing or I'll never see Susannah again. One day, dammit, one day, it's gonna be different.

I find the steamer ticket office. "You're in luck young feller! The Dime sits right over there, and she'll depart at eight o'clock sharp in the mawnin'. That'll be two dollars and fifty cents unless you want to go de-e-e-luxe?"

"Do I look deluxe, suh?"

"No you don't, son. In fact, you look like a mule rode hard and put up wet. But I tell you what, if you don't say nothin', I'll put you in a better room with a window and give you a free supper pass for each night. How's that sound?"

I'm stunned. "Better than I deserve, suh."

He nods, stamps the ticket as I give him the money, and holds on to the ticket as I take it from his hand. He eyes me just long enough to make me nervous. Maybe he's got a wanted poster on me from Choctaw County for what I did to Lester's friend Kneehigh before I left. I pull at the ticket, but he holds on tightly.

"No need to go to crawfishin' on me, son. I only got good to say to you. I got an eye for people, young man. You look like you're on a mission, and I believe God's in it. I'm lookin' for all the stars I can get in my crown on that great gettin' up mornin'. So, I'll just help send his man on his way. Just do good when you get there, son, and all along the way. Doin' good is a tough row to hoe, but you'll surely be happy with yourself when you get to the end."

The ticket master looks to be a man who's lived a hard life but with a good heart. I give him my five dollar gold piece. He gives me change and the ticket with a meal voucher. I thank him, and he prays as I walk away. I'm happy at my good fortune to have an afternoon free to make a little extra money. Down the street, two men build a boardwalk that soon will connect several storefronts.

"Need any help?"

"Can you haul boards from the wagon over there and nail them?"

"Yassuh, my Pa worked with wood just like this, and I worked with him. We built the New Zion Baptist Church buildin' just before I left comin' this way."

"So, you a church-goin' feller, too?"

"I've made it my habit all my life, except for lately, travelin' and all."

"That's good. Work hard, and I'll give you two dollars, feed you supper, and give you a rack for the night in my shed, how's that?"

I stick out my hand. "I can't thank you enough, suh."

"Don't thank me just yet, you ain't heard the rest. You gotta go to prayer meetin' with me tonight. Can you do that?" I'm not too excited about it, but

I've endured many a bad sermon in my time and bad singing that sounds like a croaker sack full of drowning cats.

"Yassuh, thank you, suh, I can do that."

"Well good then. I'm Jake, and this here's Eli. He don't say much, but he does get a bit testy if the work ain't goin' so well. The Lord's still workin' on him. So keep up! I want to finish this job by supper time." I watch them for a moment to see how they handle everything.

Eli mumbles under his breath, "Jake's always findin' fellers who don't know their ass from a hole in the ground. This one's surely a brick short of a load, and I gotta put up with it, dammit."

He says a few more things I can't understand and probably don't need to. It ain't the first time a young man like me has had to prove himself on a new job. So I set myself on doing the best I can, and with my upbringing, I have no problem keeping up with Eli.

For a boy growing up working the way I did, the job is easy. In fact, I have to slow down a bit to find the rhythm that suits them best. I guess that's one thing I'll always thank Pa for, despite his hardness. He did teach us how to work and take care of ourselves.

He'd say, "Sometimes, boys, you just gotta bow your neck and get down in the mud to make it in this ole world." Pa believed it, he lived it, and he taught us seven brothers well.

Jake paid me two dollars at the end of the day. We arrive at his modest house, and I go straight to the horse trough out back to clean up for supper. Eli, tailing behind, hasn't said a word to me all afternoon.

He bumps my shoulder and grins, "If you need to go to the outhouse, you know what the red cobs and the white cobs is for, don't you?" I've heard this one all my life, but it's a good opportunity to let Eli have his moment.

"Na-a-awsuh, sure don't!"

Eli belly laughs, "You use a red one first then a white one to see if you need another red one! Haw, haw, haw!" I thought he'd never quit laughing. He slaps me on the back and goes to washing his hands and face like a man beating out a fire. I can't help but laugh at how hard he's laughing at his own joke.

After we clean up, I stash the two silver dollars in the sock under my foot with the rest of my money. I put my little Bible in my shirt pocket and button it. At least I can catch up on my reading while the preacher rails on.

I sit down to a large bowl of brown beans with ham and cornbread that surely will quiet my growling belly. The prayer Jake says is a bit different than I've heard someone pray out loud, but a lot the way I talk with God out in the woods, alone. Jake prays as if God is sitting in the chair across the table from him.

"There's a place in Genesis where it says God spoke to Moses face to face, as man do with his good friend. That's always struck me hard in a good way. What do you think?"

I really don't want to reveal too much of what I believe, but this man seems very sincere. "I believe God still does that today. We've forgotten how to listen."

"I believe you're right, son. Prayin' ain't so much about foldin' your hands and bowin' your noggin as it is just bein' yourself with the Lord." I nod as I keep eating.

Jake pushes his plate back and crosses his arms. "Friends look at each other when they talk, eye to eye. Friends spend a lot of time together, sittin' with each other, gettin' to know each other, and helpin' each other, gettin' so comfortable with each other that soon it just comes natural. But most preachers would rather build up a big congregation than teach people how to know God like Moses did. Seems to me, that's really why Jesus came, to get us back on good speakin' terms with his Father. And about that speakin' to the Good Lord face to face? Seems to me if Jesus did it, why can't we? Jesus didn't come to make it harder to know him through a bunch of rules made up by men who only know about him by what they read or been told. That's how I land on the subject. How about you?"

This man just expressed my exact feelings. He pokes me on the shoulder. "I knowed there was somethin' different about you, boy."

Jake's wife Christine brings more cornbread. "Let the boy eat, Jake, he's gonna get enough preachin' here in a bit!"

Prayer meeting is another breath of fresh air, unlike Mt. Pisgah Baptist church on Thursday evenings. Even though things changed for the good in our move from New Zion, the church services sometimes left a lot to be desired. The pastor is younger than ole Pastor Dobbs back home and has more fire in him than I'm used to. He keeps my interest, and I pull out my little Bible to read along as he goes scripture to scripture. His sermon is short and gives us more time to pray than he gives to his preaching. All who want may pray.

Prayer meeting back at Mount Pisgah wasn't that way. It was just another excuse for Pastor Dobbs to rail and wail about the end of the world and how so few of us were going to make it when the fire comes. Imagine that, praying at Prayer Meeting. What a novel idea. It's tough to tell somebody else what they ought to be doing if you're thinking on what you're saying to God.

Well anyway, the singing is good, and the ladies prepared pies for a social afterwards. And that lemon pie with the head high calf's slobber on it. I've been eyeing all evening? Well, I almost made a spectacle of myself. After a bit, the preacher wanders over and asks if I'm new in town.

"I'll be leavin' on the Dime in the mornin'. Mistuh Jake and his sweet wife were kind enough to give me a little work, a good meal, and a bed for the night."

"So, you headin' out tomorrow for Vicksburg?"

I finish my last bite of pie. "Yassuh, and on to Looseana from there, Lord willin'." I really don't want to go any further with this conversation. It's getting a bit too personal.

"What's in Louisiana? A girl, I'm guessin'?"

I smile. "Yassuh."

He leans forward protecting the personal nature of our talk. "When you find her, treat her like a lady, save it for marriage, and love her like your own body."

"My own body?"

"Get a look at Paul's letter to the Ephesians, around the middle to end of chapter five, next time your readin'. You'll find it there."

He sits down next to me. This preacher has a way about him that just puts a man's soul to ease. "You're doin' the right thing on this journey of yours, makin' friends with the right people. Most people say it's pretty easy to fall in with the wrong kind of people. Bad company corrupts good morals. But I say a good man ain't hard to find, if you're tryin' to be one yourself. Keep on lookin' and findin' good people in the right places everywhere you go, and you'll surely do all right." He stands up and straightens his jacket.

"Go with God, Lummy Tullos, because He's surely goin' with you. That's clear as me standin' here. He's always around and with us everywhere we go. Set your heart on this. God wants you to do good for others, but also do good for yourself."

I'm stunned. "Go read about Abraham and his people. God takes care of those who bless Him back with their good livin'." This preacher has given me more wisdom in just a few minutes than all my years under Pastor Dobbs's spiritual whipping cane.

"Preacher!" He turns. "I like what you said tonight and givin' us time to pray like you did."

"I just figure the Lord has a much better word to give to the people I shepherd than I do. If I can get them talkin' to God, maybe they'll learn to relax and let him take a turn at the talkin'. Good night, my friend, and blessin's on you head to toe."

I wish I had time to know this man better.

I scrape the last bit of lemon pie with my fork so hard I make marks on the tin plate.

"Why don't you just lick the plate to get the last bit there, son?" Jake puts on his hat.

"I would if I wasn't in public, but my Ma taught me better'n that. Sure is tasty though."

"You ready to go?"

"Yassuh, and thanks for bringin' me here."

"I didn't bring you here, Lummy. God did, and I'm just His errand boy."

CHAPTER 7

YAZOO RIVER STEAMBOAT RIDE

FEBRUARY 26, 1859

A man's steps quicken when he finally gets wind of where he's headed.

THE WHISTLE BLOWS, and I'm ready to board the *Dime.* Jake and Eli wave on their way to build the next length of boardwalk down the street.

"Come back, you always got a job here if you need one!"

Eli, a man of few words, nods. All he said yesterday as we finished supper was, "Got no problem with your work, young feller."

I'll take the compliment.

I have a few minutes before we can board, so I sit on an empty hogshead not far from river's edge.

"Ho, there, Lummy Tullos. Soon to be off?" It's the preacher, and he climbs on the barrel next to mine. "Mind if we talk before you head downriver?"

I nod but wonder why he wants to converse.

"You look like a child who's been bad at church expectin' a whoopin' when you get home!"

"Lord knows I had my share, some I deserved, but most I didn't. Sorry, don't mean no harm, but most of my conversin' with preachers never seems to turn out too well for me."

"I get that. You don't mind speakin' the truth even when it ain't popular."

"I'm just careful who I talk with these days. You understand?"

"For a tall man, you carry a heavy load that needs unloadin'. That be about right?"

I hang my head. "Yassuh, but I hate to spill it out all over this ground." He puts his hand on my shoulder.

"You can trust me, son. The Lord only sent me here to lighten a burden, not pile on more."

"So the Lord sent you? And it'll just be between you and me?" The preacher nods. I gather my thoughts then start a rant. "Okay then, there's somethin' that don't set right with me and makes me want to stray from church. We Tullos's have always been good God fearin' church goin' folk. My Pa and my brother Ben, my Uncle Allen and Aunt Sarah were all foundin' members of the New Zion Baptist Church in Choctaw County back in '42. My brother Ben served as a delegate to the Baptist association, my Uncle Allen ordained a deacon, and my two sisters were baptized in the spring down the hill from the church house. Pa and my older brothers even helped build that building."

I stop. "You sure you want to hear all of this?"

He nods again.

"Okay. Later on, my Uncle Roland and his wife Catherine became members. Roland even got himself baptized again, whether he needed it or not. Ben's wife Dorcas joined later when they got hitched. But they joined McCurtain's Creek Baptist Church when they left to buy land. When they decided to come back to New Zion, they were in such good standing they didn't even need letters or references. All I know is that in 1849 Pa, Ben, Dorcas, and Rebecca asked for letters of dismission, and they were granted on the same day they were applied for. So they left." I scratch my ear.

"Then Uncle Roland made a case against Brother Sue Lopes, and it took the help of three other churches to finally get their problem settled. Not long after that though, Uncle Roland was charged with makin' false statements in conference, and then somethin' about his wife bein' disrespectful to one of the leading men who thinks he's God on earth. Long story short, they were excluded from New Zion, and on top of that my Uncle Allen had to sit in committee to make the decision to exclude Uncle Roland! Wasn't long before Uncle Roland and his wife left the church and headed to Arkansas, and Uncle Allen wasn't far behind.

"After that there wasn't a Tullos in the house at New Zion Baptist Church on Sunday. Churches and preachers, rules and beliefs, and being so overly organized, it's just too much trouble! It's too much about the right and wrong about how to do church and bein' accountable to people no better than yourself. Makes it too damn hard to find God in four walls!"

I stop abruptly, breathless but also a little embarrassed that I unloaded all of that on a stranger. I'm better having puked it up, but the words landed all over the preacher.

"Probably more than you wanted to hear."

The preacher shakes his head. "Sounds like the Spirit of God got squeezed out of that church."

"Who was doin' the squeezin', preacher? Heck, my Pa didn't even join up when we moved over to Mount Pisgah Baptist Church. He attended some Sundays, but somethin' happened at New Zion that took the fire out of him. I'm sure there were other things goin' on, too, but anyway, I got a different way of seein' on the how's and the why's of church these days. I don't see eye to eye with most men wearing black suits with white collars."

The preacher holds up his hands. "It was the church folks doin' the squeezin' all right, Lummy. But really, it's Ole Satan whisperin' in their ears and your Pa's. Just hang in there. Don't let what others do wrong keep you from doin' what's right. Your Ma found a new place to go. You respect that, don't you?"

"Easier said than done, preacher. I can't seem to connect with this organized church thing no more. Not the way it's bein' presented these days. Church has become more about who has big money, favortism, and wrong headed authority—the very things Jesus got down on the Pharisees about. Not to mention most preachers spoutin' off more politics than Bible here lately, shapin' their sermons to make their best givers happy!"

"I can't disagree with that."

"When Ma, Elihu, and Rebecca started going to Mount Pisgah Baptist, I liked how that church treats Negroes. I don't know how you feel, but I can't be with a bunch of hypocrites who claim to love God but treat his other children like a bunch a dawgs. I ain't judgin' nobody, but wouldn't I be a bigger hypocrite for goin' to church if I didn't believe why I was goin'? I just ain't havin' no part of treatin' Negroes bad no more, and thank goodness Mount Pisgah Church is some different. But the rest?" I shake my head. "Let me ask you, if a church ain't actin' like Jesus wants it to, and he ain't happy with it, does a body have to go every Sunday?"

I can tell it's not a question he's been asked before.

The preacher rubs his chin. "I see why you had a little problem with your pastor back at New Zion thinkin' that way. But the answer I believe is no, you don't have to go, not in those circumstances. A person must always be where he can find the Lord and where his soul gets strengthened. Remember this, just because a church house has a cross painted on it doesn't mean the folks inside live like Jesus. There's always wolves in sheep's clothing."

The older man drops his head, rubs his hand over his Bible, and clears his throat. "If Jesus did anythin' wrong on this earth it was givin' his authority to men. It ain't been good since he done that. Not in this fallen world. And as far as how we should be treatin' God's darker children, I believe there's gonna be a rude awakenin' come judgment day. Lotta folks gonna be surprised at who's there and who ain't on that great gettin' up mornin'. Some folks with big mansions now will be sweepin' the floors of those with no mansion now. God has a way a turnin' a thing on its head, and most people don't get that. It's all through the Good Book—first bein' the last, greatest amongst you bein' a slave, the poor inheritin' the earth, things like that. So many church folks done forgot that." A tear forms in his eye.

I hop off my hogshead and kick the dirt. "I just don't understand it. Why can't people just live and let others be enjoyin' only what the Good Lord gives them in the first place? It's like once they they get Jesus in them, they become only the hard side of him. Gettin' called into a church conference with the good brethren simply for not attendin' a meetin' and then get excluded from the church over it? That's foolishness, and you know it! Church never was about attendin' a bunch of meetin's no how. It's about walkin' with the Lord as best you can and gettin' encouraged to do good by other Christians. Those who lead the church for Jesus make it the hardest on them tryin' to walk with Him! Ain't nothin' but a bunch of foolishness, preacher!" I'm getting too loud, so I stop.

He pops me on the back. "Ever thought of becomin' a minister? Could use more of your talk around here!"

I grin and shake my head. I have a calling right now, and it ain't becoming no preacher. The steamer whistle blows, and the preacher hops down from his barrel and pats me on the shoulder.

"Lummy Tullos, it is clear to me that you seek the Lord. Don't stop. Seek His face because He's always seeking yours. God walks with a man wherever he goes, so go with God."

He shakes my hand and walks back up the river bank to town.

The Captain comes out of his cabin heading for the top of the stern-wheeler. "Ten dollars and a daily noon meal in the kitchen for any able bodied man willin' to load wood, clear logs, and sweep snakes from the deck. You'll get paid when we reach Vicksburg."

I race up the stairs.

He looks me over, up and down, noticing the lean but rounded muscles made strong by ploughing with an ornery mule and logging with a father who works like there's no tomorrow. "Damn, son, who put you on the stretchin' rack? You'll do. Get on down to the boiler room, that way, and watch your head. Find Lige and help him get the steam goin' in this tub. This ain't no half-ass, quittin' halfway down river kind of job son, you understandr? You'll finish all hundred and ninety miles of this wanderin' stream if you want to get paid!"

I salute the captain, "Yassuh!"

He stares at me strangely. "Well, get on down below and help Lige in the boiler room, hurry up!"

I take one last look at Greenwood, and the preacher sends me a wave. I wave back and duck down below quickly to find Lige, a tall Irishman black from oil and coal, laughing at my salute.

"Don't worry, son, there be a war a'comin'. We'll all salute somebody soon. But for now, I need to know you can hit a lick with a shovel. Don't worry about Cap, he barks loud but bites little. But he don't play when it comes to work. He says don't worry about the mule, just load the wagon. The man who lets that out of his mouth ought'a have to be the mule for a day, I say."

Lige works with me for a half hour to get the coal burning, showing me the ropes. When we get underway, he starts up the ladder to the deck.

"You doin' good, boy. I'm goin' up top to do snake duty, but really I'm gonna try and sneak one of sweet mamie's biscuits from the kitchen. Dang it, I'm so hongry my belly button done stuck to my back bone! Throw wood in as you need to, but keep a good eye on the steam gauge. Don't let it get too high or too low!" He laughs, "And watch your head, you're tall as a damned ole field corn stalk!"

I lay down the coal shovel and throw in wood to keep up a good head of steam. The captain walks the decks and nods at me as he looks over the boat.

I'm glad for the opportunity to see how these huge machines operate and to make a few bucks. It's good I won't be paid until the end. That'll help keep the two-legged river gators from trying to tempt me to the card tables. Taking this job, they won't think this poor boy has any money anyway. I'm not tempted, but I don't want to get cross with men in fancy suits smelling of perfume, wearing silk hats and shiny boots but known to carry knives and derringers unafraid to use them to send an unsuspecting lad like me to river's bottom without a thought or care.

I'm a bit pleased with myself. I thank the Lord that I have dinner and supper secure, a nice room in which to retire, clean up, and rest well for the next day's work. And I have a ten-dollar gold piece waiting for me in Vicksburg! The work is hard, but heck, what good work isn't?

After a good night's rest, I move wood from top deck to lower and keep the fire hot for twelve hours straight to keep a steady head of steam going. I stop only for a thirty-minute dinner break. I don't get to see much of the Yazoo but figure I didn't really miss much.

It's now the third day of our journey, and I get called up when we have to clear some logs blocking the stream ahead. I cringe knowing what the jam will be filled with. Checking the logjam for cottonmouths, I tell the other deckhands I'll swim the rope over and tie the cable to a log. Once it's secured, the captain will reverse the steamer engines and break up the jam.

My friend, Dale, trained me well during my short stint on Big Sand Creek. Doing this well will show the captain my determination to get the job done and the old deckhands my lack of fear. I remove my shirt and boots, carefully laying them on the stern, and dive in. Two deckhands throw me the big rope with a float at the end to help me swim it across the way to the jam. The current downriver carries me to the spot I need to land. I scan the logs for snakes, but I see none. Only a few turtles drop into the muddy stream.

I'm halfway when a "log" thirty yards off to my right suddenly moves. It slides into the water and disappears under the surface.

Ladies scream, and men shout.

"Gator! Swim fast, boy!"

I kick hard, but I can't see the beast anywhere. Between gasping for air and gulping down what seems like a gallon of river water, the big black "log" rises not twenty feet away, swimming directly for me.

"Hurry, boy, he's twelve feet if he's two!" The monster closes the distance quickly. I swim fast as I can, but it gains on me. I know I'm done for, but I keep up the struggle.

When the alligator gets within six feet, shots ring out, and the monster rolls over and over. It splashes its great tail up and down, his head coming out of the water with gaping jaws, as if trying to catch the bullets with his teeth. He catches them, all right. He groans as he slides close, bumping me out of the way. He lets out his last bloody foul breath, spewing water from his gullet straight into my face. He rolls over belly-up as we drift to the log jam. I wash the bloody slime off my face with river water.

A great cheer rises from the steamboat, and the organist, plays of all songs, *O Susanna!* The captain had heard me singing it while I loaded wood from top deck to lower. It never sounded so good.

I look over at the big black monster, and his eye is just a foot away staring straight into mine. I shudder. I'm just glad it doesn't blink. I crawl up on the biggest log, look down at the "sea monster" and shiver again. I watch the steamer closing the distance.

"So that's an alligator!" I've never seen one, except in a picture book. The animal starts to drift, and the men yell, tossing a smaller rope

"Tie it behind his front legs so it won't slip off!" The Captain points. "We'll have gator for supper tonight!"

I do it, though I'd just soon not. I do like the feel of the big gator's skin— rough and leathery. One of those fine gentlemen who made the shot un- doubtedly will want a pair of boots out of it, or a maybe wallet.

Two deckhands lower the loading crane and hoist the big reptile onto the front of the boat. I gasp at it's size. It surely intended to make a meal of me!

"Damn! 'Leven feet, eight inches!"

A man with a thick waxy mustache and a thick Cajun accent exclaims, "Didn't know y'all growed them this big up here! I thought these big ones only traipsed around in the Atchafalaya swamps and below."

While I get the heavy cable around a big log, the captain sends over one of the small rescue boats to pick me up. He's had enough of this kind of ex- citement for one day. He has a schedule to keep, and this isn't helping. I climb back up on the deck.

"Glad you're okay, son. You had me worried there for a bit. God's watchin' over you. Don't ever take that for granted. Just means he's got somethin' for you to do." He looks at his watch, and grins. "Since its four o'clock, take the rest of the day off, Lummy. You earned it."

Good food and a soft bed with music and laughter in the gambling hall up above puts me out like a light. I wake from napping to spend my evening sitting at the front of the steamer watching the river and the banks passing by. It's beautiful in the moonlight.

It's twilight when we swing out into the Mississippi River. I gasp at the sight of the wide expanse of water all flowing in the same direction. This river is more than anyone could ever describe. We arrive at Vicksburg just as the sun disappears, so I don't get a good look at the city. But I'm ready to get across to Desoto and on to Winn Parish, wherever that is.

With my small backpack over my shoulder and squirrel gun in hand, I start down the gangplank when the Captain yells, "Hold up there, sailor!"

I turn, pointing to my chest. "Me?"

"Been thinkin' on it. That surely was a brave thing you did back there on the Yazoo. That big gator made for some fine eatin'and will make a fine pair of boots for this captain. You get the plate of fried gator I sent down to you and Lige?"

"Yassuh, it chews like pork and just as tasty! Thank you!" He hands me an extra five dollar gold piece to go with the ten he already paid and a silver chain with a one of the alligator's big front teeth dangling at the end.

"The extra money is for doin' an extra fine job. The gator tooth necklace? Well, it's to remind you there's danger where you least expect it. I hope you'll wear it. It'll bring you good luck. See you again, son."

I immediately put it around my neck. It's a good memory I'll carry to my grave as a lesson to keep my eyes sharp for other "gators" I'm sure will come into my life.

"Heck, Uncle Silas ain't got nothin' on me with his story about him fightin' that river man, Mike Fink."

CHAPTER 8

LOUISIANA BOUND

MARCH 6, 1859

You never know what lies in the darkness underneath
the soul of a man, woman, or river.

I SIT ON the dock waiting for Hall's Ferry to make it back from the Louisiana shore. Waves from a passing steamer splash up to wet my legs. I get up on a hogshead of molasses and listen to the pipe organ as the boat goes downriver. A westerly wind kicks up off the face of the river and nearly blows the hat off the head of an over-dressed gambler smelling of cheap whiskey walking up. He grabs the black hat with a silver buckle just before it flies into the water. Rain in the air. I can smell it. Lightning flashes miles away to the west. A storm is coming.

Dark clouds hide the moon struggling to peek through a faint circle to let her light shimmer on the water. Ring around the moon. A night to be watchful, Granny Thankful always said.

She'd go through the house warning, "Trouble's comin'! Bad weather on the way! Spirits about! Hide your young'uns or the creepers'll get them! Fairies about! Cover your mirrors, guard them! Keep your eyes on what your doin' because somethin' out there surely has theirs on you!"

Granny was very superstitious, but me, I really don't believe tales from the old country. I believe God has things in hand with the help of his angels. At least when I keep my hands off them. It seems that when I take charge of my life, I tend to mess it up. Badly. I look into the black expanse revealing no stars of hope and chuckle. Granny's right, things do seem happen when the moon ain't herself. My feet are wet. A sign?

At 7:30 p.m., the ferry master makes the call and we board. No one talks. The few passengers keep looking up at the "bad moon." An older well-dressed and extremely polite couple board the ferry with help from their young slave boy. He is also well-dressed and speaks in perfect English. I can tell they have treated him well.

The boy looks up at his master. "Suh, we will have trouble in this crossing."

The lady puts her hand to her mouth. "Lamar, you know he's got the gift. He's said such things before, and something bad always happens." Other passengers watch the boy gazing intently at the moon. I believe his words.

The water rolls a bit, fat from early spring snow melt and heavy rains from up north. Eddies boil in the dim moonlight, like the Cold Hole spring bubbling up in the cypress forest where Susannah and I swam in McCurtain Creek swamp. So peaceful. This doesn't have that look.

I can just make out the Louisiana shore when a deck hand yells, "Look out!" A deep groaning sound, much like the gator made just before it died, rises from the depths of the river. It starts low but gets louder by the second. I look around, not knowing what to do. My muscles tense. Something's coming, but I can't see it. It sounds like it's coming from everywhere.

"Grab that pole and get ready!" I dash but in the wrong direction. "The upriver side, boy, on the upriver side!" Then, like a monster from the deep, a large tree roars high into the air like the Devil himself come up from the darkness of Hell reaching the extent of its leafless limbs. It rears straight up like a great dragon twisting violently to escape the depths of the dark water. Its spider-like roots aim for our flatboat. I watch the tree rise, and in a wink it crashes alongside our boat sending rail splinters flying. Two deckhands rush to join me.

The monster heads straight at me rolling and flailing like a dying animal. The other men catch the tree in mid-air with their poles and shove it with the same groans as the tree. I plant my feet against the wheel of a wagon at the end of the boat ready to take my turn, but it's too slippery. The tree shudders and rises again in the boiling mass. As it falls, I reach hard to shove it back out away from the boat when a large branch thick as my leg swings at me and slaps my shoulder harder than I've ever been hit. I go flying into the lower part of the deck flat on my back. It makes a final strike at its opponent before retiring back into the depths of darkness. The tree disappears into the deathly river swirl.

The passengers raise a cheer. I wake to the sound of the two deck hands, rudder man, and four passengers laughing their heads off.

A deckhand yells, "What'n the hell was that, boy? I guess that's what them ballerina girls look like when they decide to make one of them fancy jumpin' moves." It's like someone's hit me with a brickbat several times. I just lay still.

The blow must've knocked me out for a few seconds. It takes a minute for me to recover and clear my head. The older gentleman's wife washes my face with cool water, and the slave boy puts smelling salts under my nose.

The older gentleman asks, "What happened, young feller?"

I shake my head. I try to get up but a sharp pain wrenches through my right shoulder. I don't move. I can't. It's like I'm frozen, hoping I haven't broken anything, and at worst not be paralyzed.

"Get up, boy," a deckhand cries out, "You ain't that hurt, are you?"

"Don't touch me, not just yet. I'll be all right, just don't move me." I sound mad, but I'm not. It's just that I can't move, and I can't breathe. The tree knocked the wind out of me, and my shoulder hurts something fierce.

The slick gambler in his gaudy garb filing his fingernails says with no emotion, "Saw it all. Tree got his shoulder on its way out. His pole slipped, and that old beast got one last lick in for havin' been uprooted somewhere up north. Knocked him right off his feet and out of his shoes!" He points to my boots lying on the deck of the ferryboat. "Any closer, it would've split his head wide open, I do believe."

The older lady looks up at the gambler. "You almost got killed, son."

Her husband jokes, "Yes, but I do say, that was as fine a feat of circus acrobatics I've seen in some time!" The crew and passengers laugh, relieved that I seem to be all right. I'm not laughing.

I stand up dizzily, shaking my head, with a strong pain in my shoulder. Something's not right there. The faint blurry lights of a few small houses blink through the growing fog on the Louisiana side in the nothing of a little town called DeSoto.

The ferry master announces, "Yep, DeSoto is the beginnin' or the end of the rail line from Shreveport, whichever you prefer!"

The railroad elevators and tracks look like they're dancing. I'm weak, and my shoulder throbs. The ferrymaster gives back my fare, apologizing for the accident. I tell him not to worry.

The older gentleman set me up in one of the nicer shacks for the rest of the night to recuperate. I barely remember walking up the porch steps and falling into bed. Somebody gives me a spoonful of laudanum. About the time I lay down the storm hits, and the rain pounds hard on the tin roof. It's like music to my ears, but I don't hear it for long. I hear a strange voice that seems far away. I don't know if man or woman. I don't care. I just want to sleep.

SOMEBODY NOISILY BRUSHES the curtains open to let a burst of sunlight in that hurts even with my eyes shut. "What, where am I, what time is it?"

A stout, gruff sounding woman with a face that can turn sweet milk to clabber squawks like a jaybird, "Dinner's ready soon, honey, and you'll be wantin' it before you go."

"Dinner? Is it that late?"

"You wasn't goin' nowhere, anyway. Up 'til just a bit ago, it was rainin' so hard the animals went to pairin' up lookin' for Noah!" I laugh, but I'm stiff.

Still trying to remember where I am and how I got here, I peek through sleep swollen eyelids wondering what the commotion's about. I can't help noticing that if the loud he-man sounding woman was just two inches shorter she'd be completely round. She's cheerful enough, though.

I try to get up, but a sharp pain shoots through my right side and shoulder.

"Ain't what you used to be, are you? Hurts, don't it? Figured on that, with what Mistuh Fancy-pants told me all about what happened to you. Here, drink this, all of it."

I drink what feels like liquid fire. I cough and choke on the concoction.

"Good'ern snuff for what ails you. Guaranteed to burn the hair right off your tongue!"

I don't ask what's in the tin cup, but in a few minutes I do feel less pain.

"It's a wonder you wasn't killed dead out right! Many a good man found his everlastin' home with the catfishes in that damned ole river." She spits snuff juice into a small jar pulled from her apron pocket and grins with streaks of brown spittle staining her chin. She's so buck toothed she could eat corn through a picket fence. I can't tell if she's black, Indian, Mexican, or if a mix of all three. She sounds like a foul mouthed Cajun with a strong smell to match her language.

My Granny Thankful used to dip the light brown powder too, but always discreetly, and never like a pig wallowing in slop. This poor soul uses little discretion. Still, I'm thankful.

She whisks around the room like a happy wife. "Don't worry son, I ain't lettin' a drop get down in the cook pot. But, ponderin' on it a bit now, snuff juice might just give my possum stew a right interestin' flavor!" She cackles as she gives the stew a stir. I swear she sounds just like an old hen laying an egg.

"By the way, Lummy, I'm known around about here as Annie Fanny. That's because I got a big one!" She turns around to make her rear known. She really doesn't have to, it's all too obvious. "You get your clothes on, and I'll dip your dinner."

I lay in the bed for a moment waiting for the last of the pain to pass. Annie Fanny keeps on talking, never stopping. Dang, her mouth flops like a barn door in a wind storm that nobody can latch shut. I tune her out. I think about Granny Thankful as I dress.

Granny died when I was young. I miss her. Anytime we'd visit, she'd always reach up from her short four foot eight inch height to grab us by the shoulders and turn us around to kiss us on the back of the neck. Then she'd reach in her pocket and pull out a sweet she'd been saving for each of us children. She was a good old soul who talked to the Lord like he's sitting right here, and then him with her. It's called the mystical way—experiencing God's presence all around, all the time, everywhere, especially in the one place he wants to be found most—deep in the soul of a human being. I like that. It was the way Jake prayed back in Greenwood.

Granny also told ghost stories around the fire at night of headless horsemen, chains dragging through the house, and bumps in the attic. She scared the living daylights out of us little ones.

When she sent us to bed, she'd point her finger, "Don't forget to put a colander under your bed to confuse the haints 'cause they gotta count all them holes before they can come get you!"

I'd cover my head up for fear of seeing some sort of haint staring back at me in the dark. I'm sure I saw one or two back then. Occasionally, it'd make little Jasper wet the bed, and we'd all have to get up to change bed clothes.

But I've finally met a real haint right here in this shack on this muddy Mississippi River bank. A poor lost soul wandering into things that'll probably get her hurt one day with the wrong man.

I roll over careful not to bump my aching shoulder. I plant my feet flat on the floor and reach for my pants. I keep looking at her, hoping she'll leave so I can dress.

"Don't worry son, I've had five brothers, a husband, and a few other fellers in between, so's you ain't got nothin' I ain't never seen to-o-o many times." She grins batting her eyes.

I bet that's right. She lets go a laugh that sounds like a cotton house door hinge screeching in high wind.

"Come on, let's eat, you'll feel better."

I check for my money. "Oh, good, still in my sock."

"And nobody stole the money in your damn sock, boy!"

"Thank you, ma'am, ain't always you meet up with good honest folks." This woman has to say something about everything. She's windy as a sack full of poots, as they say.

I sit down to a fine meal of ham hocks, purple speckled butterbeans, buttered cornbread, and peach cobbler. I worried I'd be having possum stew with snuff juice. This is a feast fit for a president.

Sipping my coffee slowly, I rub my shoulder. The small rounded woman gets up to grab a can of something. She waltzes slowly, twirling around like a saloon dancer, pulls back my shirt and starts applying a strange smelling but soothing ointment to my shoulder. It burns a bit, but I feel the heat deepening into my flesh. She smiles, winking at me as she rubs my chest in a way that tells me the ointment ain't the only heat in the room. I nearly laugh out loud thinking of what Grandpa used to say about fat, lazy, overfed women.

"Damn son, if the Injuns came down on us in a hurry and she had to haul ass, it'd take her at least two trips." I ain't really looking, but that thing following behind her is hard to miss in such a small room.

Annie Fanny ain't lazy, but boy is she thick. She goes into the next room rattling around bottles when the worst perfume I've ever encountered wafts in like a skunk just showed up. She's up to something.

Annie comes twirling back with enough make up on to render her unrecognizable and perfume to chase off all the flies. Say what you will, you can't make a silk purse out of a sow's ear. You can put a high meringue on a shit pie, but it'll still taste like shit. I try to talk about something that hopefully will change the course of where I hope this isn't headed.

"Annie Fanny, did a fancy dressed gamblin' man packin' a few slaves with him come through anytime lately?"

"Sure did, my honey Mistuh Lummy, why? You be a friend of his?"

"Oh no, not really. He took a my good friend's money back in Choctaw County. I want to steer clear of him!"

"Yeah, and you know what else I be knowin', Mistuh Lummy? My man Obe won't be home for another two days. Gone to pull his fishin' traps down around Bruinsburg. Hell, even when he's here he stays drunker'n a jaybird hangin' upside down in a crabapple tree!"

Smiling, she throws her hip out and offers, "Free room and board with something else on the side if you stay a day or two. What you say there, good lookin'?" She gives a quick wink and starts bouncing her hip up and down.

"Ooo-wee, Lummy, you be fine as frogs' hair and as sweet as Cleopatra's wine!" She rubs my shoulder again, which is becoming an unpleasant experience. There it is. I knew something was up with all that prissing around.

"But what about your husband?" She gently pulls the short hairs on the back of my neck.

"Hell, he don't matter no how. My man, Obe? He's so damn ugly his Momma used to take him everywhere she went so she didn't have to kiss him goodbye!" Annie giggles like a school girl making the best grade in class. The blow of her words on my heart hurt like the tree hitting my shoulder last night.

"You just never know what lies in the darkness underneath the soul of a river, or a woman, for that matter. Anythin' might pop up and get you in ways you never expected or ever wanted." I catch myself talking out loud again. She pops me on my back.

"What'd you say? Get your shirt on boy. What's your decision?"

What am I supposed to say? What can I say? I've ever been spoken to in such a direct way about such sensitive things in all my life! I call on my bit of schooling, the poetry I've read, and the gentlemanly ways my Ma taught me. I try sweet talking her but in the other direction.

"Ma'am, that's a mighty tempting offer, with such beauty of which a man could most divinely partake. But I must regrettably decline, for I have someone special I'm to meet in just a few days. I could not honestly look her in the eye with purity of heart if I pleasured myself with a fine, ravishing beauty such as yourself!"

Annie Fanny blushes and tries to hide her smile at the compliment with three dark stained teeth showing out from underneath her hand.

I almost say out loud, "Whew, Lord, forgive me, You know I'm a damn bald-faced liar." I guess it's better to use what Pa calls "righteous deception" than participate in such craziness. I pack up fast, grab a couple of biscuits filled with fried salt pork leftover from the breakfast I'd slept through, and start out. Annie meets me at the door, hikes her leg up on a stool so that her calf showed as big as a deer's hind quarter and about as hairy.

"You best know next time I might not let you get away so easy." She hangs her head. "I respect you though, stayin' true to your woman and all. I wish I could do that with my man."

I nod politely and slide past her, barely getting by her roundness. I squeeze by scraping the door, and she laughs as I squirm out like grease from a wagon wheel hub.

"Gimme a little sugar before you go, Lummy, will you?" I lean over, give her peck on the cheek. She laughs, pops me on the bottom, and shoves me on out the door.

"Take care, Lummy Tullos. You're a good man. Follow the Vicksburg and Texas railroad track to Monroe, then get directions there for wherever the hell else you'll be goin'.' See you when you come back through, boy, and I will for sure. There's war comin', and you'll be right in the middle of it, you watch!"

She's still talking as I wave and walk at a fast pace. She yells, "Watch out for them ruffians at the rail bridges! They like to hide under 'em and shoot you in the back once you cross. And keep your eyes peeled for them damn coyotes!"

I take one last look before I go around the bend and can hear Pa saying, "Dang, I'd guess that woman to measure out to be at least four axe handles wide!" I wonder, But what's a coyote?

The land is flatter than a corn fritter, much like the delta country we steamed through from Greenwood. Every thirty minutes I turn and the Vicksburg bluffs are getting smaller. I'm still amazed at the height they command.

Annie Fanny said it was about seventy-five miles to Monroe where the track ends. That's about four good days walking. All I need to do now is find Winnfield and my sweetheart.

"I'll whisk her away in the dark of night like a dry wind picking up the morning dew, and as the fairy tales say, live happily ever after." I know it won't be that easy.

Taking a valuable piece of property away from a rich southern cotton planter is risky and dangerous business. A hanging offense. Even if this Mr. Gilmore is kind to his slaves, business is still business. And most folks don't take to another messing with their livelihood. I can't think on that right now, so I sing a few lines of Oh! Susanna.

Few people wander near the tracks. For those who get too close, I keep my hat pulled down and step up the pace making sure they see my squirrel gun. I look for no trouble and want none to find me. I pass through the few buildings at the small village of Richmond at a wagon road crossing and just tip my hat to an old lady sitting on the lone store porch with a cat in her lap. She lifts a hand to lightly wave. I keep walking. After Richmond, I see no one.

I only make ten miles first day. I'm better than this, even getting started so late in the day, but I do need to give the shoulder a good rest. I find a small cedar grove, crawl underneath a big one with low hanging branches to hide me, and wrap up for the night. It's a cool evening, but I make no fire. Too risky. I don't want to deal with any unwanted visitors. I figure anybody trailing west this way is either running from something or bent on doing who knows what when they get there.

I chuckle and shake my head. "Dang. Annie Fanny."

CHAPTER 9

ROAD TO WINN PARISH

MARCH 9, 1859

Never try to outrun a hungry coyote. 'Cause there's never just one.

SMOKE! A FIRE! How far is it? Two hundred yards, a half mile? I'm winded, sucking air like a newborn calf on his Momma's tit. They're behind me, panting. They sound like they're just catching their second wind. I'm losing my last bit of breath. It's like I have a ball and chain on each leg like the prison boys on the road building crew back home. I'm about done in. I don't know much longer I can run. My lungs are about to burst.

Coyotes, I figure. Never seen one but expect they're every bit as dangerous as the wolves we cleaned out years ago back in Choctaw County. Would coyotes do this? I don't know what they're capable of. We don't have any back home, mostly just red and grey fox, bobcat, and an occasional panther. But they never really bother anybody.

Though Monroe town lights flicker through the trees, there'll be no help from that direction. I break out of the brush and run faster on the road workmen have cleared for the new tracks yet to be put in. The coyotes follow, and I'm losing the race.

One lunges at me, snapping his jaws at my leg. I dart to the left just in time, and he rolls off into the bushes. I check my old one-shot flintlock in case they catch me. Damn! That's no good. The powder has blown out of the pan, and I can't stop to find my flask somewhere in my pack. I pull out my hunting knife.

The coyotes seem to enjoy the chase with each step I run, whooping it up and howling like a pack of Uncle George's prized blue tick hounds tracking a raccoon. I don't even have the breath to yell for help. God, is this it? I don't look back. I just keep running. The fire comes closer and closer. I can't feel my legs anymore. I'm about to throw up.

I run into the camp, fall to my knees, and somehow I get the breath to yell, "Don't shoot, don't shoot, got a pack of wild dawgs hard on my tail, and they're about to bite it off!" I puke.

The coyotes come roaring in, skidding on their heels, falling over each other, growling and snapping their teeth at us. The stranger fires off three shots quicker than a rattler strike, killing two, and the rest disappear into the shadowy night. Wiping my mouth, I look up at a pistol pointed right at me.

A stranger in fine city clothes laughs. "Relax, friend, you're safe now." I lay over on my back exhausted, out of breath, unable to form words. The stranger is patient and throws a couple more pieces of wood on his fire. The flames blaze up, and I can see my savior's long lean face, wearing all black with a gold watch chain dangling from his vest pocket. A man of means.

"Thanks for not shootin' me, suh. Them wild dawgs near about got me. I'm guessin' they was coyotes or somethin'? Never seen one, but I was warned about them. I just knowed I was gonna be ate alive out there in the dark or get gut shot comin' in here so fast without warnin', one or the other. When I saw your fire, I took my chances. Thanks, suh. I owe you."

"Yep, it was a hungry pack of coyotes for sure. Stop thankin' me so much, and don't call me suh. Suh was my old Pap back in Alabamy, and he's in a graveyard up near the Shoals. I figure we're about the same age, and dang it, sure was gettin' a bit boring out here anyway. Where you from, and where you headed? First, there's some clean water over in that pot for washing. Damn boy, you're bleedin' like a stuck pig! How'd that happen?"

I pull a small cloth from my bag and wash the blood from my arms, neck, and head. "Went through a briar patch just before I saw your fire. Thanks for the water. I'm Lummy Tullos, from Choctaw County Missip, headed to Winn Parish, that is, if I don't get killed first."

The stranger's eyes glisten in the firelight. "So what about the pistol you just seen in action, pretty sweet, huh?"

I stop washing my face for a second. "Sounds like music to my ears."

"Still sportin' your grandpa's ancient squirrel shooter, I see. Why didn't you shoot?"

"The dang powder blowed out of the pan, and I couldn't stop to prime it up! So I ran like the Devil bein' chased by Saint Michael!"

The stranger with the black hat hefts the big pistol in his hand, checking it for balance, rechecking the cocking mechanism. "Yep, eighth wonder of the world, this brand new Colt Dragoon in the much larger .44 caliber than the Colt Navy .36. Same fine weapon but the .44 sure packs a bigger wallup. Knock a man flat on his ass at thirty paces. Shoots six times, smooth and sweet. Handles soft as a whore's big titties.

"Want to hold her?" I reach out my hand, and he shoves it to me butt first. "She's loaded now, so be careful." It's amazing, smooth handle, revolving cylinder, and perfectly weighted balance. I don't dare cock it for fear I might make it go off.

"Bet you ain't never seen anythin' like it in Choc-a-taw Miss-a-ssippity!"

"Never." I hand it back, and he pulls out a small cigar.

"Maybe I'll let you shoot her in the mawnin'."

"Now that'd be a treat, for sure." The stranger is an intelligent and cultured man. He reminds me of what people have said about that Mister Gilmore I'm following, carrying refinement with him wherever he travels.

"May I ask your name?"

"Rainy Mills is my name. It happened to be rainin' frogs the day I was born, and my Momma couldn't think of no better name, so she called me Rainy. And Mills? Well, she didn't have no choice about that part. I'm a gun dealer. I sell all sorts of fine weaponry and sportin' arms you may need, ammunition, shootin' lessons, and I even tell good stories to boot. The stories are free, though. But you, Lummy Tullos, you look to have a good story to tell."

I duck my head, not used to being put on the spot so quickly by a man I don't know at all. "I got a story in the makin' as we speak, but the biscuits ain't ready to come out the oven just yet. Don't know how it'll end up, but I know what it is up 'til now." I tell him about my journey to Winnfield.

About Susannah, too, though I don't mention she's a slave. I don't know why I open up so. I believe I can trust him. After all, he did save my backside from the coyotes.

He listens intently, which is a bit unnerving. "You're a man on a mission, Lummy Tullos, no doubt about it. Don't know if it's for love, money, runnin' from somethin', or simply bold adventure, maybe all of that, but there's good in you. I see it. Don't let no one say there ain't!"

Rainy quickly reaches to scratch his back like a bug is crawling on him. "And the way you talk about God without preachin' at a feller, well, I like that about you, too. So, I want to help you on your journey. It won't be a lot, and you'll have to earn it, but you wouldn't want it no other way, would you?"

I shake my head. He pulls a monster of a gun from a soft leather case. "I'm to deliver this brand new ten gauge double-barreled shotgun to a man where you're headed two days from now. If I do that, I'll be late gettin' on over to Shreveport where I could make some profitable sales. I never miss a good profit. Tomorrow I hope to catch a northbound coach to Shreveport from Monroe. So, for a five dollar gold piece and supper tonight, I'd like you to take this scattergun to Winnfield and deliver it to it's proud owner. You are an honest man, aren't you?" His eyes twinkle, searching as he speaks.

"I am, and I'll not be lettin' another man say different, Rainy Mills."

"Don't take it personal, my friend. I am a business man, so your word needs to be as good as the gold in this here coin, and it's pure. So you best be true to it," staring at me intently fumbling the coin through his fingers.

"I done told you, I won't let you down."

He stares back like a man who's been in a scrape or two and is about to get into another when he laughs loudly, slaps me on the knee. "You're all right, Lummy, but just a bit too serious. We'll have to work on that!" He's right.

"Who do I deliver this gun, too, and how am I gonna find him?"

Rainy grins. "Oh, with that cannon in hand, he'll find you in Winnfield town, sometime Saturday week. Find Davis's Store and say hello to Mistuh Wiley, if that ole coot's still livin'."

"So, what's the name of this fella who wants this goose cannon?"

Rainy pokes the fire. "Why, that'd might be some of your kin folks, I'm bettin'. Benjamin Franklin Tullos!"

"Ben Tullos? How? When? I can't believe it. We ain't seen him in years. How well do you know him? Is he doin' all right?" My words fire off fast as the pistol he unloaded at the coyotes.

Rainy lies back on the log behind him, "Well, that's just perfect! Grab a bowl of that stew, and I'll tell you all about it. Plucked that cane cutter off a stump just this afternoon with this here pistola at thirty paces. There's a duck, a couple of puldues, and a coot in there, too. I just had to try out this ten gauge this morning. One shot got all four. I waited 'til they all lined up. Sounded like I blew up the whole damn place when both barrels touched off. Bet they heard it in Vicksburg!"

I sit down with my legs crossed like a child just handed a fresh-baked cookie. "Eat up now, you gotta be pretty hungry after bein' chased by them coyotes. Help yourself to the corn pone, it's good for dippin' in the gravy. Say your prayer first, though, out loud if you don't mind. I need some good God words. Then I'll tell what I know about your brother."

I pray a short one. I'm just too hungry to pray a Pastor Dobbs sermon long prayer and too excited to hear about Ben. "How long did them coyotes chase you?"

"I figure about a quarter mile."

"Well, I knew you had to be an all right feller, announcin' to the world how you didn't want to get shot runnin' into my camp. But I swear, I never seen such fleet of foot in all my life! You was runnin' faster'n a damn scalded dog! Like you was runnin' on your toenails."

I don't tell him that was the nickname a childhood friend gave me because I was the fastest runner at school.

Rainy lights his pipe. "I heard of a man over in Choctaw County known to be the fastest man around and the best shot. They say he even chased a deer down once after he shot at it. But when he caught up with it and saw he'd missed, he just let the poor exhausted animal go. You ever hear of anythin' like that?"

"Yep, they call him Reel, and he could knock a squirrel out of a hundred foot treetop and most times he shot 'em right between the eyes!"

The other man blows a smoke ring. "That's him, from some crazy-named place, can't seem to remember."

"Dido."

Rainy points his finger at me. "That's it. Always knew Missip boys to be good hunters, but I'm tryin' to make my livin' on men movin' in a westerly direction, you see. Huntin' goes where the game is, guns need to go where the hunters are, and Missip, sad to say, ain't the paradise it used to be, is it?"

He sits up. "Well, you've told me a good story about yourself there, Lummy, so let me tell you one while you choke down your supper. There was this old man loved gettin' up early before the sun rose so he could sit on his front porch and sip his mornin' coffee. A young feller came by about dawn one day and went into the woods across the road. About nine o'clock he came out carryin' four or five squirrels by the tail in each hand like they'd been shot, but there wasn't no blood. The old man scratched his head, wonderin' how that boy got all them squirrels, but he ain't heard no shots. The young feller came back in a day or so and did the same thing. He went into the woods, stayed three or so hours, and came back out with four or five squirrels, red and grey, in each hand. After about the third time, the old man just couldn't stand it no more. So when the young feller came out the woods, the old man yelled out, 'Hey, young man, got a minute?' The young man walks over, 'Yassuh, I do.

"The old man, scratching his scraggly beard and rubbing his nearly bald head said, 'I been watchin' you bring out all them tree rats these past few mornins. Don't mean no harm, but you ain't carryin' no squirrel gun with you, and I surely ain't heard nary a shot. How'n hell you killin' all them damn cat and fox squirrels, son?'

"'Well, suh, it's a secret, but if you keep it to yourself, I'll tell you.' The old man moves up to the edge of his rocking chair, spilling a little of his coffee on his pants as he sets the tin cup on the table beside him.

"The young man looks around, 'When I find a good hickory or acorn tree, I get real quiet like. I wait 'til I spy a good'n, then I sneak up on him keepin' a tree between us. All sudden like, I look around the tree and give him the most ugliest face I know how.' The boy makes a most hideous face, then smiles. 'I ugly him to death. Yep, that's what I do. Works every time!'

"'Ugly him to death? Can't be, but you say it works every time?' The old man rubs his chin whiskers again.

"'Yep, and I used a take my wife with me, but she tore them up too bad!'"

Rainy doubles over in laughter, howling like the coyotes that chased me into his camp. I can't help but laugh hard, tickled by the joke that catches me off guard. It's the best story I've heard in a long time, though a man might get into trouble if he has a wife close at hand. Rainy ain't the marrying type.

I eat 'til I nearly burst while Rainy tells me what he knows about Ben. I doze a little with the bowl in my hands, still chuckling about the funny story. I'm pretty spent after walking all day and running the last leg. My shoulder aches, and he hands me the rum bottle he's nursing. I take a swig, hand it back.

"Not bad for roadside cuisine and campfire stories, huh, Lummy? I always carry a few spices for the stew and a few spicier stories for the fire."

That's all I remember. I guess the rum went to my head quickly. I sleep hard. The sun flittering through the tree leaves wakes me to find a blue dragonfly sitting on my nose. It tickles as it flies away when I start to scratch the itch. I sit up to rest on my elbows, but stop, for my head aches a bit, and my shoulder is still too sore to lean on. Rainy's gone. On the log by where he slept is a note with some pencil scratching on it, the ten gauge shotgun with a two pound bag of shot and some wadding, and a five dollar gold piece.

March 10, 1859

Lummy Tullos thanks for helping me out. I'm glad to know you and expect to see you again soon. There's a war comin Lummy, and we all will be in it. When I come through Winnfield in a few months I'll sell you one of these .44 Colt Dragoons for what it cost me. Save your dollars. Believe you me boy you'll be glad you have it when the time comes. Finish up the stew

I left for you in the bowl with the kerchief over it. To make the 50 miles to Winnfield, take the southwest road to Indian Village then to Vernon and on to Rochester. After that go left when the road forks, and you'll find Winnfield town easy in two days. I now count you as a good friend Lummy, and that means a lot where I come from.

Your friend Rainy Mills.

I brush away a few red ants that found my breakfast, gulp down the tasty concoction, pack up, and set out for Winnfield at a good pace. Rainy's right, a war is coming. I need that like a man needs another hole in his head. That's what I'll get if I don't take the possibility of me going seriously. Too many people I've met on this journey talk about it. Anyway, I look forward to Rainy's visit to Winnfield. That and another one of his funny stories.

Benjamin Franklin Tullos. My big brother! Don't really know him as a man. I have mixed memories—some good, some not too good. I'm hoping for better times.

I take to the road feeling better, but I have a ways to go. "Ain't no hill for a stepper," as Uncle Rube used to say. But he wasn't carrying a ten gauge shotgun on a messed up shoulder.

CHAPTER 10

WINNFIELD, WINN PARISH, LOUISIANA

MARCH 13, 1859

Crusty ole souls have the sweetest fillin' inside if you wait 'til the pie's done.

I GET TO Winnfield town early afternoon, if you can call it a town. A farmer watering his stock as I cross the Dugdemona River laughs when I inquire about the city.

"City, ha! You got yourself six or seven damned ugly houses, two mercantile stores, and a grist mill for corn grindin'." The farmer wasn't kidding. It's hotter than normal for this time of year, and my clothes are drenched with sweat. I wonder where all the people are. I start for the largest store when a grouchy old voice squawks like a blue jay out from under a covered porch.

"Whatever you lookin' for you won't find it here, son, because ain't nothin' in this damned place to find. Hell, you can't even find trouble here. Just because you're tall as a pine tree don't mean you can't be chopped down in a hurry if you don't act right! You lookin' for trouble, boy?"

I pull off my hat and wipe the sweat. The hatband sticks to my head.

I kick the dirt. "Nawsuh, but I'd surely like to borrow some of your shade and plop down on that smooth log bench next to you to rest my feet a spell."

"Well, get on up here! It's so damn dry the catfishes are carryin' canteens! Get in the shade, boy! Never want see another man die of the heat stroke again. I did, you know, down in ole Santy Anny land back in the war. Wasn't no pretty sight at the Paller Alter battle. Nawsuh, and sure as hell won't be now neither. Anyway, it's a free country, at least for now, they say. Sit a spell, and take away my boredom if you can."

He eyes me up and down, rocking his chair with the same rhythm of a steam engine chugging down the tracks and with about the same energy. He has one leg missing from the knee down and wears an old, stained, moth-eaten Mexican War jacket with three stripes on the sleeve. He seems far away, like he's still down in those hot dry deserts fighting the Mexican army. He taps his peg leg on the porch floor like he's mashing a bug. He seems friendly enough though.

"What's new in these parts, old timer?"

"What's new, you ask? Green as a damn gourd, you danged young saplin' you! What's new, fool, is *you!* And a wise ass, to boot. And speakin' of boots, I still got one good boot, and if you keep on, you and me gonna have a three-legged race to find Doc Wesley Cockerham."

That didn't go very well. I crossed some kind of a line. He keeps mumbling about me calling him an old timer. I wonder how he could run a three legged race when there's only three legs and a peg amongst us. It ain't hard to figure out where he would want the peg. I try not to snicker.

"Now hold on! I don't mean no harm, mistuh."

"Gotcha, boy, didn't I? Neither do I, meanin' no harm. But sure, give it another go. You got the look of a feller I've become quite fond of. Naw, must be my mind playin' ticks, I mean tricks, on me. Hell, probably got a few ticks on me too, dammit!"

"Who'd that be, suh?"

"Why that'd be Benjamin Franklin Tullos, and his pretty wife, Missus Dorcas Lewis Tullos from back across the Missip River somewhere. Good people, them Tullos folks. They live back south of here on that mistuh fancy pants high rollin' gamblin' feller James T. Gilmore's place down off the Alexandria Road. They work his ground. Doin' good too I hear."

I nearly burst with excitement. I scream inside, *Gilmore! Ben's workin' for Mistuh Gilmore?*

"Gilmore just got back a week or so ago with a batch a new slaves. Don't know about that feller, busier than a two dollar whore on nickel night. But he's rollin' in the dough. Always has a stack of greenbacks folded an inch thick! I keep my eye on him though, travelin' all around, always bringin' back three or four darkies. He must be stackin' them up like cordwood in them woods of his west of here. Hell, he'll talk your damn ear off if you let him! Man who talks too much surely tryin' to hide somethin', you think?"

I don't answer. Don't have to. He's already talking about something else before I can speak. The crinkle-faced, sassy-mouthed old man rails on for a bit, but I don't listen. My heart is about to leap out my chest like a bullfrog let out of a tow sack.

"Suh, now who did you say I favor?"

"Ain't you got no ears? Benjamin Tullos I done told you! We just call him Benny Frank around here." He smiles. "Don't mind me too much, son. I had a cannonball shave my pine knot when I charged the Mexicans at Paller Alter with Ole General Zach Taylor back in the War. I fought hard, and I fought good, but hell, I didn't get no medal." He yanks off his crumpled old hat to reveal a three inch wide hairless scar on the right side of his head.

"And I been an ornery ole bastard ever since. That danged Mex cannonball must've pulled my brain to the one side when it nearly took off my gourd. Should've give me a damned medal for it." I nod. "You don't know Benny Frank, do you, son?"

"Yassuh, he's my big brother from Choctaw County Missip! And that scar on your head? That's your medal. It's an honor to know you, suh." I stick out my hand.

"Hell, don't call me sir. We ain't in no damn army now! But put her right here, my new good friend!" I thought he would shake my arm right out of the socket which isn't far from doing just that with my river injury. "I'm W.O. Wiley, from Scotland years ago, but Winnfield's been my home for some time now." The jolt of his handshake stirs up my shoulder pain, and my right arm goes a bit limp.

"You hurt, boy?" I rub my shoulder.

"Aw, nothin' really, just had a tree fall on me when I crossed on the ferry at Vicksburg. It ain't been right since. A friend I met back on the road said it might be dislocated. You know Rainy Mills, the gun dealer? Said tell you hello."

"Yeah, I know young Rainy well. Good man and a fair dealer. I like that boy. Hope he's doin' good for himself. Fought with his daddy Leonard in the war. He didn't come back, though. Sit tight, I got somethin' for that shoulder right inside." He stops his incessant rocking abruptly and struggles to get up on his one good foot using his cane but stops, "What do you go by, son?"

"Columbus Nathan Tullos, suh." It's like a bullet hits him straight in the heart. Mr. Wiley sits back down and straightens up in his chair grabbing his chest.

"Damn, you Tullos boys sure have some fine soundin' hundred dollar handles! Your Momma and daddy must've been thinkin' you boys might amount to somethin' big some day. Hmmm, explorer and a prophet. Interestin' combination. We gave Benny Frank a better name not long after he got here, but what we gonna call you?"

"Folks back home just call me Lummy, short for Columbus."

He eyes me up and down again. "A big ole name with a damn big ole gun. What is that, eight gauge? Naw, it's a ten ain't it? And where you goin' with that goose cannon?"

"Rainy Mills gave me five cash dollars to deliver it to the new owner here in Winnfield."

"And you'll be deliverin' that goose slayer to who you say?"

"My big brother Benny Frank!"

"Now aint that somethin'? God's workin' his plan all over you, Lummy Tullos. You best be about followin' to 'cause you know how the Lord wants to succeed in whippin' that ole Devil! You believe in the Devil, Lummy Tullos?" Before I can answer, he leans over and whispers, "You best be, because he believes in you!"

"I understand the Lord done already put that Satan in a big ole hole somewhere, Mistuh Wiley, when Jesus jumped up out of that grave on resurrection mornin'."

Mr. Wiley throws his arm up into the air. "For sure, and as the Book of Revelation tells it, the war's already been won. There ain't no good against evil no more, just the battle for every good man and woman's soul. That

Devil wants every soul he can steal, and believe me, Lummy Tullos, Satan is good at what he does."

"Could you just call me Lummy, please, suh?"

Mr. Wiley grins and spits a stream of tobacco juice ten feet out into the street barely moving his head. His smile disappears, and he stares at me intently for what seems like an eternity but is only a few seconds I'm sure.

"You ain't no preacher, are you?" He laughs. "'Cause if you are, dammit, I'll have to go to church for sure this Sunday and repent of all my cussin'. You ever cuss, Lummy?"

"Only when my Momma ain't listenin'!"

Mr. Wiley slaps his knee.

"Nawsuh, ain't no preacher here, but I do try to honor our Creator as best I can. I've found, Mistuh Wiley, that sometimes the only word that'll work is damn. Truth be told, I came up with a solution to that problem. I have what I call cuss days, to get it all out, all on one day, no holds barred. It generally will hold me for another week."

He rubs his chin. "Never thought of doin' that, hmmm, cuss days. Might just work, savin' all them words up for one day. One day a week, you sayin'?" I nod. "Well hell, now wouldn't that be just fine, give it all you got cussin' up a tornado storm one day a week? Sure would be somethin' to look forward to, and a bit of discipline too, like back in my army days."

"Can you point me in the right direction to my brother's place? I'd surely be obliged. I'd like to get there before dark."

"Son, you don't want do that. It's a far piece with the snakes startin' to mate right about now. You don't want to get turned around out there at night. You could be wanderin' around for days before anybody found you. Son, this ain't civilized Choctaw County. This here's Winn Parish. There ain't nothin' in these parts but wild animals and wild people."

Civilized don't always mean civil.

"You'd do well to stay on here for tonight. I'll put you up and feed you muskrat stew with some soft-shell turtle cooked like them swamp Cajuns do it. And besides, your brother, Benny Frank, comes to town every other Saturday, and that ain't tomorrow. So, you got time to establish yourself a bit here, make a little pocket change over at Davis Feed and Seed. Then, you could make it a big reunion surprise. How about we get them vittles!" Mr. Wiley struggles to get up.

"But what if he comes and I miss him?"

"Hell, boy, look around! Ain't a hundred people livin' in this here town, and you think anythin' can happen or anybody can slip in and out of here without somebody noticin'? You go on over yonder to the mercantile, ask for Mistuh Davis. See if he needs a hand for a few days. They'll want to see that cannon you're carrying anyway. Tell them you know me, and that you're Benny Frank's brother. Better tell him it's to be a surprise, or else he won't keep it a secret. Good man but a windy mouth, that Missus Davis. He was lookin' for a help just the other day. Now, he's tighter'n bark on a willow tree, but he's fair."

Mr. Wiley steadies himself and stomps his peg leg like it might be coming off. "Anyway, he'll give you your meals and a cot in the back storeroom. He'll flip you a silver dollar or two if you work real good. Come on back, and I'll have the vittles waitin' on you. I'll make you a pallet bed on the floor for the night. Oh, and by the way, go around back and wash up a bit, you smell worse than a damn polecat! I'll bring you the liniment for your shoulder."

I don't say anything about Mr. Gilmore or Susannah and won't, not just yet. That'll come to me without trying. I'm just glad to be in the right place, finally, and not far from my sweetheart. I still can't believe Ben is working for the very man who has Susannah. Wait! That means I'll be crossin' paths with Susannah sometime soon. That's good but could also be trouble.

After I wash the stink off, and apply the liniment, I hoof it across the street to the store. I slick my hair back and knock the road dust off my clothes before I climb the steps. I must look a sight. Mr. Davis is kind though. I start work in the morning and get things squared away then.

I cross back over to sit on Mr. Wiley's porch. The sun sets in the west over the tall trees. A big blue heron lights in a cypress tree a hundred yards away near a slough close to town. Old Mr. Wiley is right. I can use the rest and a few more dollars before I meet up with Ben. We sit down to his small table in his one small room, the food steams up good and makes our mouths water.

The old man's whole demeanor changes instantly. He stills himself and sits silent for a moment. He folds his hands and drops his head.

"Lord, thanks for bringin' this young man here safely to meet up with Benny Frank. Give him your strength. Lord, forgive this old worn out hateful cussin' sinner. I truly mean no harm, Lord, so give me the good grace of Jesus. I surely need it. Thank you for this good food we know comes from you, as do all good things. In Jesus' name, Amen." Best prayer I've heard in a while.

He grabs the big spoon, plops a bit of muskrat stew and a few pieces of fried turtle on my plate. "Last one to the taters gets left out, I always say. Get you a piece of that cornpone on the stove and that cayenne pepper sauce. Eat up, you look half-starved."

I pull my plate to me. "I'm so hongry, Mistuh Wiley, my belly thinks my throat's been cut!"

After supper, I lay down on the soft goose feather pallet Mr. Wiley spread out for me.

"Sorry about your beddin' and everythin'. Ain't never had no Goliath-sized man stay over ever before. I guess your feet'll just have to hang off the end. Dang, you're tall, boy!"

The liniment feels good on my aching shoulder and hanging my feet off the end of the bed actually helps my aching ankles relax. I lay still, thanking the Lord for my good fortune. I have a lot to sort through—how I'll meet up with Ben and how he'll respond not knowing I'm in town. Calling him Benny Frank will take some getting used to. I don't know him. He left home when I was just starting to grow hair under my arms. Anyway, he's just plain ole Ben to me.

Ben left home at twenty-four with his new wife to make his way somewhere else. Nearly the oldest, he and Elihu got the worst of the unnecessary beatings from Pa. Before he left for good, Ben worked jobs around the county and would come back but never stayed long. The money he made was usually just enough to get him going someplace different.

He tried settling down near the family with the sweetest and prettiest gal named Dorcas. We all fell in love with her, if for no other reason than she was Ben's wife. Dorcas fell right in with Rebecca and Saleta, God rest her soul, as a perfect sister. Ben and Dorcas tried to make a go of it in Choctaw

County, but being so close to Pa made it a prison for him. Ben was never good enough for Pa.

Pa must've said a thousand times if once, "Man's gotta get some land, work it, or he'll never amount to nothin'!"

So, the day came in '48 when Ben bought his first forty acres at twenty-one years old—no small accomplishment. Boy did we have a big celebration for him and Dorcas! Ma made a fine meal and desserts that set you to begging for more. Our good friends the Wood and Ray families joined the festivities. They'd always help us in the fields during planting and harvest, and we them. The Woods always brought the best shine, made from the sweet water drawn out of Aaron Wood's Spring.

We each brought some sort of handmade gift or tool to help Ben's family get started. The big surprise for Ben and Dorcas though, was that we all agreed to build the barn and out buildings near the one room log cabin already on the place. With everyone pitching in, it'd only take a few days once the lumber was cut.

Ben and his young family drove up in his wagon just as things were getting started. He was so proud to be what his father had always taught him to be. We congratulated them and gave them our gifts. Ben saved passing before Pa until last to receive his word of blessing, the most important gift of all. Everyone got quiet, waiting for the words Pa would say to his son.

All he said was, "Well now, here comes the big farmer's idiot, prancin' like a ruttin' buck deer thinkin' he's gonna take on the whole world." Ben just stood there in front of Pa, holding his smallest child with the other peeking around from behind his pants leg.

"Comin' from you, I'll take that as a compliment." He went on past Pa with Dorcas holding her head down. Ben told me later that day he decided to leave Choctaw County. Less than five years after that, Ben and Dorcas packed up their stuff and little ones to head west. He left and never came back. We haven't seen them since, and that was 1853. We didn't know where. Not until now. It sounds as though he and the family have fared well. Ben was always the smart and resourceful one and a hard worker.

So I don't really know what to expect when I see him. Will he welcome

me as a brother or shoo me away like a horsefly? How will I see Susannah
without him or Dorcas knowing? I'll just have to take my chances when we
meet. After all, he's my brother, and blood's blood. I hope.

I've got a lot to sort out in my tired mind. It's coming at me too fast. I
need to quiet my spirit. A single star sparkles through a crack in Mr. Wiley's
roof. Now I don't go in for studying the stars to find my life path, but I do
believe God gives them to us to wish upon. So I gaze at the star, name it
Susannah, and ask God to let me see her soon.

"Shut your trap, son, and get some damn shut eye. Mistuh Davis is expectin' a couple of wagon loads of store stuffs tomorrow, and guess who gets to
unload and store it all away? Yep, that'd be you boy. You'll see Benny Frank
soon enough, and that Susannah girlie, whoever she is, too. You just best
hope I don't snore too loud and keep you up all night! Sleep tight, Columbus
Nathan Tullos, and pray God watches over us heathens one more night."

It's not long before he's snoring and thankfully, softly. I doze, dreaming
of how things will unfold and how I so want to wrap my arms around my
sweet Susannah.

MORNING BREAKS WITH a red sun parting the trees and people stirring
about. Mr. Wiley sits out on his porch, rocking his chair sipping hot coffee
from an old tin cup. His voice is deep, like a croaking bullfrog.

"Gonna rain later today, probably be a storm. You know what they
say, red sky at night, sailor's delight, but a red sky in the mawnin', sailor's
warnin'. It's in the Bible somewhere. Anyway, get you a cup of coffee and a
biscuit before you head to the mercantile. Mistuh Davis, he'll be lookin' for
you early, to sweep up and all. I'll see you after work, and don't forget the
kindness of an old man. When you get set, bring me some sweets from the
store if it ain't too much trouble. I'm partial to lemon drops."

"Before I go, I best write my Ma a letter."

"If you get it done quick, Philip will get it in the mail before it goes out this
afternoon. Yeah, Philip Bernstein, became our new postmaster last September

and does a right fine job. Mr. Davis gives him a little corner in the store to take care of the mail." He goes back rocking his chair and sipping his coffee.

Winnfield Looseana March 14, 1859

Dear Ma, I made it to my destination though I didn't know it'd be here. I had an interesting journey, but thank the Lord I made it in one piece. I'm in Winnfield Looseana fixing to start a new job at a feed and seed store. I'm finding friends already. The biggest news I got is I found Ben and Dorcas! How this happened only the Lord knows, but I should be seeing them the end of the week. How about that! I hope all is good at home, and I will write again when I have something more. Tell the rest I miss them.

Your loving son,
Lummy Tullos

I fold the small piece of paper. I'll get an envelope at the Feed and Seed. I start for the store when Mr. Wiley talks loud so passersby can overhear.

"The good Lord's got somethin' for you, Lummy Tullos, and don't you miss church this Sunday comin', you hear? I'll be lookin' for you." He points at three women whose noses are up in the air as if trying to avoid a bad smell.

He whispers, "Them good ladies of the church are puttin' on a feed this Sunday, and boy hidey, do they do it right. Fried chicken with all the fixins." Licking his lips, "Sure makes it easier to stomach the preachin', and that good grub'll carry you at least 'til next Sunday!"

He yells as I start across the street, "Now don't you forget to be in church because that preacher's gonna get us all up into heaven this Sunday for sure!"

I cross the street, watching the old bitties clucking, shaking their heads at Mr. Wiley. Their gossipy judgment of him is worse hypocrisy than his. The only difference, he doesn't deny his. He simply asks for mercy in his prayers.

"Good" church going folks have two vices they declare acceptable to the Lord. One is good food and too much of it. You can tell by the size of the backsides of the ladies who do the cooking and the bellies of the men who do most of the eating.

And second, gossip cloaked as a need to share some news we need to bring before the Lord, sister. Granny used to say, "Gossip is anythin' told that hurts another soul, true or not. Bad talk about somebody else just means a bad heart at the source."

And it ain't just the women who are guilty. The men do it, too. Only they don't pray about it. They just cuss the fools they talk about.

It's all gossip.

CHAPTER 11

A SHORT-LIVED
REUNION

MARCH 19, 1859

Stumblin' upon a long lost brother can be like findin' gold.
Sometimes fool's gold.

WORKING FOR MR. Davis isn't too bad. Even though he's a perfectionist, I'm learning how a store operates. He thinks he's giving me too much work—tidying up the store, fixing the roof, giving the store front a fresh coat of paint, besides the unloading and loading of supplies, and filling customer's orders. It must not be easy to get good steady help. The work is easy compared to what I was used to at home. The best thing about working at the mercantile is hearing all the news drifting in with every customer.

Mr. Davis is a gentle soul who has to deal almost constantly with a tongue wagging, nagging wife whom he just can't seem to please. Heck, she's so dang irritatin' she'd make a preacher cuss. Makes me cuss, and I ain't no preacher. Mrs. Davis wheels around glaring at me.

"Mistuh Tullos, is there somethin' you wish to say?" I swear that woman must have the ears of an elephant!

"No, ma'am, just talkin' to myself about nothin', but surely is a nice store you have here. Just came through Vicksburg, and your store here can run with the best of them."

I lie about how her store can rival those in the big city, none of which had I darkened the door. Her eyes fill with pride at my compliment. I know she heard my comment, but she doesn't press it. She knows good help is hard to find around here. But she can't let it go, having to have the last word.

"Well, it's best to keep one's thoughts to himself, don't you think, Mistuh Tullos?"

"I agree on both sides of that conversation, Missus Davis, yes'um." She jerks around and goes back to straightening the shelves.

I just keep my head down and stay out of her way. I'm not afraid of her at all. Really, I'm more afraid I might set her straight if she comes down too hard about something that matters too little. That wouldn't be good. I'd get fired, and Mr. Davis would catch hell. She's pretty hateful, but I learned early to turn a deaf ear to such talk living with a Pa who never seemed happy with anything us boys did.

It irritates her that, no matter how bad the crap is she dishes out, I can simply return it with the calmness of a gently running stream of cool refreshing water. I keep reminding myself of that verse about heaping red hot coals on an enemy's head by being good to them. After a while, she just gives up and goes back to giving poor old Mr. Davis hell again.

"Thanks, Lummy, there for a bit I thought I'd get a break, but nope, you killed her with your damned kindness. Where'd you learn to do that?"

"I guess I'm more like my Ma when I want be. It's somewhere in the Good Book that doin' good to those who hate you will either cause them to leave you alone or cause you to win them over. Don't remember which, but it seems to work. And, that's really all I'm here to do is give you a good day's work for your kindness. Besides, you hired me, she didn't."

I'm not trying to be a smart ass, but the only time I see her is if she comes out of the back from her incessant eating to gripe about something that really doesn't deserve griping about. And though she gripes, she is a good cook. I'm just glad the week passes quickly.

Not much happens worth writing home about except on Wednesday night. Mr. Davis invites me to a meeting in the back room of his store. I don't know what to expect, maybe a prayer meeting or some town board gathering. I'd wash up before supper and enjoy another fine meal Mrs. Davis has prepared. She's extremely sweet, now that I agree to come to the meeting.

The small group of a dozen or so, some I've met and some I haven't, sit around a table with their palms turned up. There's an old woman with a black veil that hides her face. She calls up unfamiliar names, but it's obvious they aren't in the room. Pa told us about these "spirit rappers." The old woman, once she contacts the spirit she wants, asks questions that will be answered with raps from the table legs. The table rises and raps once for "yes" and twice for "no."

The first time the table jumps, the hairs on the back of my neck raise up, and a chill slithers down my back like a cold snake. Then I get ahold of myself and notice that when the questions are asked, four of the group sitting at the corners of the table nod almost unnoticeably, and the table does its rapping. I ask one question about something that happened back home, but I get no answer. I guess I'm not in favor with the haints who supposedly make the table rise. After that, I just play along, counting it as an experience to tell the grandchildren someday.

SATURDAY! FINALLY, THE day Ben should come to town. About noon, two wagons roll up. Mr. Davis smiles and points at me. I look across the street, and Mr. Wiley, in his full Mexican War uniform, mouths silently, "It's him!" pointing a half-hidden thumb towards the approaching party. My heart starts dancing like little girls at a church social in early May. Ben leads the way, thick shouldered and strong looking, peering around town from underneath his broad brimmed hat.

Satisfied all is well, he lays the reins pretty hard across the rears of the two mules to back his wagon up to the porch. He wears a deep furrow on his forehead and a frown like Pa used to carry. I can't tell if it is his mouth or the long moustache he sports. It looks to be both.

I watch him from the big window in the store. He's a seasoned man with years of hard work on him, his eyes sharp and piercing. Ben bounces off the wagon and stretches.

"All right, we made it, let's get the goods and get on back home. I don't want to get caught in the storm that's comin' haulin' flour, beans, and especially the powder! Bart, we best tarp down good before we head back."

A couple of young boys and their sister jump from his wagon. The older black man is a bit slower getting off the wagon than Ben.

"Come on, Bart, hell we ain't got all day. You're movin' so slow I hear your joints creakin'. I best grease them up with some hawg lard, you think?" Ben laughs.

"That'd sure do it, Massuh Ben." He grins as he slides down the side of the buckboard. Ben laughs all right, but the hardness of our Pa is in him. And, that's the one thing I remember Ben said he would never become, like our Pa.

Ben possesses the wandering foot, too. We Tullos boys get that honest, all the way back to the old country. But the anger is a family trait passed down as well. I remember when Ben left for good. After he and Dorcas married and he bought his first forty, Ben worked down on the Yazoo River between planting and harvest. Trying to get started in this world, he was putting money together, for what, Ma and Pa didn't know. But I knew. It wasn't about what he'd do with the extra money, it was about where. He planned to leave.

Pa had a good reputation around town but treated his family like dirt. Ma would leave the room or turn her head and cry when the beatings started. Once Ben stopped by on leave from his steamboat job clearing logjams and gathering wood for fuel. He hadn't even sat down good when Pa started a ruckus.

I don't remember what the fuss was all about. It didn't really matter. It was just two hard heads trying to get their way by yelling the loudest. Yelling the loudest doesn't make you right, and the one yelling the loudest usually is the most ignorant. But it struck me odd what Pa said after Ben left.

"I didn't make Ben that way. Never could do nothin' with that boy. Always the wild one. He just don't want to do right!"

A child doesn't become hatefully independent unless he's been trained that way. Pa raised us boys like he did his animals—break our spirits and remake us in his image so we could be useful to him. And never be praised or blessed for becoming good men. Each of us was too unique for that foolishness. We were never meant to be recreated into Pa's image but rather become what the Lord had made each of us to be.

Finally the words heated up hot enough to send a steamboat upriver a hundred miles. Ben spoke like lightning from a thundercloud. "You treat everybody else better'n you do your own damn family!"

All Pa could say was, "Look at you cussin' in my house."

"That's least of the sins that's been goin' in this house for years!"

Pa didn't hear a word of what Ben tried to say. He didn't want to. His self-righteous attitude of *I'm the standard in this house* always got the better of him. Obviously, he never could remember all the times we heard him cuss, out loud and under his breath. If he said a word or two and thought we heard it, he would say it again but change the words to something else.

Ma told me later that night, "When Ben leaves, I won't never see him again." And none of us have. Not until today.

Ben looks around Winnfield pushing his back forward from behind with his hands. He stomps the sleep out of his legs and pulls his hat off to wipe his brow with a rag. He starts up the steps into the mercantile. He walks just like Pa. Ben pauses to pick up a couple of axe handles and makes his way to the counter where I stand waiting.

"And what can we do for you today, Mistuh Ben Tullos?"

A man of pure business, Ben doesn't even look at me. "Well, I need everythin' on this here list if you can read. Don't forget this fancy bolt of cloth my wife wants or there'll be the devil to pay." He hands me the list, and his jaw drops. Ben just stands there staring like he's run into a friend or someone he'll need to fight.

"Lummy? That you, boy? Can't be, is it? What the hell you doin' here in Winnfield? Been too many years and look at you! You done all growed up like a weed in summer time, all straight, tall, and lean, with muscles to boot. Damn boy, you're taller'n me and look to be stronger. Wouldn't know you walkin' down the street! Thought I was lookin' at Uncle Silas!" That's a compliment I appreciate.

He sticks out his hand. I grab it and pull him close for a brother hug. I wrap my long arms around him and pick him up. I can tell he's not used to that, but I do it, anyway.

"Glad to see you, big brother!" Mr. Davis laughs at Ben's feet dangling up off the floor. I set him down, and he straightens his clothes a bit. Ben scowls at Mr. Davis.

"He's been here how long? Why didn't you send word?"

Mr. Davis shrugs his shoulders. "He wanted to surprise you. I guess he did!"

"Reckon so. Well, I hope you used him up for what you needed him for, 'cause I'll be takin' him on back to south farm. We need an extra hand." Ben looks me up and down measuring my height in a look of near disbelief.

"Figured on it, Benny. He pulled his weight well here this week. Got no complaints, and he's got a good way about him too." Mr. Davis pitches me seven silver dollars, one at a time, for each day worked. "There you go, son, you more'n earned them. You go on and help your brother get loaded, and we'll call it good. How's that?"

I start gathering the items on the list Ben handed me. "Oh, and, Lummy? come see me if you need work between harvest an plantin'."

"Thank you, suh, I will."

"Hell, give him two nickels for a dime, and he thinks he's rich." Same ole Ben, making sport of his family. It doesn't bother me much, but it brings up feelings I'd thought were gone. They're just buried. I don't laugh. Ben moves to the counter slowly, watching my every move from the corner of his eye, looking and acting just like Pa in almost every way. It's too strange.

"Mistuh Davis, that ten gauge I ordered from Rainy make it in yet?"

"Lummy, you want to get that cannon you brought in for your brother? And don't forget the shot and wadding. I'll get the powder." I return proudly with the big scattergun. Mr. Davis is telling Ben the story of how I got it.

"Really? He outran a pack of coyotes? Must've been flyin' like a bat out of hell. And Rainy didn't shoot him runnin' into his camp like that, crazy as a road lizard?" Ben looks at me strangely. "You done had a few experiences it appears, huh, boy?"

I hand him the heavy gun.

"Well, I didn't fall off the tater wagon today, just yesterday!"

Ben studies the shotgun. "Better'n havin' a panther chase after you, that's for sure. Heard about one killin' livestock in the Deer Creek country in the Missip delta. Folks there baited that ole screamer right into a barn with a cow, and don't you know that ole cat fell for it. They shut the doors, lit the barn chantin', 'Burn panther, burn.' So they named their town Panther Burn. Glad you wasn't the bait for them coyotes, li'l brother. Don't think Lummy Town has much of a rang to it no how, heh!"

Ben throws the gun butt into his shoulder, aiming it like he's leveling down on a flock of geese. He repeats the action several times getting comfortable with the fit.

"Rainy done good getttin' the stock length right. And I like my name engraved underneath by the trigger guard."

"I carried that thing fifty miles walkin'. Rainy said he'd be back through in a few months to see how you like her." Ben isn't listening. He pours over the shotgun, taking notice of every curve and notch like he's looking over a shapely woman. He puts his thumb on one rabbit ear and cocks it slowly, then the other, listening intently to the action.

"Sweet, and smooth. I'll be doublin' my duck and geese haul this year, that's for dang sure."

Mr. Davis pats Ben on the back. "I'll sell every one you bring in. Ain't nothin' like a good pot of duck gumbo to warm the soul on a frosty evenin'."

Ben sets the gun down and calls his kids over. "Talton, Wesley, Oliver, get over here and meet your uncle! Where's your sister, Emily?" The boys half-run from the candy jar counter and stand in front of me, straight and tall. Emily races out from behind the counter where Mrs. Davis is showing her a doll.

I shake each boy's hand. "I'm glad to meet you young men!" They look at each other mouthing "young men" like they've not been called that before. Little Emily hides behind Ben's legs staring at me with sparkling eyes. "Looks like I'll be stayin' with you for a spell." I bend over and grab both boys and bear hug them.

"You men are gonna have to show me all your best huntin' and fishin' spots, and we'll have a good ole time!" They laugh, and Talton looks back at the candy jars so I ask, "Be all right if they get some sweets? It's on me."

Ben nods. "Best get some for your brothers and sisters, too, or they'll have your hide. Go on, Emily, you get to pick." He gently pushes the blondehaired blue-eyed little angel, and she runs to hug me on the way to the candy jars.

I pitch Mr. Davis a dollar.

"Whatever that'll buy." I tell Talton, "Son, make sure you get somethin' special for your Ma, somethin' chocolate I believe." The two boys are as careful as they are respectful. Mrs. Davis gives them each a piece and sacks the rest.

In a commanding tone I've heard too many times from Pa, Ben barks, "All right, boy, get your stuff and let's get gone. I want to make the home place by nightfall. Storm's brewin', and dark's creepin' up on us. Enough of this back slappin' honey lovin', and besides, accordin' to the wife, we will not be late for church tomorrow." Ben rolls his eyes.

Ben walks around the wagon double-checking that everything is tied down well. "Lotta work ahead, Lummy, hope you're ready for it. We got timber to cut, salt to haul, crops to get in the field, and the boss wants to make a profit this year. I'm gonna help him make it. You came at a good time to help me do it." Same ole Ben, still bossing everyone else's life for them.

"You kids, get on up in the wagon. Hop up there with Old Bart, Lummy, and y'all get acquainted. Let's go!"

I climb up and sit next to Old Bart in the second buckboard. Ben leads with the children singing beside him. He sits straight as an arrow hardly moving with the bumps. Old Bart sticks his hand out, and I take it. He sings a few tunes between which he talks about the old country where a man might see an elephant or a hyena. Bart talks about wishing to be free to roam this country. But he also wants to go back and find the family he left when slavers took him as a boy.

"They probably all gone by now, I reckon."

Ben slaps the reins lightly. "Git 'em up, Sally, take 'em on home, Susie." He smiles. "But that Massuh Gilmore, he a good man, a fair massuh, and he takes care of us darkies good. He don't use no whip and lets us save a few dimes to get the things we wants."

I shake and have to calm myself before I blurt out the wrong thing. "Mistuh Gilmore? Heard he's a gambler and a good one."

"Sho' is, best this side of the river, and the other too. Now, don't think too badly about him, he can turn a card and roll them bones, but for good reasons. Massuh Lummy, I can't talk about that just yet." We cross another bayou, and Old Bart breathes in deeply. "Smells like fried squirrel and biscuits, Massuh Lummy." The only thing I smell is musty bayou mud.

"That be Missus Dorcas cookin' up a fine supper. She puts together a fine settin' of vittles! Oh, Massuh Lummy, she as good a Jesus woman as you find anywhere on God's good green earth. She be like the preacher talks about from the Good Book, always helpin' anybody in need. She a saint if there ever was one. You'll be likin' her. Massuh Lummy, I don't mean no harm, Ben bein' your brother and all, but he ain't always the nicest person to her, nor towards nobody for that matter. He sits with the moonshine more than he ought, and when he does, he talks about his pappy who must've been pretty hard on him. Ain't it kind of comical, we becomin' the very thing we hate the most?" I nod.

"I don't means no harm, but stumblin' upon a long lost brother can be like findin' gold, but sometimes fool's gold, if you get my meanin'." Old Bart is wise to his grey haired years. He surely would've been a village elder back home in his country.

"None taken, but I do know my brother. I've had a scrape or two with him before he left Missip. And I know Dorcas, too. Sweet as any woman God ever made."

"All right, Massuh Lummy, glad you with us."

"Just call me Lummy, my friend."

"All right, Massuh Lummy."

CHAPTER 12

THE GILMORE PLACE

MARCH 21, 1859

Only a person less than human judges another less than human.

THE ROAD TO Ben's place for the most part is dry. We take Military Road south out of Winnfield through great pine forests, crossing a half-dozen nearly dry branches.

"Best enjoy these bone dry crossin's now, 'cause the rains will start up soon enough, and we'll have hell to pay gettin' wagons through!"

There's good water in this country, even now, found in creeks with names like Little Cedar, Indian, Hurricane, and Bear, the last we cross before reaching Gilmore's south parish land holdings. We stop the wagons a couple times to rest the mules. Well-worn paths make it easier to cross these wet spots. Nearly dry in this country means nearly knee deep mud. Even so, good water is necessary to good farming, healthy livestock, and happy people.

Ben yells at Old Bart several times on the road, "Niggah, I said, keep up!"

"Yassuh, Massuh Benny, I be doin' my best." Bart can tell it bothers me.

He leans over bumping me with his shoulder. "Massuh Benny don't mean no harm. He just don't know these mules like I do. They go only so fast, but they go all day." That's not what bothered me. And Old Bart knows it.

I don't correct Bart this time. He's learned to play the part very well. I hate slavery and all it stands for. Too many years of hearing about Grandpa Willoughby owning slaves, which could have made them less than human to us. It didn't, but it's easy to take out man's frustrations on a person that a slave master thinks is less than human. I'm glad I had Temple as my Grandpa, not Willoughby. Who knows how I'd turned out living with that slave-holder. I just wish Pa had set Lucille free.

I remember Lester, the sheriff's nephew back home, singing a song every time I passed by his town perch where he cat called at the girls. "Niggahs and flies, I do despise, when I see a niggah, I'd rather have the flies!" He knew how I felt because he suspected me and Susannah.

Ma said under her breath once when she heard Lester singing that song, "Ignert ass bastard will get his one day." Ma rarely cursed, but that day it made me appreciate her more.

Until a person becomes human to you, they don't have to be treated human. Susannah surely is human, and the prettiest soul God gave a woman along with everything else too. I can't think about that too much. I just have to be patient to get her back into my arms.

Old Bart just keeps singing, almost mindlessly, but there's depth in his soul. These slaves possess a richness of heart that cannot be appreciated by a person believing them less than human. Only a person less than human can judge another less than human. Slave owners will pay for all this one day and deserve everything they get. I imagine white people in general will have to face the judge one day on that one.

Bart's songs sway my soul like a gentle breeze breathing sweet notes through the willows begging the leaves to sing. Granny often said, "Holy Ghost wind moves through a soul like soft soundin' wind chimes lettin' the song of the heart flow free." I feel God around me, his gentle touch on my arms, on the back of my neck. I hear him whispering in the wind. I feel him inside me. Old Bart's songs help.

We cross a trail, and Bart yells in perfect English, "Pacton-Alexandria Highway! We'll be home in half an hour!" I'm surprised. "Didn't know this old niggah had what white folks call edjumacashun, did you? Well, sir, I speak very well, and I read and write." I'm still puzzled. He laughs, "Go ahead, ask your question, Massuh."

"How? When?" is all I can get out.

"Massuh Gilmore, he's a good man. He frees us soon as he gets us to his place but keeps papers on us for our protection. He teaches us the three R's.

Lots of folks around here done freed their negroes. And there's lots of folks don't like it neither. That's why we can't be talkin' about it. There's enemies out in these hollows. Just got to know who they is, Massuh Lummy."

We pull up to a well-kept but rather small house facing south with a nice wrap-around porch extending around the east and west sides but not the north. A good stand of cedars guard that part of the house against the north winds. It makes sense. Ben and Dorcas can sit out in their rocking chairs after the day's work is done and catch the warmth of the winter sun or escape the heat of the western glow in summer. Ben also left a good stand of oaks on the west side to shade the house in the worst of the August temperatures. Pa always told us, the hottest sun burns at four o'clock, not noon. He's right.

Winn Parish. I don't expect it to be like Choctaw County, but the land lays much the same. We grew up in the hills near Wood Mountain, named after one of the first settlers, Aaron Wood, whom we called Grandpa. This land is not what I expected. It isn't the swampy, mosquito infested, flat delta land I came through leaving Vicksburg. It's rolling hills with nice creek bottoms. Good land.

But the delta ain't all bad. About twenty of us would gather up after harvest with mules pulling sleds loaded with supplies and go into the deep delta woods for a couple of weeks. We'd trap raccoons, shoot squirrels, take a few deer, and shoot sacks full of ducks and geese before heading back to the hills. I could never seem to get the gray mud off my boots.

The Yazoo River swamp is where I got my first deer at thirteen. It was only a three inch spike, but Pa was proud of me. We tied the deer to a pole and carried it out the longest mile walk I believe I've ever made. I helped skin it with the hunting knife he'd made me. It's one of the best memories I have with Pa.

Another good memory is Ben and I both got our first bucks that same day. His was a spike almost identical to mine. Later we both took our first antlered buck on the same New Year's Day, 1847. He got a seven point and me a six. Pa called us men, and the whole family was happy for the meat. Ben always got the bigger antlered bucks. I was just always happy to have the meat. Antlers look good nailed above the barn door, but a man can't eat them. I'm happy to take a half grown doe. Easier to carry out the meat and always tastes better.

Ma would take the deer meat, fry it up just right, make the best gravy a man ever tasted, and then seal it in jars. We ate on it all winter long, that and all the good garden vegetables she'd put up as well. But that blackberry cobbler, whew! What a taste of heaven that surely was. I miss home already.

Home rolls out the front door when Dorcas chases the smaller children out to meet their father. With her come smells making me wonder if Ma had arrived a couple hours before us.

"Bart, Lummy," Ben barks, "Let's get that first wagon unloaded. We'll take the other to Mistuh Gilmore tomorrow when we go to Shiloh church. Supper'll be on when you finish up, and make sure you wash up good. Bart, you can sleep in the barn but check for copperheads before you shut your eyelids. Shouldn't be any if that dang old cat's still around. One of the boys will bring your vittles out."

That's Ben, always in charge and wanting people to know it. This won't to be easy, but it's a good second step to getting Susannah back. Then a sweet voice from the past yells out.

"Now, just who do we have here, husband? A stranger who don't look like no stranger. He has your look, Ben, but he's a head taller'n the last time I seen him!" I don't like it, but Ma did say I favor Ben in the eyes and shape of my face.

"Lummy Tullos, get up on this porch and let me squeeze the life out you, boy! What on God's good earth you doin' in these parts, and how'd you find us? You was just a chap last we saw you! And now you done all growed up tall as a pine tree!"

"All right, Dorcas, hug his neck, and let's get on with supper before it gets cold or a coyote steals it, like last year!" Ben's actually smiling. I lean down and hug her as she ruffles my hair.

"Lummy was travelin' this way and ran into my gun dealer friend, ole Rainy Mills. You remember him. He ordered this here shotgun for me back last year." Ben proudly holds up the shotgun for all to see. His mind's working and Dorcas's too. They both turn at the same time realizing they don't know why I'm here.

"So, what *did* bring you to this side of the river, boy?" Ben asks.

I'm dumbfounded. I have no answer, but I'm coming up with one fast. I lie. "I decided to roam a bit, you know, needin' some breathin' room and all. I decided to head west. Grandpa Temple always said west is best, and Granny never let me forget that I got the wanderin' foot. So, by fate I wound up in Winnfield. I don't know if it be luck or a blessin', but I'm glad to be here. I'd like to stay on a bit and make a go of it, that bein' all right with y'all." I change the subject quickly. "Can we eat? Them good smells is about to make me lose my manners."

Dorcas just keeps looking at me. Dang, a woman is always trying to figure a man out. "All right, Lummy, bet your belly button's done stuck to your backbone. It'll turn loose here in a bit!"

Ben kicks the dirt. "You'll know in a week if it's a blessin' or bad luck bein' here. We got plantin' to do, and it's gonna take us all. Everybody's gotta earn their keep around here. Like the Good Book says, 'a man don't work, he don't eat.' So hurry up and unload that damn wagon, I'm ready to eat!"

Dorcas lightly pops Ben on the shoulder. "Said you was gonna put a cork in that cussin' jug. Ummph, that cussin' tongue of yours. I ain't never heard such in all my live long days."

"Stop all your carryin' on and leave it be, woman. We just funnin' about. Sunday preachin' ain't 'til tomorrow no ways. I'll get more'n I want then."

CHAPTER 13

AFTER CHURCH

MARCH 22, 1859

One man's lie is another man's righteous deception.

WE START EARLY Sunday morning for Shiloh church, a small gathering of good farm folks traveling from miles around for eleven o'clock preaching. Assembling with the saints isn't all that different than back home, although the thick Cajun accent of the visiting preacher is tough to understand. I get most of his sermon while Ben catches a nap.

The singing is good, and as they say back home, "We blew the shingles off the roof!" Sitting near the front row, a soul can absorb all the goodness of voices happy to sing to the Lord and each other. The sound carries me softly into the kingdom deep inside where God resides. But it's strange that no Negroes attend like at Mount Pisgah church.

Halfway through the third song, the back door creaks open, and a rather tall very well dressed gentleman sneaks in, trying to be quiet. He's extremely respectful and sits down on the back row resting his bearded chin on a brass and wood cane.

Ben elbows me. "That's your new boss. I'll introduce him after this wind-bag spits out all his words." He grins. "And he's got a damn bunch of them." Dorcas elbows him lightly in the ribs. Ben smiles bigger.

When the song ends, the fiery Cajun preacher asks, "Well, brother Ben, what's got you so tickled in God's house this mornin' when we should be contemplatin' our wickedness and the judgment to come?" I hang my head low, knowing how much Ben is like Pa when it comes to being at church. He's capable of saying most anything.

Dorcas lets out a quiet but long sigh, "O Lord, do help us in this our time of need."

Ben lifts his hands. "I was just thinkin' how thankful I am for the Good Lord's lovin' kindness on my soul." Then he stands, turns his back on the preacher, and addresses the crowd.

"The thought made me so happy, enough to put a smile on this ole sinner's face. And preacher, you know I ain't much of a smilin' soul. So thank you, thank you very much, for bringin' me closer to the Good Lord this mornin'. Maybe you ought to preach a bit more on the Good Lord's mercy than how you think he wants us all to stay up at night worryin' if we're saved or gonna get thrown in the lake of fire. Just somethin' to ponder, whilst you're preparin' your sermon, preacher."

Ben sits down and stares straight ahead. Dorcas covers her face. The children just stare at their Pa. I bite my lip so I don't burst out laughing.

Mr. Gilmore stamps his cane on the hard pine floor. "Here, here, somebody say Amen!" Several "Amens!" follow Ben's short sermon, which truly is the best I've heard in a while. The preacher has the look of a man having stomach troubles in the outhouse. He grumpily starts up another funeral sounding hymn, something about standing outside with the demons. I don't know that one, and it'll be a mercy from the Lord not to hear it again. I don't sing.

The preacher rails on for an hour and a half. I get lost in my own thoughts, except when he mentions that next Sunday, right after preaching and dinner on the ground, water baptism will be offered to all over at the big bream hole in Piney Woods Creek.

He reminds the crowd, shaking his old pointy finger, "Now you folks requesting water immersion best be repentin' this week before you get washed in the blood of the Lamb so all them sins jumpin' off you won't kill off them perches." No one laughs at his attempt at humor.

Mr. Gilmore stamps his cane again. "Surely will make for a fine fish fry, now won't it?"

Everyone laughs, and I lean over to Ben, "Ole preacher's head is about as pointy as his gnarly old finger, sharp as a schoolhouse pencil." Dorcas gives me the disapproving look this time. Ben smiles and ribs me with his elbow. It's like we're kids again.

"So preacher's gotta new name, Ole Pencil Head." Now, we're laughing hard enough to bounce up and down, shaking the entire bench up and down. It creaks every time we bounce.

Dorcas reaches over and pops us both on the hands giving a look of I gonna whoop you two when I get you home or I'll skin you right here if you keep on! I don't want either, so I settle myself down. We're getting back to some sense of normal at the end of the song when the preacher stands back up for the benediction. That means another sermon.

Ben settles into his seat dozing but accidently snorts pretty loud, half waking. It embarrasses Dorcas but brings the church back to life in hushed laughter. The preacher stops railing to point his bony finger straight at Ben.

"And what did you say there, brother Benny Frank? Bein' the talkative one this fine day?"

Ben sits up. "Oh, just—um—yassuh, praise the Lawd, and uh, add in a couple hallelujahs!" The preacher stands there hands on his hips. I figure he's about to let Ben have it again.

"That's good, brother Benny Frank. A few good hallelujahs might just wake this church up!"

For a moment, I get lost in my thoughts about my soul. "Lord Jesus have mercy on me."

Ben elbows me in the ribs. "Get up, boy, we're singin' another buryin' song which means this is over for me. Still talkin' out loud, ain't you?" After the service, Ben and I walk out with the family in tow. He wants me to help set up the chairs and tables for the Sunday dinner.

Just outside the door, the visiting preacher reaches out to grab Ben's hand. "Brother, I need to have a private chat with you."

Ben stops and bows up like a cutworm. Quick as a snake strike, he looks the man dead in the eye. "Not a prayer, preacher. Find yourself a weaker soul to deal your devilish talk to. My ears are for the voice of the Lord alone, and

He didn't speak from that pulpit today. Not through you, anyway! So back it up, crawdad. Take that sermon on down the road to the less fortunate I know who'll have to hear it. And besides, I noticed you lookin' a little too long at them three whores come through Winnfield last time I was in town. Preacher, ain't good to be a saint on Sunday and an ain't on Monday."

The preacher looks around to see if anyone's listening.

"Unh-huh, thought so." He whispers in the preacher's ear, "And if you ever call me out in front of the church like that again, I'll beat that lustin' demon out of your ass right in front of the good brethren!"

The preacher looks at me. I shrug my shoulders.

Ben walks away, leaving the preacher with his jaw on the ground.

I lean over, "And he means it, preacher."

Ben opens a small shed where saw horses, table planks, and rough benches are stored. "He ought to be ashamed of himself."

Ben sounds a little Cajun himself. I don't say anything.

He's surely said enough. I try to lighten up the moment. I know he'll say something hatefully funny. "So, Ben, how about that sermon?"

"That damn preacher's words are about as welcome as an outhouse breeze! He's so confused, he don't know whether to scratch his watch or wind his ass! I can't sit too long with such talkin's goin' on. He makes my ass itch." Ben figures out I just goaded the words right out of him without hardly trying. "I'm gonna have to keep an eye on my smart ass little brother, too!"

The good ladies bring out the food baskets arranging the items in their proper places. They throw a feast laying out everything good a man can imagine. Some good soul even made chicken'n dumplin's.

Now this is home.

A refined voice pipes up behind us. "Fine preachin' there, Pastor Benny Frank, if I say so! If you don't mind, I'd like to take up a nice collection for your well prepared word from the Lord today! I do believe you've had that gun loaded for some time!"

Ben turns from setting up the last table with a scowl that softens to a half grin. It's Mr. Gilmore. "Don't make fun of me, boss. You know how I am about all that."

"You know I'm only jokin'. But what you said is true. I like it."

I like this man.

"Well, if you want to make a donation, then give enough cash dollars to get us a new preacher for the second Sunday of the month because that one is crazy as a loon. He just won't do. Needs to go on down the road."

"Then, how about you, my friend? We could use some plain talk and simple truth around these parts, especially at the heavenly holy righteously talking behind everyone's back reverent Shiloh Baptist church!"

No, I'm convinced. I like this man. He acts as though he's playing a part in a Shakespeare play or something.

Ben turns and slips something to his mouth I can't quite see. A small flask. His head snaps back, and it's shoved into his inside jacket pocket. He's well practiced, and looks around until he spots Dorcas.

He punches my shoulder as brothers do. "See any pretty girls to catch your fancy?"

Mr. Gilmore grunts, wanting to be introduced.

Ben turns on one foot and with a wave of his hat in a bow, "Mistuh Gilm-ore, fine suh, you know me. I talk about it some, but I don't track in a straight line enough to be tellin' other folks how to run their lives. It's enough for me to manage my own, and my Dorcas says that needs plenty work. But here's the man for the job. Meet my little brother, Columbus Nathan Tullos! But we simple, plain unedjumacated folks around home just call him Lummy. He recently arrived and well, he talks a real good word about the Lord."

I kick dirt on Ben's boots, and he laughs, knowing I really don't like the attention. I gave a testimony or two back at the Mount Pisgah Baptist Church and did quote enough scripture once to win a brand new red and gold Bible in a contest, but preaching? No way. Ben embarrassed me, and he knows it. Like Pa, he enjoys poking fun at another's expense. This isn't the way I wanted to meet the man from whom I was either going to buy Susannah or steal her.

Mr. Gilmore stares into my eyes, studying every movement for any possible sign, like a card sharp reading another player's poker hand. He doesn't know that I know that about him. So I go deadpan in my expression. I give him nothing to work with like when I've had to go before the sheriff to get out of small troubles without doing too much lying. Mr. Gilmore offers his hand.

"Mistuh Lummy, I like you. I don't know you, but I do believe you have a little somethin' hidden up your sleeve. I like that in a man. Not showin' all his cards at one time. All in good time, my young friend, all in good time. But in the meantime, I'm glad to have you workin' with us. I assume you will?" He looks at Ben, who nods.

"I pay a fair wage, don't work Sundays, and only half-day Saturdays, except during harvest. A man's got to be with his family, fish, go swimming, or court a girl sometime, don't he, Mistuh Lummy? You do like fishing and girls, don't you, Lummy Tullos?" I nod. He stares at me again. His eyes brighten. He starts rubbing his chin, like he's picking me out of a crowd.

"Have I seen you before, Columbus Nathan?" He catches me off guard. Could he have when he passed through town and won Susannah in that high-stakes poker game? He studies me like a cat waiting for a mouse to move.

"No, guess not, but you do look familiar. I guess that's because you're unfortunate enough to look too much like your big brother, except you are a head taller. It's good to look a man in the eye at our height, wouldn't you say, Lummy Tullos?" He slaps me on the back, and I grin.

"That hurts, Mistuh Gilmore, sayin' I look like my dawg ugly brother!"

Mr. Gilmore brings the conversation back to business. "About that preachin' possibility...."

Ben breaks in, "You two gonna stand here and jabber all day? While you two jaybirds keep on squawkin', I'll get the rest of these benches set up. But oh, don't let me stop this all important meetin'." Mr. Gilmore nods for it's obvious his hands are pretty soft. He's a man who has the means to pay others to do his manual labor, even at church.

"I'm on the committee that evaluates the yahoos who bring God's Word to us though often in the most ignorant of ways. It's hard to get the better men of the cloth to visit such out of the way places, you understand?" I nod. "You do know you carry the name of a prophet, don't you?"

"Yassuh, my Ma talked about it on occasion, but mostly when I was in trouble or when she reminded me I should be thinkin' about the call of God."

"Well, have you heard it?"

I squint my eyes. "Heard what?"

"The call, son, the call of God? God called all great men's names to their destiny. Has he called yours, Columbus Nathan Tullos?"

"Not in the traditional way, I guess, not in the way most folks say you hear it. But I do have a special call, at least special to me, about bein' alone with the Lord of this great universe."

I start talking and can't seem to stop, like a child who needs to tell his Momma everything he learned on the first day of school. I bubble over like cool hill spring in summertime.

Mr. Gilmore sits on a chair with his chin leaned on his cane smiling. The only thing he says quietly during my short discourse is, "Refreshing, quite refreshing!" It's strange to have someone actually listening with interest to things that mean much to me. I've had no one to talk with about them, except my Susannah. And the man who's listening is her master. For now.

I talk about having a deep relationship with the Creator and that I'm not satisfied with a second hand friendship with the Lord. "The Bible I read says I can walk in the garden with him in the cool of the day."

I talk of my mystical experiences, the times I've heard God speak to me, the signs He gives in the trees, sun, wind, stars, and rivers. I speak of the spirit beings, good and bad, I've experienced, and of the dreams I've had. I tell him my goal in life is to be called a friend of God, like Moses. I stop. What am I doing? I don't even know this man. Being a card sharp, he reads me clearly and calls my hand pretty easily. I trust this man for some reason.

"You got a lot to talk about, Lummy Tullos, and you need to tell it. I bet you haven't been able to talk like this much, have you?" I shake my head. He puts his hand on my shoulder. "Just know this, you're safe here, son. I'm a fellow traveler on the same road. Your talk is good, and I want to hear more. But right now, I better get a prayer said before that preacher thinks he's supposed to preach another sermon and the flies get the fried chicken. You do like to eat fried chicken, don't you, Lummy Tullos?"

"Every chance I get!"

"Good, then sit with me. I'll make sure you get a good piece or two." He strokes his small beard. "I knew there was more to you than meets the eye, Mistuh Lummy. That's good."

We get in line, and I fill my plate to near overflowing. I almost embarrass myself. Almost.

Mr. Gilmore leans over, "They do let you go back for seconds!"

It doesn't take me long to clean up my plate, and that's enough, except for the chocolate pie I've been eyeing ever since Dorcas laid it on the sweets table. I sneak over and get a fair-sized piece before it disappears.

Most are finishing up when the preacher announces a singing will start in twenty minutes or so, and all requests will be sung until the church is sung out. It's the only thing that preacher says that people like. He's either trying to redeem himself or make sure the collection is good when they pay him at the end of the day.

Mr. Gilmore speaks with Ben out of earshot but comes back over where I'm dozing after the good meal and too much preaching.

He leans down to whisper. "Just talked with your brother, and I'll see you in the fields tomorrow. At lunch time, I'd like to hear more about your God walk, if you don't mind. You've got some special reason for being in Winn Parish, don't know what, but I'm sure it's of the Lord. You know all lying ain't bad. One man's lying is another's righteous deception. The Good Book's full of it. Think on it, and maybe you'll come to trust me with the real reason why you're here." The man looks into my eyes and sees right down into the bottom of my soul. I don't know how to respond.

"Thank you for the job, Mistuh Gilmore. As far as talkin', I don't really go on like that, but we can share our thoughts. I'd like that. I ain't found too many who know what I'm talkin' about and even fewer who understand when I try to explain it, 'cause it's a bit hard to describe."

"That's why I'd like to resume our conversation. See you tomorrow."

The saints have already gathered and hum like bugs in the trees on a warm summer's evening. I start to doze again when Ben tugs on my arm.

"Let's sneak off and catch a mess of bream before dark, unless you ain't had enough churchin'. You can bet that preacher'll fire up again, and if we don't go now, with the work this week's gonna bring, it'll be next Sunday before we can slip away. Dorcas done told me to grab you and go. Said we needed some more gettin' reaquainted time. She'll take the children home in the wagon. Old Bart is getting' the supply wagon unloaded over at Mistuh Gilmore's."

"So that's why you saddled the two mules." Ben loves fishing better than hunting and caught some real keepers back home.

Lord, make this a good time with my big brother, Ben, I pray.

It's been a long time since we've fished together. As we trot away, Ben slips a sip from his flask and hands it to me. "Ain't good as the Wood's boys make from Aaron Wood's Spring, but it'll do."

I decline. "Too soon after dinner. Won't agree with the chocolate pie."

He understands. It's really an excuse. I try not to drink, except on special occasions. I've had plenty of moonshine whiskey and know that if I drank it regularly, I'd come to like it too much.

"The bream are beddin' up in the shallows near where Piney Woods Creek runs into the Dugdemona River. Glad the baptizin's will be next week, otherwise we might hook us a sinner or two! Big pool there, not much current, and them perches just lie in wait for a big ole worm or a feisty cricket. We can dig some night crawlers when we get there and catch a few crickets too." Ben slaps his mule on the buttocks. "Let's go!"

About four o'clock, and after a half jug of corn squeezings Ben had hidden near the fishing hole, he changes. Ben becomes hateful, even cursing me when I catch a fish ahead of him. I don't say anything. From then on until dark, Ben hardly says two words to me.

Finally when I'm just getting into a good bream bed, he barks out, "Let's go." Ben's moodiness happens sooner than I wish. I hoped he'd changed in his years away from Pa. Didn't happen. The alcohol, it seems, makes him two very different people.

We rein the mules up into the yard, and Ben spits out, "You put the mules up, and I'll take care of the fish."

I take his guff, but he's already starting to wear on me like a file on a crosscut saw blade. He doesn't know it, but he's sharpening me up for whatever comes next.

I finish before he does, and I sit on the porch. Dorcas comes out wiping her hands on a dish towel taking the rocking chair next to me.

"How you doin' bein' here so far, Lummy. You gonna stay a while?"

"Yeah, I just hope it'll be all right." She knows what I mean. But I want to change the subject. "Dorcas, just curious, how'd y'all wind up in Winn Parish Looseana, anyway?"

"Well, I don't have to tell you about Ben and your Pa." Tears form in her eyes. "Your Pa will never know how much he hurt Ben. I don't know how it was with your older brothers or you, but I *do* know what little Ben's told me and what I saw when we first married. Sorry, Lummy, I know that's not what you asked me."

"It's all right, sister." Dorcas sniffs and wipes her eyes with her towel, faking a smile.

"Your Pa rarely spoke much of your uncles who stayed down in Simpson and Marion Counties with your Grandpa Willoughby and his brother, Temple. Seems like he was upset that only Roland and Burrell came with him to Choctaw County. He got mad too when Roland left and especially when Burrell did not too long after. Your Pa took it hard when Burrell died in Arkansas. Sarah came back with the girls, and she passed soon after. Your Pa wandered off to cry the day she died but was right there when it came time to take them orphaned girls in to raise. Your Pa was tryin' to make up for his hardness and meanness he'd laid on you boys. I'm sorry he and Ben never got things straightened out before we left."

She sits quiet for a minute. "Lummy, one of your uncles, Temple's son, Abraham, who married the sweetest woman—oh, what was her name? Nancy, I think—sometime around 1821. They left Marion County after a few years and made their way here to Looseana. Your Pa never mentioned him to Ben, but your Grandpa Temple did. I loved hearing your Grandpa tell his stories."

A stick cracks. Dorcas quickly looks to see if it's Ben coming to the house.

"That was before me and Ben married. Anyway, your Grandpa Temple saw what was happenin' and told Ben he ought go somewhere else to make his own way. At first Ben didn't listen. He still just wanted to be with your Pa. You remember when he bought that first forty acres back in September of 1848? He was so proud, but your Pa couldn't or wouldn't be. Never understood it. Anyway, after that, he and I started makin' plans to go somewhere else. Your Grandpa gave Ben the name of the post house closest to where he believed Uncle Abraham was livin'. Ben wrote him, and Uncle Abraham said to come on. Ben wasted no time and didn't want your Pa to know where he went. I know it must've been hard on your Ma."

Dorcas shifts in her seat. "I thought bein' away from your Pa would change him." She stops abruptly and hangs her head. The back door slams, and Ben stomps through the house. He thrusts the front door open with enough force it almost hits him when it bounces back.

He throws down the cleaned fish in front of Dorcas.

"I want these for supper, and don't make it long." He sits down in the chair beside me not saying a word. His hot breath stinks from three feet away. He scowls as he lights his pipe.

He takes another sip from the jug and growls, "You need to go take a bath!"

My ears pin back, and the hair on the back of my neck stands up. I don't move, and he repeats but in stronger tones.

I turn, smile, and look him dead in the eye like *if you don't stop, I'll be remindin' you of that cuttin' I gave you a few years back.* "I'll take a bath, Ben, when I damned well please, so leave it be. And what stanks is the fish slime you ain't washed off your own damn hands."

Ben stomps out to the barn turning up his jug as he rounds the corner.

Dorcas says in a small voice from the window behind me, "Don't pay him no mind, Lummy, he treats everybody like little children, just like your Pa."

"Well, my sweet sis-in-law, he's come to the wrong tree thinkin' he's gonna scare this 'coon down into his tow sack!"

CHAPTER 14

FIRST DAY IN THE COTTON FIELDS

MAY 23, 1859

*Church is anywhere, anytime, God's holy people gather
in Jesus' savin' name.*

IT RAINS FOR nearly a week, and Ben is restless. "Damn boy, why'd you hafta bring all this rain with you, Lummy? Hell, its rainin' frogs." I just laugh him off.

"It's true! Pa saw it in Uncle Rube's cotton field one hot August afternoon! A dark ole thunderhead came up quicker'n flies to the shit pile. A big thunder went off like Fourth of July fireworks, and little bitty frogs were layin' everywhere! Rained so hard it near about ruined Uncle Rube's cotton crop!" Ben steps off the porch to feed the hogs. "If it ain't colder'n a witch's tit in a brass brassiere in winter it's hotter'n a goat's ass in a pepper patch come summer."

"Yeah, like they say, 'If you don't like the weather around here, just stay put, it'll change.'"

Ben, not to be outdone, "Yeah, but better said, 'If you do like the weather around here, just stay put, it'll change.'" It's that way for farmers, always at the mercy of the Good Lord—rain at planting time and none at growing time. Ben and I see it differently, though.

Ben thinks about what he doesn't have and what's lacking, like a bucket half empty rather half full. I get it from Ma that a soul should always be thankful for what the Good Lord has provided, not complain about what he hasn't. Pa had a hard time seeing the bucket half-full. So Ben gets it honest. He reminds me too much of Pa. He'd hate I'm thinking that.

THE RAIN FINALLY stops, and the ground dries enough to start ploughing. We wash down our last biscuits with gulps of coffee and head out as the sun breaks through the trees. Dorcas kisses Ben and hugs me. She follows us out onto the porch. Ben and I walk like we're going to a fight.

"Y'all be careful now! Watch out for them copperheads and rattlers! See you at dark, and don't you be late!" She's still talking, but we get out of earshot. When it's time to go to work, it's time to go to work. Besides hunting with Pa and my brothers, working together always seemed the better of times back home. I hope it'll be that way now.

We get the mules from the barn, and Old Bart arrives with two more from Mr. Gilmore's place up above the Dugdemona River near Shiloh Church. Being half way across Winn Parish, Old Bart and the field hands will stay in the barn and take their meals out on the porch. Ben treats the field hands well, but he doesn't mix with them.

On his way in yesterday to get supplies, Old Bart stopped by Davis Feed and Seed and picked up my first letter from Ma. I stuff it in my shirt to read it later. Old Bart gives me hellos from the Mr. and Mrs. Davis.

We're ready and excitement fills the air. Good men like good work. We trot the mules down the trail to the first field. The hired hands are cutting the larger grasses and small bushes that have grown up since last harvest. Mr. Gilmore's three "slaves" gather the cuttings to be burned later. Ben explains Mr. Gilmore freed his "darkies" but keeps them on, providing room and board and wages.

Ben shakes his head. "What's this damn world comin' to?" I'm not sure what he means. Ben calls the men in close and looks up in the sky this early morning. "You men are chompin' at the bit to get goin', and I appreciate it. Before we start I want the Good Lord in on this. We want a good year. Lummy, talk to God for us, would you?"

"Sure, brother. Happy to do it." The Negroes put their hands together under their chins.

Ben kneels down, the white farm hands stand with hands folded, but the slaves bow down low behind me already talking, "Yes, Lawd! Yes, Lawd!" I start, and so do they.

"Lord, you're a good God, and we praise your holy and righteous name, for Jesus savin' us and your Holy Spirit livin' in us."

The slaves rock back and forth, "Yes, Lawd! You a good God, you always been good!"

"Hear this feeble prayer comin' from feeble and weak lips. Forgive our many sins. We know you do, 'cause you love us and gave your Son just for us."

"Yes, Lawd, thank you!" one slave cries.

"Hear us, Lord, for right now we need Your kind blessin' on us today and through the rest of this plantin', growin', and harvestin' season. Give Your children good gifts, rain when we need it, sun when we need it, with no harm comin' to any of us, and good prices for the crops. You make things grow. Thank you for Mistuh Gilmore providin' a good place to work, but we depend on you, Lord."

The slaves start to moan in a kind of singing. "Help us, Lawd! Oooh, help us!"

I start winding down lest I start a revival. "Be with us, bless us, Lord, as we walk in your way. Thank you in advance for what you'll do for us, amen, in Jesus' holy name."

The slaves stand up and shout, "In Ja-a-azuz name, we sayz A-a-amains."

Ben stands up. "Damn good prayer, Lummy, but I didn't know you was gonna preach and get the black folks all stirred up!" Everyone laughs. I grab a dipper of water and start for the field.

The head Negro yells, "We ready to get on with the workin', Massuh Benny! With Massuh Lummy's prayin', we gonna be fine, don't you think, boss?"

"You betcha." The three freedmen jog back to the field where they left their tools. These black men have been treated well. Their clothes look good, and they wear good shoes. I'm glad. But even though these men are free I still hate slavery. With a growing passion.

While I prayed, Mr. Gilmore had eased up behind me. His eyes are still closed, his hands folded in front of him. "Lummy, somebody done taught you well, son. I want to see you about noon."

Ben yells, "All right, boys, let's get this crop laid in! Don't be lookin' for your Momma's titty to cry on 'til Sunday! We might have to put time in after Sunday meetin', too! We got work to do, and I'm sure even Adam had to tend the Garden every day. Ain't no cryin' now! It's on! And we gonna be busier than a one-eyed bobcat watchin' two rabbit holes. Let's go to work!"

We laugh, glad for the sunshine and the work. It'll be hard, but at day's end we'll enjoy a good tired. With a supper in his belly, a man can settle down and go straight into dreamland.

We slap the mules on the back with the reins and start busting ground. I help Old Bart, taking turns at the reins and then switch to keep the plow on course. Working together, I'm right at home. Ben farms just like Pa taught us. Two men working the plow keeps things moving, stopping only to water the mules or remove rocks.

I start up a chorus of my favorite song, *Oh! Susanna.*

> *Oh don't you cry for me,*
> *For I come from Mississippi*
> *with my banjo on my knee.*

I sing it all day long. It makes the day go faster and the thoughts in my head sweeter. The sun rises hot early in the day and shirts come off. Old Bart fetches a water bucket, and when he comes back, I'm staring at the freedmen. Two have terrible marks across their backs. I know why. It hurts my soul to see it.

He hands me a dipper of water. "Now, Massuh Lummy, you must know they got them stripes somewhere else, not by Massuh Gilmore's hand. Nawsuh, Massuh Gilmore, he don't go in for such. See that young'un over there? Ain't got nary a stripe, do he?"

I shake my head.

"That's 'cause Massuh Gilmore raised him from a pup. Found him in the swamp where his mammie hid him when they hauled her off to Nawlins to be sold. She knew Massuh Gilmore would treat him good, raise him on up in the Lawd, givin' him a chance in this ole world. And the best thing about that? He's been free all his life. Ain't that somethin'?"

What I've heard all the way here from Choctaw County is true. Mr. James T. Gilmore is a good man who treats Negroes as human beings. That gives me comfort about Susannah.

The morning passes quickly. At straight up noon, a Negro woman drives up in a cart, rings a dinner bell, and yells for us to come eat. I've never been happier. It's been a while since I've plowed and forgot how it works muscles a body forgets he has. Blisters are already popping up on my hands.

I walk with Old Bart and the freedmen to the wagon. "Is she free, too?"

Old Bart nods with a smile. "Massuh Lummy, what's that song you been singin'? I kinda likes it."

"Oh, just a tune I learnt on my way here, that's all. So all Mistuh Gilmore's Negroes are free?"

Old Bart smiles, and that's my answer.

I want to know Mr. Gilmore more than ever now. My, my, how a soul's estimation of another man can change getting the right information. I'd written this man off as a gambling, lustful slaver. Turns out he's on a mission, taking slaves by a what some call a sinful sport and turning his winnings into something truly godly.

"Lord forgive me for my judgin' another."

We gather around the cart, wash our hands, splash water on our faces, and Mr. Gilmore says a short grace over the meal. Slabs of ham, thick bread, and cheese lay in piles with a pot of roasted potatoes and a couple of boiled eggs each. This is home.

A new hand, Mose Cockerham smiles. "Hellfire, boss, I don't eat this good in my own Momma's house!"

Mr. Gilmore snaps, "Watch your words, young man! I don't mean no harm, but let's refrain from usin' language that might upset the Good Lord watchin' over on our work. We want blessin's on this crop, not cursin's." Mose is embarrassed.

"Sorry, Mistuh Gilmore, won't happen again, I promise."

"Don't sweat it, son. The Lord forgives, and He forgets. And, I try to be like him every chance I get. Think no more about it. Just be a better man from now on. Lummy?"

"Yassuh?" Mr. Gilmore waves for me to follow him out of earshot.

"I hope you'll attend prayer meetin' this Tuesday. I've wanted to ask you, but I needed to see if you are what you say you are. Now I invite anyone wishin' to gather with the saints, but you have to know some folks don't cotton to white and black folks congregatin' on equal terms. I know now you're fine with that. I'm invitin' you, but I also got a favor to ask."

I draw back, not knowing this man well enough to agree to any favors just yet.

"I'd like you to talk to us about the Lord." I start to object, but he throws up his hands. "I understand you might not be ready just yet, but who ever is?" My heart drops a little.

"Just go for fifteen minutes and don't do a lot of preparin'. Speak from what's deep in your soul. That's what you do best anyway. I been listenin' to you talk with the hands, sharin' with them about the Lord. Tell us about an experience you had with the Lord or some scripture special to you. Ponder on it, and the blessed Holy Spirit will guide you. You do believe in the Holy Spirit, don't you, Lummy Tullos?"

"I do."

"Good, 'cause the Holy Spirit surely believes in you, son!"

"Yassuh, that, too, but I ain't always been around people like you. So, I'm free to speak what the Lord puts on my heart?" He nods. "Ok, I'll do it."

"Next Tuesday, instead of going back to Benny Frank's for the night, you can stay at my place. I'll have you back in the field by the time your brother gets here, if you don't mind an early mornin' mule ride with Old Bart." I nod. "Good, it's settled. I'll speak to Ben about it. You all right? You seem a little fidgety."

"Understand, I ain't got a problem with it, but people back home say havin' church anywhere but in a church house nowadays is like those crazy end of the world predictin' folks who don't follow God's way."

"Hold on now, Lummy, I see your point, and the Lord knows nobody knows when Jesus is comin' back. But I've come to believe church is anywhere, anytime God's holy people gather in Jesus' savin' name. Even the Good Book says the first Christians met in each other's homes." Mr. Gilmore leans on his cane. "I did hear you mention somthin' about two churches didn't I? One with walls and the other out here. Seems to me church went down hill once the men who claim to be smartest amongst us started teaching church had to be in a building at certain times on certain days. And besides, ain't it about time you start livin' what you preach?"

"You're right, it is time I do."

Mr. Gilmore stomps the mud from his boots. "So talk about whatever the Good Lord lays on your heart! Can you do that?"

"I'll be ready Tuesday night and do my best to let the Lord speak."

"Look forward to seein' you then. Prayer meetin' will be in the barn next to my house. All are welcome, if you know what I mean?" I nod. "So be prepared to get a little help from the darker skinned children of our Blessed Creator!"

That means Susannah will be there.

We finish just before dark, satisfied with the day's work. Ben and I settle into rocking chairs on the porch after a fine supper of fried chicken, potatoes and gravy, greens, and fresh bread. We're happy as dead pigs in the sunshine.

Ben lights his pipe. "So, you get a letter today?"

"I did and done plum forgot all about it." I carefully slide my knife under the flap sealing the envelope and pull out the two page message like a kid opening Christmas presents.

Bankston Mississippi May 1, 1859

My beloved son, I am so glad you finally made it safe to where God wants you. Do you like how well I write this letter? I had Mary write it for me. She's going to school and has a gift for the letters. Anyway, I am so glad you have found Ben and Dorcas. Are they doing well? How are their children? Do they have more? What are they doing these days? You must write and tell me all about it. Please tell each one I love them and give them hugs and kisses for me. All is well here. Elihu, George, Amariah, Jasper, and James work hard to get the crop in. Pa made a deal with the Wood family that we work our farms together. They have plenty of help like we do and working together Pa believes we will all fare better. We'll see. Some of those

Wood boys can be pretty mean. But they are good men and hard workers. Rebecca, me, Mary, and little Emaline stay busy keeping them fed and in clean clothes, milking the cows, putting in my garden, and doing our church work. Mt. Pisgah Church has grown due mostly to Pastor Dobbs preaching more positive sermons. Pray for your Pa, he doesn't feel well these days. He never says anything, but I know. That's all for now but know I never stop thinking about you all. I love and miss you all, Ma

I stare at the letter. Ben has his head turned away. A tear rolls down his cheek. He fakes a cough to wipe it away. I don't say anything. We just listen to the hum of the night bugs, and Ben tends to his pipe. I like the smell. I like where I am right now and who I'm with. I'm glad Ben still has a heart to find a tear.

CHAPTER 15

SUSANNAH!

MAY 24, 1859

Talk to the Lord like you're talkin' to me.

I HAVE A week to think about what I'll say at prayer meeting, and still nothing steals my mind. I don't want my words to sound like a sermon out of some book. My prayers tonight are about Ma, my brothers and sisters, Ben's family, his drinking, our work, and Susannah.

Lord, keep her in the palm of your great and lovin' hand.

I give thought to how I pray. There it is. I'll talk about prayer, since it's a prayer meeting. I rest peacefully now.

WE WAKE TO a beautiful sunny Tuesday morning that begs good men to do good work. Mr. Gilmore comes by at dinner to see if I'm still good to speak tonight. I assure him I'll be there and that whatever comes out will be of the Lord because I'm certainly not good enough to say anything worth hearing.

"Don't talk like that, Lummy Tullos. Give your soul and your tongue to the Lord, then expect that He'll come through for you. I'm expectin' something good!"

My heart swells like a father blessing his son as he sets out to build a life of his own, like an officer stirring up his men before a charge. It's the word of encouragement I need. I start singing one of Bart's songs, and he joins in.

Bart jumps in to take the lead, "All up in my prayer meetin', Lummy gonna let it shine, let it shine, let it shine, let it shine!" He bursts out laughing, "You gonna preach tonight! Done heard it from the boss man!"

At first I think he's laughing at me, but he's happy.

"Can't help it, Massuh Lummy, I knows the Spirit of the Lawd is all up in you! I believes you gonna find somethin', or better yet, somebody in the crowd when she shows up."

I act like I don't understand.

"Can't fool no ole fool, Massuh Lummy. Done heard you singin' that *O Susanna* song too many times with more soul than your mouth lets on. That's all I got to say!"

Oh my, am I caught? So I go to praying. And hard.

"So's what's the preacher got for us this evenin'?" The only word I get from the Lord in the moment is exactly what I'm doing in the moment.

"Talk to the Lord like you're talkin' to me."

"Ummmph, I likes that!" He grins like a man who just walked into the house smelling a good meal and can't wait to eat. How am I going to contain myself seeing Susannah and speak a word for the Good Lord all at the same time? I go back to praying as I work.

We quit around two o'clock to make the trip to Mr. Gilmore's place. Leaving comes at a natural break as we finish a field on the upper end of the property.

Ben yells as we drive away in the wagon, "Y'all don't forget where you left from today and be back when the sun rises! Don't forget the tools and supplies Mistuh Gilmore promised!"

By the time we arrive at Mr. Gilmore's house, I'm nervous as a cat in a room full of rocking chairs. I wash up, eat supper with Old Bart out on the back porch, and try to keep my thoughts focused on the talk I'll soon deliver.

Susannah's face keeps popping into my mind. I'm only a few feet away from her, and she doesn't even know it. I guess she doesn't but will soon enough. In minutes, I'll be reunited with Susannah, but I won't be able to hold her, tell her how I've missed her, caress her soft dark velvety skin. I need to stop. Mr. Gilmore asks us to split kindling and gather firewood for the barn stove before prayer meeting.

He sits down at the end of the porch, takes out his pipe, and lights up a smoke. "This little cool snap feels good, but I hope it'll clear out before we seed the ground. Anyway, the ladies will appreciate us takin' the chill off tonight."

As we chop wood, a lady pulls back the curtains in the window. It's hard to make out who. There's something familiar about that shapely girl. Did she just wave? I can't be sure, and I don't want Mr. Gilmore to catch me staring. It's hard not to. He almost catches me looking, but I turn away back to splitting the smaller sticks. I look again when Mr. Gilmore goes behind the barn, but she's gone.

I fool Mr. Gilmore, but Old Bart has been watching me the whole time.

"Best be watchin' that little bitty hatchet, Massuh Lummy, it be razor sharp. It can get you quicker'n a stumptail moccasin!" He rubs his head looking towards the curtained window. "Well, you don't know this, not manys does, but that's Massuh Gilmore's daughter."

I'm still not sure what he knows about me and Susannah. "Daughter? But she's—well, black!"

"Yep, black as axle grease! Massuh Gilmore and me brought her from Missippity not long ago. Calls her his sweet angel."

That worries me. I still don't fully know the intentions of this seemingly fine gentleman.

"Now, son, it ain't nothin' like that. Massuh Gilmore, he a good man. He don't do nothin' to harm her. He lost his daughter to the fever three years ago, not long before his wife Miz Nancy died. Lawd, that man wailed like a haint in a graveyard, moaned for weeks. I cried with him, too. When that girl in that window came, it eased his soul, and mine for that matter. I never had no growed daughter, but I left a young'un, and my woman back in 'Bama when the Massuh there sold me down the river. My heart broke in two pieces that day." Old Bart wipes his eyes as a lump grows in my throat. "She keeps house good for Massuh Gilmore and ain't never been nothin' but good to me."

He leans in close. "She even slips me sweets when Massuh Gilmore ain't lookin'. She ain't been here long, but she done captured all our hearts. She's like the Balm of Gilead!"

Oh, how I do miss that girl. I start chopping larger pieces with the double bit axe, splitting the red oak with every stroke. I need to work off my excitement.

The shadow returns to the window. She waves! My heart stops.

"So, what's her name?"

"Oh, it's a pretty name. Sounds like cool, sweet spring water runnin' slow over smooth flat creek rocks. Susannah." Bart looks like he just called the name of an angel. "But, Massuh Lummy, you already know that."

I'm caught. I can neither hide the excitement in my eyes nor the trembling in my knees.

He cocks his head sideways peering at me from the side like a squirrel's eye. "Said she was about to run off with some white boy over in Missippity. Massuh Gilmore don't know that. He won her in a card game and brought her here. I don't mean no harm, but I believe you come from there, too. Same place as Massuh Ben? You ain't angry with me, is you?"

"Heck no, I ain't mad at you. I'm just worried I'll get busted out about why I'm really here. Bart, I need a friend right now, and I need it to be you. Can I trust you?"

Bart slaps his leg. "Massuh Lummy, the Lawd done told me you was head over heels in love with that girl. You be safe with me."

I trust him. He can see into a man's heart, and he sees into mine.

Torches are lit on stakes outside the barn doors to guide in the good folks coming to be with God and each other. Then the door swings open wildly, and Mr. Gilmore strides in with the fanfare of a Shakespearean actor. I saw stage actors act that way once when a traveling show stopped at Bankston to perform Shakespeare's Julius Caesar. He waves in those following him. Five freedmen—two men and three women—wander in with three of the new Negroes, who are still healing from lashings and poor health. Mr. Gilmore treats these people with such respect. And it ain't for show.

In walks Susannah, graceful as a princess and even more beautiful. My heart melts. She wears the prettiest purple dress, and her hair is put up in a way I've not seen. She cuts her eyes my way without turning her head.

Old Bart pokes my leg with his knee. "Whoa now, boy, time will bring all good things."

He's right. But, I still want to run hold her close, her heart pressed against mine.

Mr. Gilmore stands. "I truly hate to break up such good fellowshipping in the house of the Lord, and we know that anywhere God's people gather in Jesus' holy name, it's His church!" He sits down. The freedmen and the new Negroes sway a bit and break into a chorus.

It's such a good sound, and the words get me ready for my little speech. I sway in rhythm with the rest who wave their hands. A couple of older Negro women get up and dance, caught up in the Spirit. Though I didn't grow up doing this, it's just right for these people. It's right for them to worship as the Lord leads them. When the song ends, it's as if I've been doing this all my life.

Mr. Gilmore stands again. "We are blessed tonight. A new young man from Missip came here followin' the Lord's lead and now finds himself workin' with his brother, Benny Frank Tullos. Y'all know Benny Frank and his good wife, Dorcas. This is Columbus Nathan Tullos, but those that know him and love him, as we all will find very easy to do, he's just called Lummy."

Several men and women welcome me, "Glad you here, Massuh Lummy, what a blessin'!"

Mr. Gilmore interrupts, "I mean no harm to you good folks tryin' to show respect, but there ain't no Massuhs in this house of the Lord, unless it be King Jesus himself!"

In one voice and with big smiles, the slaves belt out, "Amains, Lawd, amains!"

"Brother Bart, please pray for the man of God sent to give us a word."

"Yassuh, be pleased to." Bart waves me up to the front. He turns me to face the crowd placing his hands on my shoulders. I hardly hear a word he says except when he asks the Holy Spirit to fill my mouth with the sweet honey of God's Word. I can't keep my eyes off Susannah, who blushes and smiles with tears running down her cheeks. Her smiling eyes are like God himself looking back at me.

Bart closes his prayer, and I've never felt more ready to speak for the Lord. I start out slowly, but with the help of the freedmen and women, I get louder as I go.

When I sit down, there's a clap, another, and then the whole group shouts and starts singing loudly. I don't remember much of what I said when I sit down.

"Did I make any sense at all?"

Old Bart shoots me a surprised look. "Make sense? Is you crazy, boy? You talked like God was right here amongst us. In fact, you talked to God more than you talked to us!" We stand up and join in the singing.

After the service, Mr. Gilmore introduces me to all his workers and the few whites who've come from farms around. "I saved the best for last, Lummy. Meet my sweet daughter, Susannah."

My knees start shaking.

"That was a fine talk about the Lawd, Massuh Lummy. I hope we'll be hearin' more from you soon."

I take her extended hand to kiss it gently, and she blushes. "I do hope so, and please, it's just Lummy. Like Mistuh Gilmore said, ain't no masters and no slaves in this house of the Lord, only people who love each other in his name." I squeeze her hand and softly let it go. She nods, never breaking her stare into my eyes. I'm about to melt.

Mr. Gilmore clears his throat, "Bart, please see my daughter to the house. I'd appreciate it." Old Bart hustles over and takes Susannah's hand. Halfway to the house, she gives me a wink.

"Interestin', very interestin' indeed, young Mistuh Lummy. Don't recall hearin' such an impassioned yet so personal a speech in all my days. It's like you was talkin' not only to the group and with the Lord but also to someone special."

I don't know what to say.

"But I liked what you said, a lot. It's what our people need, a real God they can talk to. It was good when you said God spoke to Moses face to face, like a man does with his good friend. These are good God lovin' people. For too long they've had to respect masters who claimed to be God himself."

I don't hear much of what he says after that. My mind wanders back to Susannah, and without thinking I say aloud, "I'm so glad she's here, thank you Lord!"

Mr. Gilmore stops talking. "Say wha-a-at?" Fortunately, he got rather animated and didn't hear what I had said.

"I'm so glad to be here. Thank you for tonight." I start to leave, and Mr. Gilmore waves.

"Oh, okay. Well, thanks again for such fine words. Can I expect you to be a regular for us?"

I nod. I wander towards the small barn where I'll bunk with Old Bart for the night.

Mr. Gilmore yells with his hands cupped, "Coffee at four, biscuits at four fifteen, then off to south farm by four thirty!"

"We'll be ready, and thank you again, Mistuh Gilmore."

He walks away mumbling, "That man has more than love for the Lord in his soul. He's got love in his heart for someone special."

Things are unfolding and I have little control, much like my feelings right now. I'm just about to burst with excitement. Like Ma used to say, "Lummy boy, you ain't been able to hide your feelin's from nobody, so just live them." She's right, and I will, however this story goes.

CHAPTER 16

HARD WORK CURES MANY A BAD THOUGHT

JUNE 20, 1859

Sometimes you just gotta bow your neck!

WORK ON MR. Gilmore's farms suits me just right. Plowing with the two new oxen he just bought strengthens my injured shoulder muscles. Work brings back good memories.

Back home, Pa's two mules, Sandy and Kate, would only work hitched on the same side every time. Kate, the black mule, had to be on the right. Sandy, a reddish colored lop ear, had to be on the left. If they weren't hooked up that way, neither would budge. They'd just patiently wait until one of us got smart enough to switch them to their proper places, and then you didn't even have to smack them with a plough line. They'd turn the ground pretty as you please.

At day's end after we wash up, Dorcas applies ointment on the "rubs" where plow lines blister our shoulders and hands. Its funny how calluses go away in the short time between harvest and breaking ground. But it doesn't take long for them to show up again. The pain is good knowing good work is being done.

There are two happy times every day on a farm. First, coming in out of the sun for dinner, cooling off, eating a big meal, and laying in the shade like a fat lazy old hound dog for an hour. Mr. Gilmore provides the supplies and usually shows up about that time to see how the work is coming along. He likes Dorcas's cooking, too. Then about one o'clock, we go back and work until until dark.

The other happy time is at the end of the workday—gathering tools, trudging in at sundown, tending the animals, and taking stock of what's been accomplished.

By the first part of June, we have all the plowing done and the crop in on the larger south farm. We move to the smaller piece of ground near Shiloh Church. Once that's done, we clear land on the plot Mrs. Gilmore left her husband. Working both farm plots and cutting timber to send down the Dugdehoma River at the same time runs us ragged.

With everything caught up, Mr. Gilmore gives us a rest. I'm ready for a break. The bream are bedding up. I suggest we take the boys fishing and catch a mess for a fish fry. And of course, Ben caught the biggest one.

Ben announces as we're cleaning the fish, "Let's go to town Saturday and catch up news about how things are shakin' out around our country."

Dorcas agrees, "Yeah, and let's get the kids some sweets. They've been a big help totin' water and such." It's a happy time and a prayerful time, a time to thank our Creator.

Two kinds of people are especially close to God. First, the hunter/trapper knows the ways of the woods and critters nearly as good as the One who created them. Not the sportsman type whose only goal is to kill the buck with the biggest antlers or the most squirrels for the sake of numbers and sometimes leaving the meat to rot. No, it's they who thank the Creator each time an animal is taken using the meat and hides for good, often for the survival of the family. This man lets a doe pass when trailed by two little spotted fawns and never shoots a squirrel nest.

The other are farmers who trust the dirt, wait on rain, and pray for more when needed. Farmers like Ben must talk to God quite often when gully washers take away planted seed or when drought burns everything up. But it's the women on both counts that really have the greatest faith, first in God, and second in a husband and what he's chosen to do.

I look up into the blue sky. "Lord, You know best, and You know what this family needs. Into Your hands we give ourselves." I fully believe in the One to whom I pray every day that He'll answer. At His blessed and wise discretion, of course.

The best part of my day is washing off the sweat and sitting on the front porch with Ben. It's when he's at his best, until he tilts up the brown jug a little too much. We sit in rocking chairs eating cornbread and sweet milk out of big tin cups Dorcas keeps cold in the icehouse.

On this Thursday evening, the air is warm but not unpleasant. A steady breeze keeps the sweat from rolling down my legs and mosquitos from landing. We just finished supper when Ben pulls out a couple of cigars he's saved for some time.

"We need to celebrate, Lummy. You're doin' real good here, brother. I appreciate your hard work. When payin' time comes, Mistuh Gilmore will take care of you well. Just keep it up."

Was I day dreaming, or did Ben just give me a compliment?

He hands me a cigar. "Made from that good sou-u-uthern tobacco!"

We smoke in the silence of a day well spent. I never smoked much, really only one cigar in my life, except for those grapevines which no one likes. I puff it and like it. It's quiet. Two doves light in a poplar tree at the edge of the yard and begin their mournful song.

Ben reminisces, "Granny Thankful said mournin' doves call for rain. Could use a good'n on our plantin'."

"Yep." Cigar smoke hangs thick in the wet air like fog as the gray feathered duo sing high up in the tree. I love my brother and being with him. The cigar smoke smells good.

Dorcas comes out wiping her hands on her apron, and the kids follow in a straight line like ducks swimming behind their Momma. It's a special treat for them to sit with the grown folks. Dorcas brings out teacakes fresh from the oven covered with muscadine jelly.

"Been savin' this last jar for just such a special occasion!" The tin plate of cookies gets passed around, and they disappear quickly.

Ben snickers. "You remember working that big garden for Mistuh Garland back home? Can't remember, were you old enough to pick beans on his place?"

"Sure was, that was where Pa first taught me how to 'gee haw' with that old gray mule."

Ben blows a ring of smoke, and Talton tries to catch it. "Yeah, that's right. We made good money working that ground for him. But I remember Mistuh Garland spittin' tobacco juice on our bare feet and always laughing at us. But for 'sproutin' bucks,' as he used to call us, he was trampin' on this one's territory."

Dorcas gives Ben a look of, *Don't be too hard, remember the children.* Ben nods. It's funny how husband and wife communicate without speaking a word.

"You remember ole Mistuh Garland would come down from his big house, always in the hottest part of the day, wearin' his fine clothes? There we'd be with our shirts off and ringin' wet with sweat. He'd laugh and call us women 'cause we had to pick beans, which for some people was women's work. I never felt that way, not after sittin' down to Ma's good cookin'everyday. Well, this one hot August day, he...."

I burst out laughing remembering the story he's about to tell.

Ben looks aggravated at first, but when I roar again, he understands. "Let me tell it from here Ben, come on!"

The children scoot closer, shaking with excitement. "Please, Daddy, let Uncle Lummy tell it. We ain't heard this one yet!"

Dorcas pats Ben on the arm, and he grins, "Then tell it good."

"Ain't no other way to tell it, big brother! Well, Mistuh Garland not only spit 'baccy juice on our feet and make fun of us for bean pickin', he'd come down with the bi-i-iggest stone pitcher of cold, fresh-made lemonade you ever saw! It was strong. You could smell it before he got to us, like stickin' your head in a jar of lemon drops at Mistuh Davis's store!"

Four year-old Martha giggles. "Oooh, I love them lemon drops, don't you, Uncle Lummy?"

"They sure is good, ain't they? Mistuh Garland, well, he'd sit himself right down on the end of our wagon where we all could watch him take his tin cup and fish out his lemonade from that stone pitcher. He drank it ever so slowly, winkin' at us, but never offerin' us a drop."

The children shrink back like they'd walked up on a snake. Little Nancy—named after Mr. Gilmore's deceased wife—blurts out, "Bad manners, huh, Momma?"

Dorcas nods.

"Well, your daddy tried to do the right and best thing for us younger children. He was the oldest and all since your Uncles Elihu, George, and Amariah were off with Pa cuttin' timber. Well, Ben decided to speak up for the rest of us. Your daddy was becomin' a growed up man. A real man don't take kindly to bein' called no bean-pickin' sister boy. No harm intended, Dorcas." She winks. "So your daddy caught Pa in the hog pen and told him what was happenin'."

"Pa didn't care much about other people's feelin's and told Ben, 'Boy, sometimes you just gotta bow your neck. There's always gonna be somebody on you about somethin'. Just bow your neck, take the heat, and put up with the ignert asses you gotta work for.'"

I cover my mouth.

Dorcas cuts me a look that reminds me of Ma. The children hold their hands over their mouths, "Oou-u-u, Uncle Lummy gonna get lye soap for breakfast, huh, Momma?"

"Well, he just might."

Ben leans up, "It is in the Bible, you know."

"Yeah, but thems the four-legged kind, so don't be a two legged one in front of the children!"

Ben shrugs his shoulders. The children giggle at their ma chastising their pa. He sticks his tongue out when she turns back to listen to the story.

"Anyway, before me and your daddy get into worse trouble, Ben done had ju-u-ust about enough of ole Mistuh Garland. One hot August day, I mean it was a scorcher and not a lick of cool breeze anywhere, we was down on our knees pickin' purple-speckled butterbeans."

Nine year old Oliver whispers to little Elihu, "Boy, I hate them speckled butterbeans, ugh!"

Ben pops him lightly on the head and shakes his head.

"And don't you know, Mistuh Garland sauntered right on down the hill, pretty as you please, all dressed up with that lemonade jug and his one tin cup with no plans to share?

"Before he even got to the gate of the garden patch, he yelled, 'What a fine bunch of lilies in my field of garden growin's! I might have to pick a few for my wife's supper table. You lilies sure look pretty out there in the bean patch. What? You forget your aprons, sister boys?'"

"Unbeknownst, that's a good word ain't it, unbeknownst?" I rubbed young Talton's head. "Unbeknownst to Mistuh Garland, your daddy done had enough of his lemonade jug, fancy clothes, and sassy words. He slipped into the corn stalks unseen. All I heard your daddy say was, 'This lilly is gonna pick himself a daisy today!'"

"Mistuh Garland was steadily mouthin' off, when"—I double over laughing with tears in my eyes—"I seen this huge rotten tomater sailin' in a perfect arch high enough to reach the angels. If I didn't know better I'd say one of them caught it and carried it right on top of Mistuh Garland's head! It exploded like a bomb! With his big ole sassy mouth wide open! The red juice from that old nasty tomater splashed all over his head and went right into his pickle sucker. He went to spittin' like he done sipped turpentine. I betcha turpentine tastes better!"

Everyone roars while Ben hangs his head, knowing now one of his children will surely pull that or a similar stunt one day. Maybe on him.

Dorcas does the motherly thing of covering her mouth, like she disapproves but snickering all the same, and then bursts out like a big sneeze and laughs with the rest of us.

It's good to hear this family laugh. Ben's happy.

"The funny thing was Mistuh Garland didn't know who done it! We all would've taken a beatin' with Ben, or for him, before we'd tell on him. And you know what? We never could understand why that Mistuh Garland never back came around the garden patch no more!" The kids laugh at the whiny little old man voice I make.

Dorcas asks, "What'd your pa do after that? He must've got told about that happenin'!"

Ben looks at me. I don't know.

"I told Pa, and he ceremonally gave me three licks with the leather strap out behind the smokehouse so he could tell Mistuh Garland he whooped me. Easiest whoopin' I ever got." Ben chuckles, "When he finished my butt strappin', Pa told me, 'Tomorrow at church, you sit down easy, like your butt's been on fire and just put out. Let Mistuh Garland see you, and whatever he says, you take it and say you're sorry.'

"I remember bristlin' up sayin', 'But Pa, I shouldn't have to.' Pa held up his hands, and I stopped. 'Me neither Ben, just do it. We need that garden patch. Sometimes you just gotta bow your neck and take it.' I dropped my head. Then Pa playfully pushed me on my shoulder. 'And by the way, how'd in the heck did you make that shot? It was a good'n I heard. Wish I could've seen it myself!'"

Ben laughs, and then his face expression changes. "That's one of the few happy moments I remember and the only whoopin' I remember gettin' that didn't leave purple welts on my ass or blood in my drawers." His eyes glass over. He's gone to a far off place in his head. He takes another swig from his brown jug mumbling. "But Pa, he was all right. I wished I'd seen him before we left."

A tear trickles down his right cheek. He turns away so the kids can't see. Dorcas takes the cue.

"All right, children, bedtime, and I don't want another word!"

The kids wail, "Aww, Momma, we want more!"

Dorcas stands up. "I said you best get on. We got work tomorrow, and you're gonna be right smack in the middle of it. Kiss your daddy and Uncle Lummy good night. If anybody needs it, you best get to the outhouse and back quick before that headless horseman gets you!" The kids scamper into the house. After that scare, I imagine slop jars will be the order of the evening.

I sit quietly, leaving Ben to his thoughts. My stomach's a little queasy, and I'm dizzy. I look at the short stub of my cigar and then at Ben.

"I'm fixin' to throw up." I swallow hard, and my guts start to heave.

"Well, go on over behind the catalpa tree, away from the house." I barely make it before I puke up my cornbread and sweet milk supper, some of the cornmeal grains blasting through my nose. That ain't good. I wash out my mouth at the well then come back to my chair.

"Dang, didn't know I'd do that."

Ben sniffs. "Noticed you puffin' that thing way too fast. Saw it all along.

Knew what would happen."

I want to say, *Why didn't you tell me? You dern'd fool!* But I leave it alone. I guess there's some things you learn by doing once and twice if you're stupid. I ain't stupid.

Ben sighs, taps his foot a few times, and looks away for a moment. "You know, Lummy, we didn't grow up like other boys. Not everyone got beatin's from their Pa like we did. I been around lots of people in a lot of different places and met many a man who had a peaceful home, where the father wasn't so damn hard on his children." There's sadness in his voice but also hardness. I can't tell which.

"Yeah, I'm figurin' that out and tryin' to get on past it."

Ben looks me in the eye and fakes a smile. "I can't seem to, brother. I'm too much like Pa, becomin' everythin' I ever hated."

Another tear rolls down his face. He wipes it quickly, thinking I don't see. He doesn't need to know that I do. It's hard to reconcile love for a father who only returns hardness. Ben's right. He's too much like Pa. He knows it, but it's hard for him to see it in himself, and not a person can tell him different. Not even Dorcas.

He takes a draw from the jug. "But Pa did teach us to work, didn't he? And how to take care of things. I love my wife and the kids, would die for everyone of them. But anymore, the only joy I get out of life is what I can accomplish and maybe a little too much shine. I find hard work cures many a bad thought. Is that a bad thing, Lummy?"

I shake my head.

We sit in the silence of past memories. "I wish I'd worked things out with Pa before I left. Hope he gets well soon. Maybe we could go visit him and Ma. Maybe not. Don't think things could've ever been set right between us. I love Pa. Just have to do it at a distance."

"Yeah, I learned that, too. Didn't know I'd wind up here, but I do appreciate you takin' me in, makin' a way for me. But I think a bit different. Work don't cure anythin' for me, but it does help take my mind off of things."

I try to lighten the mood. "Yeah, work never bothered me none! I can lay down right beside it and go to sleep!" Ben chuckles and then grows quiet.

He stares into the dark of the night, listening to unseen sounds. His eyes follow lightning bugs floating about. The silence brings peace to our souls.

"I'm glad you're here with me, brother. Didn't know if I would, but it's good. I like the way you talk. Do me a favor and pray for rain. We need it now that plantin's done."

"I will, brother." And for other things, too.

I TAKE MORE interest in how things are done around the farm. I know a lot about surviving in the woods and some things about running a farm but not so much about how to be settled, stay settled, not just to survive, but thrive. Ben thrives on a farm. He may have been of the moving kind, but he surely is of the settling kind now.

Me? Heck, not sure where on God's good green earth I'll finally land for good, if I do. Only He knows. My settling place will have to be somewhere different than I've ever been before, given my love for Susannah. Anyway, I pay close attention throughout the summer and over the next couple of years to the way Ben runs things. I watch how Dorcas gets her work done and handles the children. I expect to have my own place one of these days and I want to be prepared to care for my family.

Living on the south farm I rarely see Susannah, except when we have business up at the main house. I don't get to attend prayer meeting very often in the summer. There's just too much to do and not enough time to do it. We don't want to hire on extra hands. That'd cut into Mr. Gilmore's profits. So we do double duty, like back home, hoping for a better pay day when harvest is over.

Old Bart visits once a week to drop off mail and see if we need anything from Davis's Store. He takes butter Dorcas makes to be sold in Winnfield. We get an occasional letter from Ma, and I respond back. But that's not the only mail I get.

I pass Susannah messages scribbled on newspaper Bart brings us weekly. In turn, Susannah writes me sweet notes on nice stationery with a splash of flowery perfume that stirs my heart. Old Bart grins when he hands them off to me discreetly.

"Sure had a hard time not readin' that one, Massuh Lummy. Must be some powerful love words floatin' around on them papers to smell so sweet!" He teases me trying to hold them back. He knows they are worth more than my pay. I read and reread every one down by the spring out of sight of Ben and the family.

I help Ben with hog killing and learn how to prepare hams and bacon for the smokehouse. I watch Dorcas can everything from string beans and black eyed peas to stewed venison and sausage for the winter. I especially like when she boils blackberries in summer and muscadines and possum grapes in the fall to make jam. We tan hides—hog and deer—to sell to Mr. Davis.

I learn safer and better ways to log timber and get it to the river. I haul salt in wagons to the Red River with Old Bart and learn the names of steamboats docking there. I watch how Ben treats the men who work for him well, especially Mr. Gilmore's freed men. We learned that, too, from Ma and Pa. Pa may have said bad things about Negroes on occasion, but he always treated them with respect.

I watch Dorcas bring a story from the Scriptures and have the children say their prayers. She won't let them say the same old words. She teaches them to pray from their hearts. But everyone can repeat Ben's breakfast time prayers without thinking. I believe he means what he says when he bows his head.

When it comes to the basics of life, Ben and Dorcas surely are a good pattern to follow. I'm a better man for being here. I'm in a good place, and I thank the Lord.

CHAPTER 17

THE BIG COUNT

SEPTEMBER 3, 1860

King David counted his fightin' men, even after the Lord said, "Don't!"
It did not go well for him after that.

WE TULLOSES HAVE all been counted before by the government. I remember the excitement of getting my name written down in a big ledger by some man out of Jackson in the 1850 Census. Pa talked about being counted in the 1820 Census in Pike County after he and Ma got married. Not everyone back home got counted or wanted to be. Some hid up in the hills, and other families weren't counted together. Ours was one of those in 1850—a sign we were older and scattered about.

The government man from Jackson recorded Ma and Pa, Elihu, Rebecca, Amariah, me, and Jasper together in 1850. But not Saleta who'd gone to be with the Lord back in '47. We still talked about her like she was with us though, at least Granny and Ma did. I don't remember, but somehow James didn't get his name in the big ledger. It was a big day for me, proud to be recorded as a farmer along with the other men. I felt grown, but I was still far from it.

Ben didn't want to get counted back then and doesn't want to this year either. In 1850, he caved in to Dorcas who wanted it recorded that she was married, had four children, and that their family had five hundred dollars in personal property. Dorcas wasn't bragging. She was just so proud of what they'd accomplished together.

Our brother, George Washington, a year younger than Ben, had joined him to farm and cut timber. He got counted with Ben because he lived on their forty acre farm at census time. Those two always got along fine and together could turn a cash dollar pretty easily. Ben was no nonsense when it came to working on the farm, and George Washington just fell right in line with him.

Pa sent me to help them when they had to reseed a field after a gully washer or get the last bit of cotton before a rain. I liked the work, and at sixteen I could pull a cotton sack or limb a tree with a double-bit axe with the best of them. I liked the way Ben and George worked together without a lot of mouthiness or meanness. Ben's changed since then.

But this 1860 Census? Ben resists even more this time, saying the Federal government just wants to get an accurate count of possible fighting men in the southern states should war break out. I don't disagree. He finally gives in to Dorcas and goes to the Goodwater Post Station to see the census man. He stands in line, shifting one foot to the other, visibly unhappy.

Ben steps up to the census man and motions for Dorcas to do the talking. She has no problem saying that she and Ben have seven children and eight hundred dollars in personal property.

"That weren't so bad. I guess we don't look too bad on paper, huh, Dorcas?" She smiles, puts her arm under his, and they stroll away the afternoon. He stops by the store to buy her sweets. I watch from a distance. They enjoy a rare moment from farm work and raising seven kids.

I'm not very far away talking to Mose. Dorcas reminds Ben she's so proud of him but most especially of how the Good Lord has been very good to them.

Ben kisses her lightly. "You know I don't express my feelin's on the Lord very often. Our Pa laid religion on us boys way too hard, on others way too easy, and not always for the right reasons. Ma said that under her breath a hundred times, 'That preacher needs to hear his own words.' He often used religion like a whip on us boys." Ben shudders. "If we done wrong or tore up something, he'd tell it out in the church yard on Sunday after service just to shame us. Truth be told, that's why I don't cotton much to attendin' church or puttin' up with some hard talkin' preacher. 'Cause when I look at it, Dorcas, Pa wasn't the only self-righteous bastard talkin' bad about everybody else. Got some bad thoughts I can't seem to shake from back then.

But I go to church 'cause you want me to, and the children need example. I love the Lord, Dorcas, and I praise him in my own way, a lot like the way Lummy talks about it." He waves his arms out into the air as if he's becoming part of the wind. I've never heard Ben talk or seen him do anything like that.

Ben, embarrassed, tries to change the subject. "Hell, it's hotter'n an egg in a fryin' pan!"

Dorcas pulls him close and puts her arms around his broad shoulders. "You ain't gettin' away that easy. I gotcha hawg-tied for sure, husband! The Lord is patient, and so am I, Ben Tullos. I ain't goin' nowhere and neither are you!"

Ben grins shyly enjoying every minute of it. "I don't know who's more in charge, you or the Lord, Dorcas Tullos."

She giggles like a school girl, "Then, me and the Good Lord'll just have to keep you guessin', won't we? What you think about that, Benjamin Franklin Tullos?"

I slip away, but I needed to witness that. I have more compassion on a brother who may never get over the wrongs done to him he never asked for. I'm not sure I ever will either. But we can be together and have a home together, here in Winn Parish.

I already got counted at the Post Station in Winnfield back on June 25th, along with Mr. Gilmore's family and Moses Cockerham, who lives on the place. Our postmaster, R. B. Williams, formed up the lines, making it easy for the government man with the big ledger to do his recording. I was staying out on Mr. Gilmore's at the time, mending about a half-mile of fence with Mose when it came time. It didn't matter where a man lived, I just had to declare a residence to be counted. So I chose to officially reside at Mr. Gilmore's. Mose did, too.

Mr. Gilmore gave us the day off today after milking the cows to join in the festivities here at the Goodwater Post Station. There's a band, flags everywhere, a few soldiers, and lots of laughter. It reminds me of when Jefferson Davis gave a stump speech at Greensborough a few years back trying to get votes to get elected governor.

There's a few long winded talkers this afternoon too, but after I watch

Ben and Dorcas those few minutes I head for the free food. I wave over to Mr. Wiley who happens to be in the small village visiting an old army friend. He waves back, and I get them a plate. I carefully carry the loaded tin pans across the dusty street and sit on his friend's porch.

"Lummy, meet my good friend, Hugh Maroney." I hand each of the old men a plate, and I shake Mr. Hugh's hand. "Hugh was the one who dragged my ass to the doctor's tent when the cannonball about took off my head. Sure glad he was there."

I nod and wait.

"Oh, yeah, this is my good friend, Columbus Nathan Tullos, from Choctaw County, Missip. He's a good'n and works for Mistuh Fancy Pants Gilmore."

Hugh looks up from his plate. "I like that man. He has his head on straight about the darkies, I believe."

I go back to get a plate for myself and settle in on a rough oak bench to enjoy the fine food. We watch the festivities, and I listen to Mr. Wiley rail on about the coming war.

"If the government don't back up off us soon, there's gonna be hell to pay! Damn 'em, ain't got sense God gave a goose!"

I try to change the subject. "Mistuh Hugh, don't mean no harm, but what kind of name is Maroney?"

Mr. Wiley butts in, "I-i-i-taliano, and the best damn cook you could ever experience. He came in by ship at New Orleans years ago and joined up when we all took the long walk south with General Taylor back in the Mexican War. Good man and damn, his vittles are the best—that is, when he can get them good spices."

I look at Hugh, and he shrugs his shoulders. "That's about it."

The day lingers on slowly, a good break for hard working farm and logging families. We catch up on the news, talk about crops and livestock, and hear the latest gossip. A few of the older boys try to impress the giggly girls while the younger boys chase the little girls with frogs and lizards. It's a strange thing how boys change into men, if they ever really do.

Old Bart waves me over from the back corner of a building. I take our plates and say my goodbyes to Mr. Wiley and Mr. Hugh.

Old Bart and the other slaves get counted behind Mr. Davis's store, as does Susannah. They have their own little gathering, and Mr. Gilmore has provided good food and sweets for them. I'm ashamed of the separation, but I stay with them the rest of the afternoon.

Susannah rubs her elbow on mine. I shiver with excitement, and she grins. I can't believe it. I am standing with the prettiest woman in the whole world, side by side, like two people about to be married—the day I wish for.

Ben yells, "Lummy, where are you, boy? Let's load up and head out."

I don't answer. I forgot I was going to their home this evening, having finished my work on north farm. I rub my shoulder once more gently against Susannah's.

Old Bart sees the love in my heart all over my face. "I gots her for you, Massuh Lummy. Ain't gonna let's no harm come to my li'l sister, so's don't worry nairn."

"Thanks, Bart. You're rapidly becomin' my very best friend."

"I likes that, Massuh Lummy."

Two government counts in this parish—white and black. Two states in Louisiana. Two countries in this United States. Two different ways of thinking in the minds of men headed for a crash. And, here we are counting up the number of people who will either get hurt or killed in that crash.

I remember Pastor Dobbs telling one Sunday at Mt. Pisgah Church how King David thought too highly of himself and broke the Lord's command by counting up his fighting men. The Lord told David not to do that. He did it anyway. It didn't go well for him after that. Or for seventy-thousand Israelites God struck down with a plague. David did repent of his mistake but not until after he heard the number of fighting men. A census. Just like now.

It's interesting that God didn't take David's land or riches. He took away the very thing King David believed was his property, what would make him secure—fighting men. King David forgot that those fighting men were never his in the first place. King David got too big for his britches, and everybody else paid the price.

It seems to always go like that. Some big shot, thinking he has the power of the Almighty, does something to provoke the True Almighty, and those who didn't have anything to do with it are the ones who get punished. I'm going to have to ask the Lord about that one day.

Have we forgotten that all people are God's people? When did one man get to decide who is, and who ain't, God's child? Where does that come from? Not from God. Color never mattered to God, or we wouldn't have all come from the same Ma and Pa—call them Adam and Eve, or Noah and Mrs. Noah—however you want to do that.

Ma said God made people different colors because he likes variety. For me, the most important thing is that Negroes never were ours in the first place, no more than the land, water, or sky ever has been. Anything we do have, whatever we're blessed with by God's good hand, is only given us to bless someone else.

God might just send a plague sent down on us. I wonder if we'll be smart enough to repent now, before the count is final and the plague of war comes upon us. It will be us, Louisiana, Mississippi, and the other southern states God sends the plague down on, hard and fast. Then our plague will hurt the Yanks too because they can't stop the war.

Uncle Rube told me once that the Yankees yell about southerners having slaves, but are happy to buy all the cotton we can grow to help fatten their wallets in their cloth factories up north. This war will surely set somebody free—maybe all of us—from the evils of greed and slavery. The cost will be bloody and heartbreaking, though. God will watch as many of his white children lose their lives and property. Many a Yankee will never go home to his family or sweetheart for being cheered on by fat merchants wearing tall hats, sipping glasses filled with fine whiskey. God will take southern rights from rich planters who buy and sell Negros like cattle. It'll be painful. It will be grisly.

It will be liberating.

It'll be because of the two counts. One white. One black. We won't repent. It's too late for that. None of us will. We're too proud. All of us, north and south. We put too much faith in our belief that slavery makes us secure, south and north.

I repent in front of Old Bart, Susannah, freedmen, and those still slaves. I fight back the tears. They say a prayer of peace over me. I hug Susannah and start for the street.

Ben climbs up on the wagon looking for me. A mail rider trots his horse into town and stops at the Feed and Seed. Though letters are few and far between, I always hope to get one from Ma. Today I do. As I open it, I'm pressed down in my spirit. I read the letter, and my feeling is confirmed.

Pa is gone.

He's with the angels. His labors are over. His work on earth is done, and he won't be counted in the 1860 Census for Choctaw County, Mississippi.

I follow Ben and Dorcas on a mule back to south farm. How am I going to tell Ben Pa is dead? He won't take it well, but he won't show it either. Just like Pa. Hard men living hard lives rarely show soft-heartedness.

We put the mules up, and after Dorcas gets the kids into bed, I ask her and Ben to join me on the porch. I lean on a post and pull out the letter.

Dorcas blurts out happily, "How's Ma and Pa? They doin' okay?" I shake my head. Her face turns solemn.

Ben knocks out his pipe and refills it from his drawstring tobacco pouch. "Go on, read it. Can't be all that bad."

I fumble the two short pages and read slowly.

Bankston Mississippi, June 7, 1860

Dear Lummy, Ben, and Dorcas, I hope you are well and in good spirits. We are doing much better now that the drought has ended. We weren't sure we'd have a crop this year, but the Lord pulled us through. But with that good blessing, I do have some very bad news. It saddens me to write that your Pa has crossed river Jordan and rests with his fathers. The flux swept through the hills and with his other ailments, he wasn't strong enough to overcome it. It was so bad. We had a burying nearly every day, and many a good person went to be with the Lord. We laid my Archibald high on the hill above the house with the rest of our dearly departed family. I know you boys didn't like Pastor Dobbs much, but he gave a good service for your Pa. Know that Pa loved you boys and always said good things about you to other people. Try to remember the good things if you can when you talk about him to his grandchildren. Anyway, whatever was not right for your Pa in this world is made right now that he's in the arms of Jesus. This is all I have the heart to write just now. I will send another letter soon. The boys, Rebecca, Mary and little Emaline send their love, as do I, your Ma.

Ben gets up slowly out of his chair and walks to the barn. He turns up a jug he's hidden on the shelf above his work bench.

Dorcas grabs my hand. "Lummy, he'll never be all right, will he? He can't fix it with his Pa now, and I fear he will grow more bitter with age. I don't know what to do."

"Ain't nothin' we can do but give him time."

Things will get worse with Ben now.

"How you doin' with all this?"

I sigh. "I'm glad I got things straight with Pa 'fore I left. He didn't understand everythin' I said, but he hugged me and said he was proud of me. That was enough."

We sit in the dark night, listening to a whippoorwill call for a lost friend. The loss hurts. Worse than the beatings and hateful talk. He was my Pa. I'm glad he rests and sees the Lord.

I ask Dorcas for pen and paper to write Ma a letter. Funny, I don't have the words.

CHAPTER 18

BACK TO WINNFIELD

OCTOBER 20, 1861

Some things are too broke to fix this side of heaven.
Don't try to fix what ain't yours to fix.

T HE REST OF 1860 flies by like windy thunderstorms headed east. I hardly look up from my work most of 1861, and now that harvest is about over, most people are in a good mood. But things are changing. The war is on and many have enlisted. Some have already given their lives for the southern cause. Gray or blue—doesn't matter, death cares not what color uniform you wear.

We don't feel the effects of the war much this far out. Rich planters, merchants, and a few lawyers raised $80,000 to help build up the Red River defenses. That might hold back the blue army if they decide to come here. The Confederate Army whipped the blue bellies pretty sorely at some place called Bull Run in Virginia. The papers said they ran like rabbits, as did all the pretty ladies and fine gentlemen who went out to picnic and watch the Yankees win.

That's what the fine folks up in Washington City thought. It'll be a big show and the Rebs will back down. We haven't. The important people who started this thing didn't figure it'd go on this long. Ole Abe thought they'd make quick work of a few backwoods ridge runners and bayou bushwackers. He was wrong, and should have known it, having bragged so much about his country upbringing during the election. Maybe he forgot.

This disagreement has festered for years, and it'll take time to sort it out. Meanwhile, men in tall hats by warm fires smoke fine cigars and shake their heads at the losses, feigning insincere sadness. Lincoln and his armchair generals will devise another way to win their war. And, many more good boys, with very bright futures, will die.

We finished harvest a week ago and give ourselves time to rest to take stock of how God has prospered us. I'm thankful for the past two years—working two farms, trapping, hunting and fishing, clearing land and cutting timber, and delivering a load of salt occasionally when Mr. Gilmore secured a contract for his wagons. Bart and I had good times on those journeys to Week's Salt Works and the steamboats on Red River. We made good this year, especially with the growing need for foodstuffs and supplies for the Confederacy.

At year's end, Mr. Gilmore made a reckoning of what was accomplished to pay his hands fairly and give his due to the Lord. The added thirty acres of improved land we farmed coupled with the timber we cut off the one hundred and ten unimproved acres makes for a profitable year.

Mr. Gilmore lays it out. "Just in case something happens to me, the cash value of the farm is six hundred dollars and one hundred twenty-five dollars for farmin' implements and machinery." He records in his ledger two fine horses, nine milk cows, three farming oxen, twelve cattle for meat, and ninety-five hogs, worth five hundred dollars. It's not as much as I thought, but his generosity makes that so. He doesn't mention the value of his personal property. That's not our business anyway.

We'd slaughtered a few animals selling for them eighty-five dollars and harvested two hundred bushels of Indian corn for grinding. We picked five bales of high quality cotton, weighing out at four hundred pounds each ginned. We picked twelve bushels of peas and beans to put up for winter, and made eighty–five pounds of butter, half of which was sold at market. Not a bad year, given we ate off what we grew all along the way. With Mr. Gilmore's occasional gambling trip and the timber sale, it's enough to keep us going. His goal is to help folks who want to work hard and do right. That's for white folks and Negroes. I like that. It's good to be a part of something productive and successful and right in the eyes of the Lord.

Mr. Gilmore takes off his spectacles. "You men have done me very well this year despite the drought that cut us short. We produced about half of what we normally do, but I am thankful for the Lord's kindness. I wish it could be more, but Ben, here's your pay with an extra fifty dollar gold piece for your family. You led this crew well. Lummy, here's yours and an extra twenty dollar Liberty Head to stow away for another day. I'll give Mose one and Old Bart, as well. We're headed for some tough times, and soon a gold piece will buy more than paper money."

Ben stuffs his in his pocket. "Good advice, and thank you, Mistuh Gilmore. Always a pleasure workin' for you. My family has a good life here. We're always ready when you need anythin'."

"I know that. It's a pleasure to have good friends like you Tullos men."

I chime in, "Mistuh Gilmore, thank you for this generous gift. I'll save mine like you said. Thanks for givin' me the opportunity to work for you and all the spiritual wisdom you share."

Mr. Gilmore stands to shake our hands. "I expect to see you men here and there, hopefully at church, but for sure come plowin'and plantin' time next spring?"

Ben promises, "Count on that, Mistuh Gilmore."

I nod.

"Lummy, you still comin' to prayer meetin' I expect?"

"Yassuh, wouldn't miss it." It's too long between times I get to see Susannah not to go. With harvest over, I hope to see her more often. I have a plan cooking to make that happen.

We pack up our mules with the extra food and supplies Mr. Gilmore gives us and wave to all as we take the last turn in the road back home. I take a long look back at Susannah, who's standing on the porch. I'll see her at prayer meeting Tuesday, but also we plan to slip away into the woods like we did as kids. Old Bart warns me not to get caught, but said he'd watch out for us, as long as we stay right with the Lord. That's always been the plan.

It's been a good year, and I have money saved. I want to explore a different road than living with Ben through the winter. I have a good job with a good reputation with a good boss and friends in town who respect me. This year, I want to move forward to be on my own with Susannah. I don't know how that's going to happen, so I pray.

Ben told me earlier this year that when harvest was over, I could either work in town or duck and goose hunt with him and trap. Over the two years, Ben's drinking at night got worse when he had more time on his hands. He acts like he doesn't want me around and wants me to feel bad if I decide to stay.

At the supper table last night Ben barked, "Hell, if you gotta stay, I guess we'll just have to put up with you."

I know I'm valuable to his work here. I work like I own it all, treating everything as if it was mine. I love my brother and want his family to succeed in every way, but he's too unpredictable, making things unnecessarily difficult. Ben has become too cantankerous to be around, bossing my every move, complaining when I don't do things his way. He drinks too much, but rather than saying anything, I bear it for the sake of making a living and keeping the peace.

A man can take most anything if his goal is worth taking somebody else's crap. I've had my share of crap from Ben and need to take a break. Fresh air does a man good. I've had enough of Benny Frank Tullos and his gassing.

I'll get my old job back at the Feed and Seed with Mr. Davis in Winnfield and help out Mr. Gilmore for the winter. Being in town will put me closer to Susannah. I'll ask to stay with Mr. Wiley and help him out a bit. He's going down fast and can't get around well.

Dorcas agrees, when I announce my intentions at the supper table. She believes it will salvage what little of the relationship Ben and I have. There isn't much left. Ben isn't pleased with my decision but has way too much pride to ask me to stay. He doesn't say a word to or from church today. I'm liberated knowing I'll be on to newer things tomorrow morning.

We get home from church, and Ben just huffs about the house like an old black bear letting the whole world know he's unhappy. No one is giving him much attention though. Everyone avoids him. He sits alone by the fire, chewing his tobacco, watching the flames flicker. He grunts as he gets up from his chair and stares at me like the devil himself.

Ben wants me to speak first but only with what he wants to hear—me staying because that's what's best. What's best to Ben? Is what's best for Ben. He
cares little how anyone else feels. He pulls the plug of tobacco from his mouth,
throws it into the fire, spits the leavings, and gives me that devilish stare.

"No sense wastin' time hangin' around here. Get the hell on down the
road, and tomorrow mornin' ain't too soon." He drinks from his brown jug
to wash out his mouth. He spits in the fire, which flares up a big flame. He
walks away without looking at me. "And to hellfire with you."

I give a little snicker of contempt. But on the inside, I ache that my
brother never can seem to get it right. And, I want him to. Some things can't
be fixed this side of heaven. As Granny Thankful used to say, "Don't try to
fix what ain't yours to fix."

I'M UP EARLY this morning to find a fine breakfast waiting. Dorcas is
always too good to me. I sit down to a steaming cup of coffee and stir in a bit
of cane sugar with fresh cream. It always seems to end like this. Ben has to be
an ass to get some point across that doesn't make sense to anybody but him.
Mostly he just enjoys the meanness.

I sip my coffee, thinking about a deer I took a few weeks ago. Dorcas
asked me to get her some venison. So I took my old flintlock Grandpa Aaron
used when he served with the South Carolina militia fighting the British
back in the Revolution and, gun in hand, planned to bring some meat back
before sundown.

As I stepped off the porch, Ben spoke gruffly from his rocking chair. "Go
down that trail, cross the creek, make a hard left at the big oak, climb up in the
forked dogwood tree, and watch the trail twenty feet or so down the hill." Sure
enough, I hadn't been there forty minutes when a nice fork horn came feeding
along. His crunching pin oak acorns sounded like corn popping.

I checked my flint, powdered the strike, aimed for the front shoulder,
slowly pulled back the hammer. When he turned broadside, I touched the
trigger, and a huge cloud of smoke belched from the barrel. At first, I couldn't

see if I'd hit him or not. The wind wasn't stirring, so smoke hung in the air. I waited a few minutes to let things settle down, my heart pounding loud and fast, and then slid down out of the tree.

My heart was still racing when over near a cane break I saw the last flicker of the buck's tail. The shot had been true. I reloaded, cocked the hammer back, and eased over to the buck. I jolted him with my gun barrel to be sure he was dead. I sat knees down and rubbed his beautiful cape. I was glad to provide meat for the family but sad that I had to end the life of this woodland child of God. I thanked my Creator for this blessing that would feed the family for a month. I could already taste Dorcas's biscuits and gravy.

I cut a branch, slipped it through the tendons of his back legs, and dragged my prize to the house. The children came running yelling, "Uncle Lummy got a buck!"

Dorcas came to the door. "Fresh meat for supper tonight. You're a good'n, Lummy."

Ben came around the corner smiling. "Fine buck, little brother. Deer meat sure sounds good, if we can get a little biscuit and gravy to go with it." Ben winks at Dorcas standing in the doorway.

"You know I will, husband, but you best be gettin' them chores finished up. I want an early supper tonight!" Tapping her chin, she mumbled, "Maybe I'll make a blackberry cobbler."

Ben and I looked at each wide-eyed, like two men who just found gold in a creek.

"What should I do with the guts? I know you'll want to save the hide, liver, and heart, right?" Ben was still daydreaming about the blackberry cobbler. Maybe that or the shape of his pretty wife as she went into the house. It was a good moment, and I hated to spoil it for him. "Your a lucky dawg, Benny Frank—pretty wife, a great cook, and a tow sack full of children. The Good Lord done surely blessed you, big brother."

"Yeah, yeah He has." He's obviously only half-listening me as he eases up the steps after his wife. He reeks of moonshine. "Put the guts in the hole behind the smokehouse. Save the heart and liver for eatin' and the brains for tannin' the hide. Save the bones and hooves, we can use them. Save the hide, we gots lots of uses for it. It's worth a couple dollars in Winnfield if I need to sell it." Ben had something else on his mind and wasn't making much sense. He shut the door behind him.

Dorcas leaned out the window. "You children stay outside and don't run off. Talton Wesley, since William is off runnin' his coon traps, you're in charge. I'll let you know when you can come back in." The children start up a game of hide and seek. I take my deer to the skinning tree, hoist it up, and go to work.

I just finished washing my hands to bring the meat to Dorcas when Ben stomped out of the house with fire in his eyes. The children scattered like chickens on killing day.

"All done, Ben, the meat's ready for Dorcas. Want give me a hand?"

"Give you a hand? Hell no, you ignert bastard. What I ought to do slap your damn face! And another back hand for good measure!"

"What?"

"I didn't want you to throw them damn stinkin' ole guts down that hole over there. It's gonna bring every critter in the country side, especially them blasted buzzards that puke all over everythin'! You should've known better, you dumb ass. Use that damn head a yours for something more'n a hat rack!" My face got hot, but I wanted to control myself. It was like being with Pa all over again, but I wasn't going to take this lying down.

"You told me to take them guts there, and that's what I did."

He gritted his teeth, "Then you're gonna go down in that hole, fish 'em out, and take them somewhere else, you hear me?"

I don't move. "No, I'm not."

I thought Ben's red eyes would pop out of his head.

"You will too, dammit, or I'll beat you like a damned red-headed step-child!" He started towards me balling up a fist.

I held up my hands. "Here's what happened and here's what ain't gonna happen. You're drunk, and probably don't remember what you said, but I asked you where to put them guts, and you told me in that hole behind the smokehouse. That's what I did. What ain't gonna happen is me doin' anythin' more with them guts. What *is* gonna happen is if you come any closer and try to lay a hand on me, I'm gonna throw you down in that gut hole. Do you hear me?"

Ben stared at me for what seemed like an hour, but it was only a few seconds. I'm ready for him. It doesn't matter if I'd get whipped or not, because when my big brother, Ben, walks away from this fight, he'll be limping.

"All right, dammit!" Ben turned and stomped up on the porch to sit in his rocking chair. I gathered the meat and took it to the house. In that short time, Ben had passed out and snored softly.

Dorcas shook her head when I came in the door with the meat.

"You done the right thing standin' up to him, Lummy. He shouldn't treat you that way."

"Aint nothin', my sweet sister."

"I'm worried about my boys. They already show the signs. He's always been like that, hasn't he?" She hangs her head. "He ain't all bad. He just likes that damn ole shine too much." It was the only time I ever heard Dorcas cuss. But it wasn't the shine that made Ben that way. Whiskey just opens the door to what's deep inside.

Ben was the last one to the table for supper. Dorcas laid out the finest fried venison meal a man could wish for. He sat down and smiled at everyone.

"Brother, would you thank the Good Lord for this fine meal and that he bless the hands that prepared it?" It was as if nothing had happened. Too much like Pa. He'd get so mad you'd think he was going to tear the world apart, and then, in just and hour or so, he'd be perfectly all right. But the rest of us weren't, still reeling from strain of a very angry and sometimes violent man.

Supper went well, all laughing at my funny stories. Dorcas brought steaming bowls of blackberry cobbler with fresh cream. I ate 'til I was nearly sick. When all finished, I ask Talton Wesley to help me clear the table.

Dorcas looked at me funny, as did Talton, but he smiled, "Sure Unc Lummy, glad to."

Ben laughed, "Dang, Lummy, you gonna spoil these women if you keep this up. Talton, get your Uncle Lummy to teach you how to go after a buck deer tomorrow. He's the best hunter around here."

Ben was trying to clear the air of the trouble that afternoon. It was too late, these young boys had already been trained.

Talton tossed the scraps to the yard dogs. Ben and Dorcas relaxed on the front porch while the children chased lightning bugs in the dark. Ben lit up a cigar, and Dorcas slipped her arm under his and drew him close.

My mind slipped away to a hopeful thought. *Why can't my big brother be a good big brother?* That's all I really want. I'm ready and willing to be a good little brother. Makes for a good story in a book, I guess, but heck, this sure ain't no storybook. Anyway, those guts stayed in the hole where I put them that day.

As as I sip the last of my coffee, I don't expect to see Ben before I leave for Winnfield this cool Monday morning. I don't want to. I hate this—too much like being with our Pa, God rest his soul. I hope he has peace now in the arms of the Lord. My hope is dashed when Ben criticizes one of the children outside about something that doesn't really matter. It brings back bad memories.

Dorcas pats me on the back looking at me funny. "Sorry, I was in some far off place for a moment there, Sis." She wraps her arms around me from behind, squeezes hard, kisses me on the back of my neck like Granny used to do.

"You're doin' the right thing. Ben's a good man, you know that, don't you?"

"Yep, he's a good man, just like my Pa. Ben's become everythin' he hated and the very things he said he was leavin' home about. I hope he'll get over it one day, but that shine jug keeps him stuck in the past. Me? I can't stay in what I already done left behind me, and I won't carry it any further than I have to. It's taken a long time to shuck it off. Bein' here with Ben showed me what I never wanted to be but could be."

I set my coffee cup down. "We Tullos boys got a mean streak, but it needs temperin' and used only when needed. Which is hardly ever. We like the power of anger too much. It's creepin' back on me. It's been hard to fight it off bein' here. I need to go somewhere else for a spell."

"Then get gone early before Ben comes in for breakfast. It'll be better that way."

Earlier, before the sun rose, I'd packed my things to leave before breakfast. I finish the quick cup of coffee and my conversation with Dorcas. I take
a ham biscuit for the road. I head to the door, having kissed each child and
Dorcas too. I pull the door latch as Ben stomps up the porch steps. Hard
steps, like someone wanting to be heard.

I open the door, and Ben stands in the doorway, blocking my path.

"I don't want you to go. You're gonna stay. That's what I want, so go un-
pack your stuff. I need your help this winter, startin' today."

I don't move. He wreaks of moonshine. I won't cower to a big brother
who still won't act like one. I'm leaving.

He just doesn't understand that yet.

"Ben, it's always this way with you, and that's too bad. You have to be
an ass about most everythin.' No, I ain't stayin'. I'm puttin' some yonder between you and me." I stiffen, and my eyes become narrow slits. "I'm gonna
walk out this door, either 'cause you step aside, or 'cause I move you. Your
choice!"

He's dumbfounded. Finally, he ducks his head. "Okay."

He slinks back, his shine jug in hand.

Dorcas cries, "Lummy, we'll come see you in town!" I turn my mule towards the road.

A small crackly voice from behind the smokehouse whines, "Come on
back Christmas, Lummy, I'll do better."

I act like I don't hear him. Will I ever see Ben again? I'm not sure I want to.

CHAPTER 19

A LONELY ROAD LEADS
TO NEW FRIENDSHIPS

OCTOBER 21, 1861

*Bein' who God wants you to be sometimes means leavin' some people behind.
If they're supposed to be in your life, they'll catch up.*

THE ROAD TO Winnfield winds lonely through dark and shady woods. I've made this trip several times the past two years for supplies, mostly in the spring and summer. But with the leaves gone the land's easier to see. The road is good, the weather cool, and the hills aren't as steep as in Choctaw County. The money I received from Mr. Gilmore wasn't as much as he wanted to pay with the war on, but I believe things will get better.

I look back once.

Ben's in the road waving wildly, like, *Come back!* I keep riding. I have no complaints about working with Ben or staying with the family. They treat me well. But Ben's ways remind me too much of me.

That is, too much of the me I want to put away.

I leave wishing things were different. They could have been. It just isn't to be. You never know when you leave if you'll ever see that person again. Ben left never getting things straight between he and Pa. Maybe it just wasn't possible. I'll not do that with Ben, at least I hope. He did say come back Christmas. I walk the mule slowly.

Me, that hidden man inside, somehow becomes the great enemy. Often too much credit is given the Evil One, and I'm happy to give him his due, but truth is, he ain't got no power over me I ain't give him in the first place. I say it out loud, and a squirrel starts barking thirty feet into the woods. If I was going to camp for the night, I'd make that squirrel my supper. I want to make Winnfield by late afternoon. That cat squirrel gets to live another day.

"Lummy Tullos, you've come far in your short years, but you're still your own worst enemy." I remember Granny Thankful's words, "When you figure out who the problem is, you can get on the right side of things quicker." I look around to see if anyone heard me. I talk out loud too much. It'll get me in trouble someday.

Granny also said, "The hardest thing to do is set your self free." I figure it's never about what others have done to a person. It's more about what a person does to others, and to himself, because of what others have done to him. I call it, *E-N-E-M-E...* meaning, I'm my own worst enemy. A man's got to cut the ropes of the past and press on like the Apostle says. Easier said than done, though, I've found.

I miss Granny's wisdom and her singing to us at night when we were little. She sang all the time, mostly without noticing. Ma said it was her way of dealing with Grandpa. I sing one of her tunes. The mule seems to enjoy it.

THE RIDE TO Winnfield is peaceful. I hitch my mule to find Mr. Wiley grinnin' like a possum on his front porch. He tries to stand up but drops back down into his rocker.

"Well, knock me down and steal my teeth, looky at what the dawgs drug up! You look to be six pounds of flour in a five pound bag! Miss me too much, Columbus Nathan Tullos?"

"Well, glory be Mistuh Wiley, you know I ain't never been the last hawg to the trough! You know I missed you something fierce but mostly that good Cajun cookin'! I thickened up a bit, but I can still move quicker'n a swamp cat!" I hop off the mule in one bound, get up the porch steps in a leap to bear hug old Mr. Wiley.

"Hell, boy, last time you was here, you was so poor you could've fell through your ass and hung yourself! Damn boy, your squeezin' the crap right out of me! Folks gonna think we was family or something!"

"Mistuh Wiley, I got a proposition for you." He kicks his peg leg at me.

"Now, boy, I ain't the marryin' type!"

"I don't me-e-ean that, dang it! I'm bein' serious here. I need a place to stay for the winter. Mistuh Davis said I can work at the Feed and Seed. I plan to help out on Mistuh Gilmore's farm on slow days, but could you let me stay at your place? I'll pay."

"Hell, keep your money, just bring food into the house, shot or bought, I don't care, and keep things tidied up for me. And oh, yeah, keep the wood box full. That'll do it. You don't want to stay in the stock room like you did before?" I hang my head and smile. "That double-wide skirt lady store keeper too much trouble?"

"Ain't got no dawg in that hunt and don't want none. I just want a peaceful place at night, you understand?"

Mr. Wiley tries to jump up out of his chair. "Well, hell, yeah, Lummy Tullos, I want you to stay. I need a good domino player to keep me sharp so I can beat Mistuh Davis, and maybe even your Mistuh Gilmore, if I can cheat when he ain't lookin'. Sharp man, that James Gilmore."

"Sounds good! A good game of dominos by the wood stove on a cold winter's night with some muskrat stew all spiced up. Ummm, I can taste it already."

"Well, get your gear in here and go see Mistuh Davis. Hey, get me a plug of that new 'baccy he said just come in. Should be good'n fresh. Here's two bits. Get some sweets for yourself."

I reach for my wallet. "Now why don't you let me pay?"

"Put your money up! Call it your homecomin' celebration."

Mr. Davis is glad to see me. "Just in time to help with the shippin' of grain, cotton, and salt. I'll work it out so you can help Mistuh Gilmore, and oh yeah, I'll need you here when I go to Shreveport for my Christmas shoppin' trip with the Missus. We always pick up special items folks around here ordered for their children, wives, and sweethearts. That is if the Yanks don't get in our way. Could you work that out with Mistuh Gilmore?"

"Ain't nothin' to worry about. The Reb Army's got them Yanks pinned back all the way to the river. Ain't no Yank gettin' very far on this side of the Mississip. There's too many boys willin' to grab a musket. Go on and make your trip. I'll guard the Feed and Seed better'n if it was my own. Mistuh Gilmore knows I'll be workin' with you. It'll all work out, suh."

"I believe you, son." I unload the seed wagon into the storehouse out back and then spy the catalogs in the store.

"Mistuh Davis, is it too late to place an order for Christmas?"

"Naw, Lummy," peering down his nose over his spectacles. "You done found a sweetheart?"

"Aw naw, just somethin' I want to get Dorcas for takin' such good care of me whilst I stayed with them. Just a thank you, that's all. And a few things for the children."

"Uh-huh, I see. There's some catalogs on that there counter. Take a couple with you when we close up, and make your order tomorrow. But don't you dare let Mistuh Wiley get ahold of 'em. He'll have them in the outhouse, and he won't use them for readin' purposes!"

"I'll guard them with my life, and thanks."

I appreciate the Good Lord placing good and interesting people in my path who believe in me—Dale, Jake, Annie Fanny, Rainy, Mr. Wiley, Mr. and Mrs. Davis, Mr. Gilmore, Old Bart, Dorcas, and even Ben at times. The Lord knows I need something extra Pa couldn't give.

I'm glad I squared things with Pa before I left, now that he's gone. But he surely knew how to keep us boys down. There's a bad spirit roaming inside of each of us. Sometimes it takes every bit of the good spirit doing battle with it to keep the bad at bay. I don't know if it was Pa looking down on himself, but he always had to put us down, and in front of people too.

Pa told us many times, "You ain't never gonna amount to nothin' if you don't finish school." He only went three years but could read and write fairly well. Big sister Rebecca and brothers Elihu and George didn't get much chance to go to school. They finished four years, but Ben, well, we were all so proud when he finished eighth grade. After graduation, we had a celebration. Ma made a cake. In comes Ben, proud to be the first Tullos to make eight years, enough to do some teaching, if he wanted. We congratulated Ben, backslapping and whooping it up.

Pa sat in the corner, leaning back in his chair, finally spoke, "Ye-e-e-up!"

The room got quiet as a church mouse, all of us hoping for a good word for a well-deserving son. "There he is, the educated idiot!" His words sucked the happiness right out of the room. Pa did that sort of thing too regularly. The cake wasn't so sweet after that. Ma cried. Ben got angrier.

I'm sorry Ben is too much like Pa to stomach for very long. I knew it would come to a head, so it's best I left before the top blew off the kettle. I won't be going back. I don't know what's going to happen, but the Lord has me headed somewhere else. It'll be somewhere Ben won't be.

Granny used to say, "Bein' who God wants you to be sometimes means leavin' some people behind. If they're supposed to be in your life, they'll catch up." I leave Ben behind. I'm not sure I want him to catch up.

Mr. Wiley and Mr. Davis are kind men though tough as any. Mr. Davis is a hard worker and gets his due if you work for him. I always feel good about the day's work when it's time to close up shop. But Mr. Wiley, his kindness seeps through the cracks of his rough outsides. He talks tough, but he's soft as fluffed cotton, once you get to know him.

Days are long at the Feed and Seed, but after work on Saturday I head to Mr. Gilmore's house and bunk with Old Bart. Sunday's I go to Shiloh church and work at Mr. Gilmore's until Tuesday so I can make prayer meeting. I confess I want to praise and pray to the Lord with His saints, but the real reason is to see Susannah. It's difficult being so close to Susannah. I enjoy our encounters, occasionally slipping off into the pines for a walk when we're careful.

It's time for a change. I feel it in my heart. It's in her eyes. The Lord is giving me direction. It's time to take the next step.

CHAPTER 20

WINNFIELD, A PLACE NOT LIKE HOME

NOVEMBER 16, 1861

Home is where peace is found, even if it is split between two places.

EARLY WEDNESDAY MORNING I start out to make the Feed and Seed to sweep up before it opens for business. I've settled in easily at my old job and staying with Mr. Wiley. The seventy-five cents a day I make doesn't sound like much, but it adds up over time, especially when I have nothing to spend money on. It's not the dollar a day I got when I first came to Winnfield, but times are hard, and so is finding a paying job. I keep Mr. Wiley in coffee, tobacco, and lemon drops, but I won't buy his whiskey. I let him take care of that.

The trip back and forth to Mr. Gilmore's is tiring but worth it to get a few moments with Susannah. I can leave after work Saturdays and get to Mr. Gilmore's place by nine. I help Old Bart get enough done so that he can take care of things until I get back the next week. On Sunday morning, the Shiloh church bells ring way too early, so I get up and be presentable for preaching.

It still bothers me that Negroes aren't allowed in the Shiloh church for worship, but Mr. Gilmore makes clear it's for their protection.

"Heck, Lummy, you know they can't stay still enough for a white folks church meetin' anyway!"

He's right, and he makes a way for his Negroes to have worship in their own way. A man ahead of his time.

The three days at the Gilmore place I make sure the animals are cared for, enough wood is on hand, and that the foodstuffs stay in good shape. I work the hay to feed the livestock, slop the hogs, and fix the barn roof but never see inside Mr. Gilmore's house. Chopping wood and kindling is always my favorite because it gets me close to the house. I catch a brief look at Susannah who always pulls the shear curtains open just enough so I can see her smile. That's not all I take notice of.

Sometimes I can see her through the curtains. It's hard to make out her features. One afternoon she waves but turns quickly. Mr. Gilmore saw me. I go back to splitting kindling. I take another look when Mr. Gilmore goes behind the barn, but she's gone.

Does he know?

Mr. Gilmore let me stay out in what looks like an old slave shack. Inside it's furnished better than Ben's home. I bunk with Old Bart and the other freedmen. Though different, I get to know these men who impress me with their kind hearts and integrity.

With half-day Saturdays and Sundays mostly free, I can get my work done and fish or hunt a little after church. But, I always hope to get a glimpse of Susannah or sneak away if we can.

Mr. Gilmore plays the part of an eccentric gentleman planter and gambler perfectly, but he has been accused of what staunch slaveholders call a dark secret. Mr. Gilmore says it's not right to own a man or woman like a mule, but in this country that's how it is. So, he "owns" Old Bart and others, but you'd never know they were slaves. I've watched him, and he lives up to his reputation. He keeps them dressed and fed well, pays them, and only holds the paper on them for show. His dark secret of making Negroes human is a bright shining revelation of God to me.

Mr. Gilmore keeps the land close around the house in cattle rather than cotton. That's for Old Bart's sake. He's getting up in years and stays close to keep up the place and care for the cows.

Old Bart and I sneak off when we can to take a few ducks and geese, some squirrels, or a deer. We set lines in the creek for catfish and always have a couple waiting when we return. It's a good change in diet, and the old Negro ladies can cook wild game and fry fish as good as Ma.

In those days before Christmas, Susannah says she wants more for us.

It's time, but I just don't know how we can bring our lives together, save slipping off into the night. Mr. Gilmore doesn't deserve that. After getting to know him, I give up the idea of stealing her. I can offer to buy Susannah's papers, but I don't expect he'd do that. So we hatch a plan that'll work for all.

It's time for my life to change. I'm twenty-seven years old and life needs to take shape. I don't want the whole world like some men, but I do want what the Lord has for me. All I want is a good wife, some children, a bit of land, a job if I don't farm, all under God. Not too much to ask. But these are hard times to be asking, and they look to get harder. I'm saving my money for the future I hope for with Susannah. But the waiting is about over.

I believe I could make my home in Winn Parish. I've found home is where peace is found, even split between two places. The two places used to be Winn Parish and Choctaw County, but that's changed. Now it's Winn-field and Mr. Gilmore's home. Soon that'll change. Moving and settling. I've done enough moving, and now I'd like to settle for a while.

IT'S FROSTY THIS November morning in Winnfield. I want to curl up in the sack just a little longer, but Mr. Wiley snorts. "Lummy, you awake? Could you put another stick on the fire for an old man? If you do, I'll make biscuits and gravy from the squirrels we had last night."

I'm up quickly, throw a couple pieces of wood in the pot belly stove, and scamper back under the quilts. "All right, I'll be expectin' biscuits and gravy about anytime you're ready!"

"Give me a few more minutes, boy, and I'll have this shack smellin' so good your covers'll sneak up to the table for a bite!" I doze for a bit getting the courage to get up.

Saturday's always a good work day at the Feed and Seed with lots of folks in town to spend money and share news. Wagons start rolling in before daybreak. I hope it's not another army train coming through. Some of those boys have yet to learn manners about catcalling women and taunting Negroes. The other day, a gray uniformed soldier driving a wagon headed to Monroe sang a tune that raised the hackles on the back of my neck. I've heard it before.

"Niggahs and flies, I do despise, when I see the niggahs, I'd rather have the flies!" He sang it louder when he passed two Negro men loading supplies at the store. I couldn't help myself.

"Yeah, and shit always enjoys the company of flies! These Negroes wouldn't know what a niggah is if they hadn't seen a white one in your wagon first!" The gray soldier gave me a death stare, but kept riding. The two Negro men, Jack and Sam, waited until the wagon turned the corner and burst out laughing like two schoolboys letting farts in the back of the schoolhouse.

"If he didn't have a gun, I would've chunked a rock at him. And I'm a pretty good shot!"

People stream in early this morning, and Winnfield buzzes like a beehive in spring time. A loud noise off in the distant darkness thunders like hundreds of voices.

"What in the heck is that? Sounds like an army comin' down the road from every direction!"

"It's hawg killin' time, son! Always happens the first killin' frost in November. Town folks never know when hawg killin' will be, but farmers do. They just show up, and that's today!"

The men from around the community drive their sale hogs from their farms to holding pens in town. The women come early to boil water in large black cast iron pots. A few men come with them to sharpen knives and rig up skinning racks on a hill so the blood will drain away.

The pigs? They just squeal bloody murder, as Granny used to say. They know their time has come. I always hated hog killing time, but I don't like killing anything anyway. When I kill a deer or a mess of squirrels, I always go somewhere else in my mind when I lay my knife into the skin and flesh. It bothers me if the meat still quivers when I cut it.

I hope Susannah will come in for the festivities, but that will only happen if Mr. Gilmore makes a trip to town. Mr. Davis steps out on the store porch and waves me to come over. I choke down my biscuit, take my last swallow of coffee, and head that way.

Mr. Wiley yells, "Get us some hawg liver and some hawgs feet if you can. Oh yeah, and as many chitlin's as they'll give you!"

I wave as I jog across the dirt street and up the store steps where Mr. Davis stands.

"Thanks for comin' in early, Lummy, it'll be long day, but a good one. Never know when these boys will kill their hawgs. But today's the day, so I need you to go to my house and fetch them two big sows I been feedin' all year so they can be slaughtered. I'll give you the livers, chitlins, and the eight feet to Mistuh Wiley for doin' it. And your pay too, how's that?"

"Sounds good."

Mr. Davis squints to see Mr. Wiley in the window. "I knew that ole coot done already asked!"

"You bet he did, and he'll be happy as a buzzard on a gut wagon to get 'em."

"And they'll be comin' in today, too!"

The two sows don't give me any trouble, so I get back pretty quick to the store. I scan the growing crowd, and who do I see? Old Bart hanging around the skinning racks. He looks sheepish but brightens up when he sees me.

"Lummy, some of these men don't like niggahs hangin' around whilst they clean their hawgs. I guess with the war and everthin', they afraid of a niggah with a sharp knife."

I march to an empty skinning rack driving my two hogs and Old Bart's four. "Bart, you're first."

Men mumble down the line but I pay it no mind. A couple of men stare, and I give it right back, not blinking until they do, then I go back to work. I ain't in the mood for bullies.

At noon, everyone takes a break and just in time. Mr. Gilmore, Susannah, and few of the other slaves ride into town. I hustle to the store to have the appearance of being on duty, but really I want to see Susannah. Mr. Gilmore's hair has grown longer, and he sports a stubble beard.

Mr. Davis good-naturedly says, "You lookin' to provide the Injuns out West with a good scalp, Mistuh Gilmore?"

"With the way things are goin', leavin' my beautiful mane of gray on some well deservin' redskin's lance would be a sight more than I'll leave be-

hind anyhow!" Mr. Davis grins polishing the glassware. My glances at Susannah are discreet, and she gives me the sweetest smile.

"Lummy, you best go get your vittles before you miss out. Take Mistuh
Wiley his trimmin's along with these lemon drops. Tell that ole man that I
sent them over to remind him we all know he's a sour puss but hopin' he'll
turn sweet!" I grab the bag and wink at Susannah.

"Sure will, be back in a bit." I invite Old Bart to Mr. Wiley's for a dinner.
We cross the street with four large wooden buckets full of things most "re-
spectable" people won't eat.

"Here comes my hawg cuttin's! Boy hidey, I'll cook somethin'good for
supper tonight! What do you say there, Bart? Doin' all right? How's the
ole leg o' yours?"

Old Bart sets his buckets down breathing hard and sits on the bench to
stretch out his left leg. "Looks to be all right, I reckon. These ole bones sure
ain't what they used to be but thanks just the same. I don't give much thought
about what happened back then."

"I know, but I'm a'gonna tell it, whether you like it or not!"

"All right, if you have to."

Mr. Wiley had our dinner laid out, so I settle in for a good story.

"Old Bart here thought he was much of a man when he was just a pup.
He was strong as an ox. Problem was, that's what most people thought of
him—a dumb ox. Ain't so, he's a fairly smart individual. Now mind you,
he was still fresh from wearin' the chains of his slavery when General Sam
Houston came through back in '35. Ole Sam Houston stayed at the Prothro
Mansion not far from the Red River where he plotted to take Texas from the
Mexicans. Funny thing, I went to that same mansion to join General Zach
Taylor on the long walk to fight the Mexicans in '46!

"But, that's another story. Anyway, I was just a chap myself, but I heard
every word Sam said while I sat under the table playin' with the wooden
soldiers my daddy carved for my birthday. Sam plotted 'til he and them men
landed on a plan they believed might work.

"Sam had set Bart free back in Tennessee and him, bein' only twelve at
the time, had the opportunity to go to Texas. 'Come help me take Texas, and

I'll make sure you stay free. You'll get your land just like the other men who sign up for militia.'"

"Young Bart scratched that nappy head of his 'cause I was watchin'"—Old Bart starts chuckling—"stood up, saluted like he'd done become a soldier, sayin' 'Yassuh, General Houston, sir, I'm ready to go to war with you when you say go!' Bart was rearin' to go, except he came down with the rickets. Couldn't walk for two weeks, and his leg ain't never been right since. Ole Sam was sure sorry about that. He left Bart fifty dollars and went to Texas without him. Well, you know the rest of that story, the Alamo and all. But not Bart's.

"There were some men who didn't like Sam or his plan to take Texas. They wanted it for themselves. To hurt him, they grabbed Bart, chained him up, and made him start walkin' to Nawlin's, bad leg and all. He pert near died, but when they reached the Missip, one of Sam's friends recognized Bart on a steamer and yanked his ass loose from them damn cheats. But Bart never saw his fifty dollar gold piece again."

Old Bart cuts in, "And I've been livin' here ever since! Me and Massuh Wiley been friends a long time, huntin' and fishin' together, workin' as farm hands and such."

Mr. Wiley has many sides to him, and I like them all.

"So what you got for me in the buckets there? I can't wait for supper, and Bart you're welcome to stay over. We'll have us a good ole time."

"I surely will, thanks. But you knows I gots to ask, Mistuh Wiley, do you like the pig?"

Mr. Wiley throws his chin up into the air like a hound baying at a possum in a persimmon tree. "From the rooter to the tooter, and you know that better'n anybody!"

We laugh, and Old Bart is just getting started, "And Mistuh Wiley, whilst we was cuttin' them hawgs, I heard a feller tell it, 'Yeah, that dang old boar had such a bad case of hemorroids, we ate chitlin's off him for two weeks before we brought him in for slaughter!'" I have to catch Mr. Wiley from falling out of his rocking chair he's laughing so hard.

"Massuh Wiley, you ever seen such a thing?"

Mr. Wiley wiped away tears. "I never even heard of such a thing!" We have cold salt pork biscuits with left over coffee and help Mr. Wiley with the hog trimmings before we go back to work.

Mr. Wiley cuts the liver into several pieces and starts soaking the feet in a brine solution. But the chitlins? They require a special touch.

"Now boys, y'all go on back to your knifin', I'll take care of these chitlins!"

Old Bart jokes, "Now Wiley, you ole fox, you get them cleaned up good now, and do's I need to remind you how to take care of them chitlins?" Mr. Wiley stands up steadying himself on the rocking chair like he's about to preach a sermon.

"Hand slung, stump whooped, creek washed! Makes for the best damn chitlins in the world!"

Old Bart cries out, "Amains, brother Wiley, amains!"

I enjoy a certain contentment living in this small but blossoming town. This place is growing on me, and I guess I'm growing on it. Being well thought of, and gaining a good reputation without the shadow of Pa, or Ben for that matter, surely makes the difference.

Life is finally settling down, shaping into something good put together by my own hands, under God. Even with the war, I trust God's plan for me. Good friends, good work, the best girl in the world gives a man a peaceful outlook on life. Old Bart reads my thoughts as we cross the street back to the hog killing.

"God is good, ain't He, son?" I sneak another peak at Susannah.

"Sure is!"

CHAPTER 21

LIVING AT THE GILMORE PLACE

DECEMBER 21, 1861

Some have mansions now, some will later. Some only now for the good done for themselves.
Some with mansions now will have greater ones later, for the good done for others.

THE WEEKS DRAG on slowly, but two jobs in two places keeps me hopping. Staying with Mr. Wiley is always a hoot, and trying to catch a glimpse of Susannah shoos away boredom. The occasional encounter at prayer meeting and glimpses at the main house only build the fire in my heart for the woman I believe God has given me.

Christmas is just a few days away, and I have a decision to make. I want to be with Dorcas and the kids, but I'm not ready for Ben again. I haven't seen him since I left. I have men around me, white and black, who treat me better than my own brother. I need to come up with a reason to be somewhere else. I hate it, but I didn't make it this way.

More people visit Davis's Store full of cheer about the holday ahead but more so about Confederate Army successes. Special foods and even some luxuries people order from catalogs are still available out of Texas and New Orleans.

Mr. Gilmore comes to town today to pick up holiday gifts and foods. New shoes and clothes, tins of sweets and presents have been wrapped for each person living on his place. The shipment includes the things I picked out for Susannah. I sneak mine to the back when Mr. Gilmore spies my clandestine attempt. Mr. Gilmore admires the large stack of sundries he purchased and asks Old Bart to load them in the wagon.

"Now just who are those things for, son?" I shy away red-faced.

"They're for"—I clear my throat—"for Dorcas and the kids, suh."

"I see the children's things, very nice. But Ben might think you're a bit too sweet on Dorcas givin' her such dainties!"

"Beggin' your pardon, Mistuh Gilmore, but I don't have to tell you everything I do."

"No you don't, but if you'll follow me out to the wagon, I have a proposition for you." My stomach turns over. We get to the other side of the wagon, and he wheels around on one foot with a fire in his eyes.

"Those things ain't no more for Dorcas than they're for me, are they? They're for someone else, and I believe I know who it is!"

My knees wobble. I'm actually frightened a bit. Not a feeling I've had in years, but Mr. Gilmore has the power to send Susannah away, and me for that matter, in a heartbeat if he's unhappy that Susannah's my girl.

"I know what's been goin' on, Lummy, and I for dang sure want to know your intentions."

I hang my head. I'll just have to trust him.

Lord, if You ever been with me, please be with me now.

"My intentions, suh, are honorable, and my plan is to marry Susannah. There, I said it! I want her for my wife. I've known her long before you took her away, since we was kids, and we have become one in all ways God allows before marriage. I've refused myself only two things with Susannah. Knowin' her as a wife and gettin' a preacher to make her mine. There it is. The truth."

"Why, Columbus Nathan Tullos, didn't know you had such a command of the English language! You should become a teacher of young minds." I'm startled at his response. "Now don't get all lathered up. I had to come at you hard to get the best out a you, and I did." He studies me for a moment. "I believe you." I sigh in relief.

"So what now, Mistuh Gilmore?"

"What's now, is my proposition. I spoke to Mistuh Davis, and after Christmas things will slow down. He's willin' to cut you loose to work my place fulltime. That's half the proposition."

"And, the other half?"

"Are you ready to fulfill your duties to a fine young Christian woman, to have and to hold, to love and protect, 'til death parts you, Columbus Nathan

Tullos?" He stands staunch with his hands on his hips. "What do you say? You look shaken to me."

"Sorry, Mistuh Gilmore, it's like I been stung all over, like I fell into a swarm of yellerjackets. I never imagined you askin' me that question."

"Well, you surely don't know everythin', now do you? Susannah told me about you two back in the summer. Besides, I noticed the looks you two have had for each other ever since that first prayer meetin' back in '59. When did you ask her?"

I kick the dirt. "When we both turned twelve back in Choctaw County down by our secret swimmin' hole on McCurtain Creek. She said yes before it came out my mouth good. We decided then to do things God's way. I ain't never looked back nor looked at another woman like I do Susannah. Mistuh Gilmore, it's time for a change, and I hope you don't stand in our way, 'cause right now I believe I could knock you in the head so her and me could run off together!" He raises his eyebrows.

"But we can't do that. We won't do that. It wouldn't be fair to you and all the good you done for us. Susannah and I love and respect you too much to treat you such. We want your blessin' before we go farther on this long road we've been on for so many years."

Tears form in his eyes. "She told me you followed us here all the way from Missip, not even knowin' your brother Benny Frank lived in these parts. That says a lot, and I appreciate you treating her as a lady. A father takes note of such things. I'll make it plain. I'd be proud to have you as a son-in-law. What do you say?" My words are stuck for the lump in my throat. He grabs my hand to pull me close.

"I love you both for who you are. This union is hope for a new world. I'm just thankful to the Creator for allowin' me to be a very small part. We'll just have to be careful."

WE SET THE date for Christmas Day. Susannah flitters around like a butterfly, and my heart wants to explode. Then it hits me. I won't go back to

Ben's for Christmas. But, I never said I would. So no promise made. I won't worry with that now.

With only a few days to the wedding, I catch Mr. Gilmore on the side of the barn. "What am I gonna do? I got no preacher and no ring. Lord knows we don't want a circuit rider, and I ain't got time to order no ring!" Mr. Gilmore grabs me by the shoulders.

"There you go, Lummy Tullos, worryin' about things the Lord is very capable of handlin'. Mistuh Davis is a legal servant of the State of Louisiana and one of us. He'll perform the ceremony." I don't want to ask. He removes a silver chain with a gold band from inside his shirt.

"I've worn this ever since my sweetheart died. She'd want it to live on in the lives of good people like you and Susannah. Take it and let it be the symbol of love that holds you two together." I don't know what to say.

"Thank you, Lord." Tears dripped from my eyes.

"That's exactly right. If it wasn't for the Lord, I wouldn't know to do what I'm doin'. You just keep livin' for him. That's enough thanks for me, son."

I leave for Winnfield early Wednesday morning. Christmas is only a couple days away, and I still haven't seen Ben and Dorcas to say I won't be with them for the holiday. I can't tell them I'm getting married. They won't understand. I must give a good reason. I'm out of time.

Time drags on for the good and the bad—good for getting my heart set for the wedding and bad for having to face Ben. Bittersweet. Seems that's been the taste in my mouth for too long.

Saturday morning comes with a big frost covering the windows of the Feed and Seed. Mr. Davis smiles and pats me on the shoulder every time he passes as we sort through Christmas orders. Mrs. Davis waltzes around the room in the happiest mood I've seen yet. She even gives me a peck on the cheek as I stock the can goods on the shelves. Mr. Gilmore already told them.

About noon Ben and Dorcas arrive with the children. The kids run for the candy jars marveling at all the different kinds and colors. Dorcas gives me a signal that Ben's mad. I shrug it off. I have to be a man about this. After all, this time next week I'll be a husband.

Ben asks, "Guess we'll be seein' you next Wednesday? Come stay the night, won't bother us none." He's trying to be kind, as much as Ben can be. I'm in a bind. I've thought about what to say, but nothing sounds right, no matter how I phrase it. I take a shot at splitting the difference.

"I'll come Tuesday, but I'll head back to Mistuh Gilmore's early to help with his plans."

"Heard you was workin' his place full time now. I want you to stay for the day, to be with me and the family on south farm, and that's that." Dorcas sends the children out to play, each with their favorite piece of candy.

I take a deep breath. "No, brother, it ain't, that's that. You heard my plans. and that's the end of it."

"Well, maybe you ought not come Christmas Eve, neither, boy," Ben stares, inviting a fight. I'm just about to invite him outside when Dorcas steps in and pats Ben on the chest forcing him to look into her eyes.

"Now, dear, Lummy has responsibilities, and he's gonna tend to them just like you would. Let's just enjoy the time we'll have together Christmas Eve, okay, husband?"

"See you Christmas Eve then, boy."

"Sounds good, what can I bring?"

Dorcas pats her foot. "Why don't you bring the candy? And make sure you bring somethin' chocolate, you hear?"

"Gotcha." Ben loads his supplies trying to hide the children's Christmas presents. They're out the door quickly wanting to get home for the holiday.

Today is my last day working at the Feed and Seed. Mr. Davis nearly shakes my shoulder out of joint, thanking me for the good work I've done over the years. He gives me my regular pay, and then he grabs my other hand in his.

"Ain't much but hope it helps." It's a shiny new ten dollar gold piece.

"Oh, no, Mistuh Davis. I can't take this. You're gonna need it with hard times comin'."

"Won't have it no other way, son. Take it, let it make a better life for you, and you know who! See you Christmas Day! Things get slow on the farm, I can always use an extra hand." I throw on my coat to head out the door. A clay jug breaks on the porch of the empty building.

"Somethin' special, ain't you, livin' in the home of a fine gentleman like
Mistuh Gilmore. Too good for Tullos' folks, ain't you, boy?"

"Ben, what are you doin' out here in the cold? Dorcas and the kids leave?"

"None your damn business, boy, my sons'll get the women folk home.
Don't worry your special little head, boy!" If he calls me boy one more time I
believe I'll knock him down.

"If you don't want to come for Christmas Day, then damn you, don't
come at all!"

"You're drunker'n a skunk, you ignert fool, and don't know what your
sayin'. Go home and sleep it off! I'll see you Tuesday evenin'." When I turn
to walk away, Ben takes a swing at me with little power and less control. He
falls down. He yells how he always hated me because Ma doted on me and
cries about never making peace with our Pa. It's a pitiful sight.

I care for my brother but have no room in my heart for his sobbing.
Sometimes a man must leave certain people behind. They'll show up again if
they're supposed to be part of my life.

But still, I wish Ben and the family could share the joy I will have soon.
If he came, I believe he'd make the whole thing about him. I can't deal with
that right now. I refuse to let anything steal what God's doing in my life
with Susannah.

Mr. Davis pushes open the door. "Go on, Lummy, I'll get him inside
where it's warm. He'll sober up with some strong black coffee. I'll make sure
he gets on home." He pulls Ben to his feet. "Can't win a pukin' contest with a
buzzard. Buzzard always wins. See you soon."

As Mr. Davis drags Ben inside, I leave the things Dorcas asked for and
the gifts I'd purchased for the family with Mrs. Davis.

"Please pack these things on Ben's mule. Dorcas will find them."

"Don't worry, I'll take care of it. I know I'm a cranky old biddy sometimes, Lummy, but you done us good, son. You're always welcome." I always
knew Mrs. Davis had a good soul.

"You know that Mistuh Gilmore is a strange bird, but God's usin' that
man for good. He'll surely get his reward." She looks out the window.

"Lummy, some have their mansions now and some will later. Some only have mansions now for good they do for themselves. Some with mansions now will have greater ones later for the good they do for others." She bats her eyes and covers her mouth like she's embarrassed, "See you Christmas Day!" I start out the door and untie my horse from the hitching post.

I whisper, "That just might be the last words I ever get to speak to Ben."

Before leaving town I check on Mr. Wiley. He's sitting perfectly still in his rocking chair covered with a couple of heavy quilts. He saw and heard everything that just happened. He waves me over. Mr. Wiley speaks in the softest tone since I've known him.

"You know, son, history tends to repeat itself if a man don't learn from it. To live on this earth, a man must remain eternally hopeful. Otherwise, you best put a bullet in your head."

"Well, I ain't doin' that. Too much good ahead to be worth only a bullet." I find the small package in my pocket.

"Here, gotcha little somethin' for Christmas. Hope you like it." His eyes light up.

"Ain't got no Christmas present in many a year! What you gone and done, boy?"

"Open it and quit fussin'!" Mr. Wiley carefully unfolds the paper from the package to find a box. He slowly lifts the lid to find a shiny new pocket knife with letters engraved on both sides.

Teary-eyed, he hands me the knife. "What's it say, Lummy? You know I can't read." I can hardly get the words out.

"W.O. Wiley, Christmas 1861."

"And the other side?"

My voice cracks, "Your son, Lummy Tullos."

Mr. Wiley drops his head. "Lummy, if I'd ever had a boy of my own, I'd want him to be just like you. When the Lord gives you a son not yours, his blood makes us more family than our human kin. Thank you, my son." I grab the reins of my mule and hop up on his back.

"I like the spring in your step boy! Maybe you'll tell me about it next time you come? Stay eternally hopeful."

"See you again soon, old timer!"

Mr. Wiley struggles to get up. "Boy, I'll whoop your ass all the way back to Gilmore's place!" He throws his tin cup at me. "Don't be a stranger, and have a good Christmas, son!"

CHAPTER 22

THE BIG DAY!

DECEMBER 25, 1861

Some days are meant to last longer than others,
but this day will last a lifetime.

CHRISTMAS DAY! WEDDING day! Day of days, and I'm nearly beside myself! Even though the ceremony is a secret, there's no shortage of excitement around the Gilmore place.

This wedding will be different than back home, with kinfolks and friends wishing a newly married couple well with gifts and kind words. Mr. Gilmore advised we keep it quiet. He doesn't want to cause a stir among slave holding secessionists. We don't need any extra attention.

I missed Christmas Eve with Dorcas and the kids last night, but I want no sadness today! I soak in the joy that comes at the end of a long journey. Even though Ben owns no slave, he doesn't believe the races should mix. "That's like crossin' man with an ape!"

I just kept my mouth shut when he would spout off like that. Besides, a fool is a fool, whoever he's related too. And I don't need to correct everyone I disagree with in this world. Biting my tongue—a price I'm willing to pay for the love that's captured my heart.

I can't wait to see her all gussied up for the wedding! A few of Mr. Gilmore's friends arrive. Children run and jump, stop and giggle at me singing an unfamiliar tune.

"Massuh Lummy and Miss Susannah, dem two in love, dem two gettin' hitched, dem two gonna have bebies, ooh ooh!" Their parents smile at me. A mother shoos the children away.

"You know it's true, Massuh Lummy, and, Lawd, what pretty childrens you be havin'! Mix childrens always the best lookin'!"

We gather outside on the porch on this warm Christmas Day. Mr. Gilmore spared no expense for decorations and food. Cedar greenery surrounds the house and porch. Cinnamon candles burn in the main rooms. The ladies have been cooking for two days, and the aromas can melt a man.

Someone plays a familiar tune on a flute, an old song Granny hummed at weddings. Old Bart sings a sweet melody about true love and God's hand in bringing two people together. Then I see Susannah like never before. Mr. Gilmore gently walks her up the brick path to the porch steps. My knees shake. My heart beats nearly out of my chest.

Mr. Davis steps up, Bible in hand, as Susannah slowly climbs the porch steps. Her eyes are down until she reaches the place where I am standing. She turns to face me. She lifts her chin, and her dark eyes meet mine. For a moment, I believe I see God.

No, I'm sure of it.

Mr. Davis nods, and at first I don't notice who it is hobbling up to the front. Mr. Wiley! Clean-shaven, wearing a borrowed jacket Mr. Davis lent him. He shakes my hand like he's gonna take my shoulder off. He turns to the crowd, removes his hat, and prays the prettiest prayer I've ever heard out of the mouth of man.

Susannah and I never close our eyes. We stare deeply down into each other's soul. Mr. Davis let's us have the moment. He finally clears his throat to bring us back from our dreamy state.

"Now y'all know I ain't no preacher. I'm just a civil servant of the great State of Looseana with the power to make people legal in marriage. But I love the Lord, and I can't help it. I must read from the Good Book about what it means to be husband and wife."

He reads solemnly from the Song of Songs and then talks about a man loving his wife as his own body, and a wife caring for her husband. I hardly hear a word for being lost in the beauty of Susannah's dark eyes. She blushes and grins, only to look away for a moment, embarrassed at my relentless attention.

"Lummy, you here with us?"

Everyone laughs for they know what's happening.

"Yassuh?"

Mr. Davis pats his Bible. "Well, do you?"

"Do what?"

Mr. Gilmore nearly falls from his chair laughing. "Do you take Miss Susannah to be your lawful wedded wife?"

"Why sure I do, that's why I'm here!" The small crowd roars with laughter.

"Well, I asked Miss Susannah, and she said 'yes,' but I've asked you twice, son."

"Sorry about that. Uh, yeah, I do!" Everyone laughs, sighs for the joy in this place far removed from the war, bigotry and hatred, bad memories, from all the anger and violence. It's a moment dropped out of heaven, and I don't want it to end.

"You gotta ring, son?"

Susannah whispers, "It's okay if you don't. Old Bart said he'll make us some." I reach into my pocket, nod to Mr. Gilmore, and hold out the most beautiful gold band either of us have ever seen. Susannah covers her mouth, crying.

"No, suh, Massuh Gilmore, this is your beloved's!"

Mr. Gilmore holds up his hands. "Missus Gilmore wouldn't have it no other way, my daughter."

I place the ring on Susannah's finger and stare into her eyes.

"Well, boy, you gonna plant one on her or what?" The kiss I've waited on forever finally comes. We kiss long and passionately, until Mr. Davis says, "We ain't done yet." He clears his throat.

"By the power vested in me as an official of the great State of Looseana and more importantly as a follower of God, I now pronounce you man and wife! And don't nobody even try to give a reason these two can't be together, or we'll be havin' words." A shout rises from the small crowd.

Susannah and I turn to face the group, and everyone claps. Music plays and everyone starts dancing. We sit as the honored guests at a feast fit for a king and queen, laugh, toast, share good words with each other, cherishing this precious moment God has given us.

IT'S NIGHT, AND Susannah and I settle into our new little cabin not far from the main house. I had been fooled into believing we were building this cabin for the new slaves Mr. Gilmore just acquired. Lying on the bed we see stars from our window. We are now husband and wife. We can now, in the sight of God, enjoy each other as God planned so long ago for Adam and Eve.

Susannah starts to undress by the window's light. I watch her unbutton each button, untie every ribbon, brush back her hair with her smooth silky hands. I wonder what Adam must have thought when he saw Eve for the first time in the Garden of Eden. What went through his mind? How did he feel? Whatever it was then, I surely feel it now.

Oh, Susannah and I had skinny-dipped a few times at the Cold Hole where no one could see. It's beautiful clear water spring bubbling ever so slightly in the middle of a cypress swamp just off from McCurtain Creek. But that was nearly four years ago.

My heart skips several beats. She's no longer the skinny dark-skinned girl I fell in love with years ago. Susannah has blossomed into a woman, and what a beauty!

"Lord, let this moment stand still." Some days are meant to last longer than others, but this day will last a lifetime. We lay together on the soft goose down bed, my arms wrapped around her. Susannah sighs, and I can tell she wants to talk.

"Remember when we used to play What's in your head? and you always made me go first?"

Susannah giggles, "I do."

"Well, you start." Susannah squirms trying to formulate her words.

"Lummy, I wish your family had been here. I want to know Ben and Dorcas better. Missus Dorcas is so sweet when I see her in the store." Ben acting an ass yesterday and my missing out on Christmas Eve with Dorcas and the kids grabs my heart. I unleash a tirade about Ben.

Susannah lets me go on for a bit until I say, "If it hadn't been for that damned ole Pa of ours, none of this would've happened." We sit silent for a moment.

Then like the voice of God speaking through the sweetest angel voice, she whispers, "At least you knowed your Pa, Lummy."

It hits me. "Susannah, I never knew anythin' about your Pa. Or your family, for that matter."

"That's 'cause you never asked."

"I thought it'd be too painful."

"I'm glad you knew your father. Mine had already died when ya'll first came to Mount Pisgah Baptist Church. He was cuttin' timber in the swamps near McCurtain Creek. Just one swoop from a cypress tree killed him. I was only nine."

"And your Ma?"

She shakes her head. "Too hard to talk about."

"It's all right, you don't have to."

"No." She holds up her hand. "You're my husband, and I need to tell you everythin'. Her name is Sophie. Mistuh Gilmore told me it means wisdom. Sweetest woman ever walked this earth"

I nod.

"I growed up fast seein' too many bad things when I was way too young. I stayed with my Momma before we came to Missip from Alabam. I saw all the meanness a man can do to a woman. What them overseers made her do no child should ever see. One white man took a shine to Momma, so he run off the others. He was the meanest and treated her the worst."

Susannah sobs, "I'm so sorry, Lummy, I just couldn't take that man hurtin' my Momma. I'm so sorry I ain't told you before now. I'm afraid you wouldn't love me no more."

"Go on, get it out, I ain't goin' no where."

"He made me watch all them nasty things he done to my Momma! And oh, the beatings!" Susannah cries uncontrollably. I hug her tighter.

"I understand, darlin'. Go on, get it all out, and we'll be done with it."

"That man came to our shack, run off the other women and children so he could have his way with my Momma. Then he'd make me cook for him. So I took some arsenic from massuh's store room and mixed it with a stew I made for him one night. I spiced it up real good so he couldn't tell. It killed him deader'n a door nail lyin' in his own bed two days later. Everybody just thought he got sick and died. I never said nothin'. Neither did Momma." She bawls.

"I'd done the very same thing Susannah, and we don't need to discuss this ever again." Susannah's tears drench my night shirt. She needs to cry out all her pain, a long overdue purging.

"Lummy, I love you, my darlin'."

I hold her face between my palms. "But I love you more!"

Susannah tells what she knows about her family. Her mother, Sophie, shared it with her not long before Mr. Gilmore took her away. She was named for her master's great grandmother, but it wasn't her real name from the old country. She said I couldn't pronounce it even if she told me. She hasn't seen or heard from her mother since leaving Choctaw County.

I love her more now for defending her mother. I love her even more for the sense of justice she carries in her soul. I have no problem removing the raper of women and the destroyer of children from this earth. Susannah falls asleep, wrapped in my arms.

WE WAKE THIS morning to Mr. Gilmore ringing the bell. We dress quickly and stumble our way over to the porch, wiping the sleep out of our eyes. The tables are set with a fine breakfast. Once Susannah and I sit in the places of honor, Mr. Gilmore taps his coffee cup with a spoon to get everyone's attention.

"Yesterday marked the most important day in my life, second only to my marriage to my dearly beloved wife and the birth of my daughter, God rest their souls. I do look forward to seein' them again. But today, I present my personal gift to the newlyweds."

"Now, Mistuh Gilmore, you've done enough already!"

Mr. Gilmore barks out comically, "Sit down and hush up, son-in-law! I got something to say!" Everyone laughs, and I ease back down in my chair. Susannah leans over to kiss me on the cheek, shivering with excitement.

"Mistuh Lummy is a fine, upstandin', hard workin', trustworthy, and faithful man of God."

The Negroes chime in with their affirmations. "Yeah, uh-huh, amains, you gots that right!" I hang my head and hold Susannah's hand tightly.

"I've waited for this day a long time, and God has allowed to see it. Lummy and Susannah!" We stand for what we don't know is about to happen. "My gift to you today, against all who unlawfully set themselves up as God himself to enslave people, is to grant you, my darling daughter, freedom from the chains of slavery. I do this first for God, because he gave you to me, and second, against wicked men who make such laws. But more importantly, for this fine couple choosing to live life God's way. Can I get an amen, somebody?"

The newly arrived slaves and freedmen jump and shout, dance and celebrate as if Jesus himself just returned. For them it's the Year of Jubilee. Mr. Gilmore hands Susannah the papers Mr. Davis drew up to make her freedom legal. We look at each other and both hug Mr. Gilmore.

"Guard these papers like you guard her. If they get them, they can take her away. Mistuh Davis made two copies. Keep one handy, and hide the other." Mr. Gilmore kisses me on the cheek.

"Take care of her, my friend. God couldn't have provided a better son than you."

It's a blissful time, these days before New Year's Day, 1862. No work, no responsibilities, no worries. Just the quiet of a warm bedside fire, snuggled under warm blankets, losing ourselves in each other, losing all sense of time. I wish the Lord take us all back to the Garden of Eden right now. But as the Scriptures say, some people can't be happy with what the Good Lord provides.

I'm trying to be eternally hopeful, as Mr. Wiley told me. I believe if more of us learned to live as true human beings, we might just have that peace someday. But in this world, there are always those who want to take peace away.

CHAPTER 23

THE RECRUITMENT

JANUARY 1, 1862

Moses said a man stays home for a year with his new bride.
The Confederate States of America don't agree with that.

T
HE CALL COMES Christmas Day. Fast riders in gray uniforms drop leaflets in every village and town making a plea for men to volunteer for the Confederate Army. I knew it was coming. We all did. A war like this will go longer because it's already gone this long. It's not like the Mexican War Mr. Wiley fought back in the '40s. That war would've ended sooner had the army not had to go so far to end it.

Nope, this war will go for a while. No short and quick rolling up of the enemy. No marching into Washington victoriously demanding the South be cut loose from the Union. And the bluecoats haven't taken Richmond either. Both sides thought it would end quickly. Both sides thought they'd win easily because each still believes they fight for God Almighty himself.

Some folks in Winn Parish ask, "With the Yanks invadin', how can the Rebs not be victorious?" Others ask, "With the Rebs breakin' up the Union to keep slaves, how can God allow them to win?" Who can honestly claim God's blessing? Neither. Today it goes further than just asking questions.

Happy New Year, 1862. Church bells ring loudly, and our nation is split in two. Where are you in all this Lord? Can you even call us Your children now?

Winn Parish is just as divided. Two differing political points of view vie for the souls of men. One is loyalty to one's home state, and the other is loyalty to the Union as a whole. It just ain't easy as white and black, or gray and blue, for that matter.

Last year, David Pierson and the other six delegates representing Winn Parish voted against secession at the Louisiana State Convention. They wanted the parish to become the Free State of Winn but was ignored completely by officials at home. Even though David Pierson voted against secession he organized the Winn Rifles when the fighting broke out. Mose Cockerham, who worked with us on Mr. Gilmore's farm, joined up then. I wonder how Pierson lives with such divided loyalties—pro-Union but taking up arms against it. What can I say? I'm against slavery but joining up to fight for home and family.

It's a struggle not knowing which way to turn, but it's a decision that won't wait. Me? I'm joining up before the Confederate States of America conscripts me. At least I'll get a bounty to give Susannah before I go.

In town, men shout at each other, taking sides that sometimes ends with fistfights when too much moonshine is consumed. I've stayed away and let fools be fools. But today, it's not the moonshine that has stirred the souls of violent men. It's the war.

A call to arms isn't my kind of New Year's party. Today I should be in Mr. Gilmore's house, sipping rum eggnog by the fire. Mr. Gilmore told us that President George Washington had crafted his own eggnog recipe spiced with rum. Mr. Gilmore uses that story to justify the generous portions he drinks but shares with others as well. No complaint from me. I wonder if Old George would have turned down the offer of head Yankee General like General Lee did.

It's cold this morning, standing in the street with a bunch of men, listening to the pleas of the stump talkers waxing eloquent about our great Southern Cause. These boys are too excited to miss out. Fit to be tied, truth be told, but ignorant of what's coming. I'm concerned about what this will do to my new life. There will be no escaping it. I'm a log in the middle of the Mississippi River wandering here and there wherever the current chooses to take me.

A crackling voice like a crow cawing rises above the hum of the crowd. Mr. Wiley yells from his rocking chair waving his old sidearm from the Mexican War. I always enjoyed hearing the old men back home tell their

stories sitting on saloon porches, reared back in straight chairs spitting tobacco into the street, telling mostly embellished stories of battle and glory.
Mr. Wiley never did that.

Mr. Wiley, wearing his threadbare, moth-eaten jacket, pokes out his
chest. "Yeah, war is comin'! I'd go myself, but my head ain't right. But by
George, if the Yanks come here, I'll shoot everyone I see. No crawfishin'
here, boys. Stand tall and get your pinchers up! Bring 'em on!"

I know him better than that. Though I've never heard him say so, Mr.
Wiley is really against any war. It's just an act of support for his town, I reckon.

It's strange how men get so excited about the prospect of getting shot at.
It won't be a buckshot load of rock salt from Mr. Sidney Whisenant poured
on us the night we stole pears off his tree. This won't be funny.

Battles have been won up north at places I've never heard of, except
in the papers—Bull Run, Ball's Bluff, and Belmont. There have been a few
skirmishes in Louisiana but nothing near Winn Parish. Every time news of
another battle hits the papers, the boys want to rush off and shoot Yanks. I
don't join the shouting, but when I think of the Bluecoats as bullies trying to
take our homes, land, and hurt our families, I do get pretty stoked up myself.

I don't want anybody ruling me or my state, like Grandpa Aaron fighting
with the South Carolina militia against the British. I agree with that. But I do
scratch my head when stump speakers cuss Northern domination but in the
same breath say slavery is white man's God given right. It just don't add up
anyway a man argues it, unless you say another human is less than human. I
ain't buying that one. Never have.

As recruiters rail on like brush arbor preachers trying to gain another
convert, an old Indian leaning against a post at the Feed and Seed nods me
over. I met Choctaw Charlie in Mr. Davis's Store soon after coming to Winn
Parish. I respect his simple yet profound wisdom. A quiet man who stays out
of sight to avoid the talkers. Choctaw Charlie covers his mouth.

"White man wants everythin' and everybody under his control. How
much is enough, Lummy? When does a man find it in his heart to say he
has enough? When was it ever his to own it in the first place? It wasn't ours
when white folks came to Missip and stole it. Don't mean no harm. I'm really

talkin' about that demon Greenwood Leflore." I don't know what to say and probably shouldn't say anything.

"Must've done it in a fever."

He looks like he might scalp me.

"Hell, no, that man had way too much time to think on it! He plotted with the government, and we got the damn short end of the stick." Choctaw Charlie straightens up.

"When I was just a boy, I went with my Pap to the Dancing Rabbit Creek gatherin'. A lot of Choctaws waited for the men in black suits and tall hats to stop talkin', but them squawkers railed on for hours sayin' how proud they were of such good citizens of the United States of America. We waited for the hammer to fall on our heads, and it did. We was dumb as a bag of rocks, givin' away our land that way. Damn shame that was." The crowd grows louder.

"We Choctaws remember comin' to Missip and that somebody came before us. The ancients who left the big mounds were there long before us. Damn that Leflore, the shame of bein' removed as chief just wasn't enough for him. He arranged his stayin' and our leavin'. Heard he had a fine mansion built on the best of huntin' grounds, happy as a tick on a fat dawg. Chief of all the Choctaws, shit, sure as hell ain't chief of me. Never was. Man like that, if his lips are movin', dammit, he's probably lyin'." He shakes off his feet like it says in the Bible and slips into the alley with his bottle. That's how they keep the Indians quiet.

There were a few Indians around when I was boy. Some hid out when the soldiers came to round them up for the removal west. They blended in with the half-breeds like Greenwood Leflore who asked to become American citizens. Ma said it was a shame to take their land so we could buy it cheap. Ma secretly fed some hiding in the woods. Dan Creekwater! I haven't thought about him in quite some time. Wonder how he's faring?

It's all about domination—who wants the most, has the most, who can take it away from someone else, and who's willing to sell their souls just to get the most. And the damnable misery of it all? It's always at the expense of someone else. They have the gall to use God and His good scriptures to make their case.

I walk over where men stand in line like they're ready to march off at the drop of a hat. Men ready to plunge off a cliff without any thought if there's a bottom waiting for us to hit. There will be for many, if the papers are right. The bottom of a six foot deep hole in the ground.

The loudest of the bunch wearing a Rebel cap yells at me, "Why the hell you hangin' around that old drunk Injun for, anyway? Injuns is worthless as tits on a boar hawg! What do you say, plowboy?"

With some men, they get so wound up that they yell about whatever they see. And a bully's strength lies in his sorry bunch of friends.

The heat rises in my face, so I grace him back. "You're a loud-mouth sorry son of a bitch. That's what I say."

About my size, he bows up like he might take a swing.

I look him dead in the eye. "Go ahead. What's holdin' you, boy? Ain't nothin' between you and me but air! And I say that's pretty thin with all your gassin'!"

His friends wait for a response.

The loudmouth looks around, making sure all can hear him. "I'm fixin' to cloud up and rain all over you if you don't shut the hell up!"

I keep a steady glare into his eyes. A sweat bead rolls down his face.

"Don't think so. You're sweatin' like a whore in Sunday mornin' church service, boy!"

The bully's reputation weakens by the second.

"Back down or I'm fixin' to be on you faster'n a one-legged man in an ass kickin' contest!"

I step forward, and my nose touches his. "When you get to feelin' froggie boy, you hop!"

The world around me disappears, and all I see is the man in front of me. I'm ready to spring like a cat on a mouse. His eyes betray his fear, but he's too far in to quit now.

I lean forward pushing his nose with mine. "Hop on anytime, boy, 'cause when you get done, there'll be a helluva lot left over!"

A loud deep-voiced man pushes his way through the gathering crowd.

"Hold on, boys! Break it up! This ain't the time! Save your fightin' for the

Yanks. There'll be plenty of opportunites to take somebody's head off soon enough!" A sergeant steps between us.

The loudmouth stops, and though nobody else notices, there's relief in his eyes. He tries to save his worthless pride. "If you can't run with the big dawgs, then stay under the damn porch."

"That's all you got, you damn cur dawg, is talk and worthless pride."

I step toward him again, but the sergeant grabs my arm.

"Son, he talks tough, but he'll be cryin' for his Momma when cannonballs start droppin'. But we need him, even if only to stop a bullet. Stay with me, lad, and fight for the Cause."

I don't want to fight. A man has to be too angry to fight. But what I just felt toward that loudmouth will get me through whatever's coming. To do what this recruiter suggests, a man must have rage like a tornado wind in his soul to survive.

I've experienced Pa's rage too many times. I don't want it in me anymore. I want peace. Anger and rage is mostly unfounded and unnecessary. It's just in the Tullos blood to gut wrench about things that ain't right. I guess we got pushed a little too much through the years. I'm not in the mood to be pushed today.

I was taught to be angry and lived it nearly all my life. When I had to fight, it was just to be left alone. Fights come looking for me without me ever inviting them. Ben told me after I tripped Lester with the jump rope at school those many years ago that someday I'd regret standing up to a man bigger than me. He stopped saying that when I cut him that Sunday after church.

I think about Lester, the Sheriff's nephew, who made it his business to torment me. He stepped up his constant punishing after I laid a rock squarely between his shoulders that day. Ma said it was because I refused to kowtow, even if he did have a pack of mongrels to back him up.

Lester and his buddies hung out by the stables in Bankston most days, throwing knives and betting on just about anything. One day, Pa sent me to the blacksmith to get a horse fitted with new shoes. I walked the horse down the dirt street to the corral next to the black smith shop.

Lester and his cronies started calling me hayseed, dirt farmer, shit shoveler, and names a man can't say out loud. The closer I came the louder he yelled, drawing people's attention. I knew there would be trouble when Lester hopped off an empty hog's head barrel and planted himself right in front of me.

"You gonna have to go around me, boy!" He looked around and laughed with his friends.

I waited with the reins in one hand, a fist drawn up with the other.

"You gonna move me, sistuh boy? Try it, and I'll beat your ass to a pulp, bitchy boy!"

His friends howled like mongrel dogs. People in stores and shops moved our way.

I didn't move. It was like first year of school all over again at play time, except we weren't children anymore. "You will try."

Lester, loud and boisterous, yelled, "But I'm bigger'n you!"

I sighed, knowing he'd probably whip me. But I was resigned to the fact if he did, he would leave with a bad limp. I spoke that day with the calmness of the dawn but with the strength and fire of the rising sun.

"Yeah, that's what the giant said to young David. Difference is, I ain't gonna use no rock and no sling shot, neither."

Lester looked like a man who just stepped on a timber rattler. I stood still. He fidgeted around and looked at his friends who were dumbstruck. There was something in his eyes I'd not seen before.

Uncertainty.

Then fear. Uncertainty because he realized his world just changed. Fear because he realized this wasn't the school yard anymore. That day he understood that bigger might not always win. And he wasn't willing to chance it. I'd grown since he'd seen me last. He cursed and kicked dirt on my shoes, but everyone knew Lester's day was over.

Ma said these troubles come because I am too different from most folks. "Lummy, there's people that just don't want people livin' peaceful in this world, so they get them in on the violence by startin' it. Instigatin', it's all about instigatin'. Riling people up for no good reason except for the joy of seein' them fight. Don't believe the Good Lord is happy with that. Blessed are the peacemakers, for they shall be called sons of God."

In my mind I can see Ma speaking the words, but I say, "Yeah, ain't that the truth," out loud. The men standing out in this street just think I'm agreeing with the gray uniformed recruiter hoarse from yelling. Maybe he'll stop his squawking and let us go home.

I'm tired of the anger, tired of the fighting, exhausted with people who just do not want to get along. I want to be free of people who wake up grouchy in the morning, hold a grudge all day, and stay mad at anyone who don't do things their way. Some even lay down at night hoping to have a new problem to be upset about the next day. And if they don't have a problem, they create one because they don't know how to live without being torn up about something. I've had enough of defending my beliefs about my love for all people.

I just want peace, a simple life, and my wife, Susannah. I want to be a schoolmaster, teach kids the three R's but also some history, showing them how we can stop making the same mistakes. That, a modest cabin, a few acres for logging and hunting, a garden, a few cows, and lots of children, all under God as I have come to know Him. That's not too much to ask in this short life.

But this loudmouth joker won't leave it alone.

"That's right, let the Sergeant fight your battles, sistuh boy!"

The Sergeant shakes his head. That I can't let go by.

"You must be one a them niggah luvin', Yankee-minded bastards who want to free slaves and make them equal with us! I bet you got a pretty little dark thing you been tappin'!"

The Sergeant knows I have to take care of this or I'll be taunted from now on. He whispers, "Get him! I've got your back."

I march in a stride strengthened through years of pushing a plough. I tighten my shoulders and arms made strong clearing land with axe and crosscut saw. I set my gaze on the man wearing the Rebel cap.

One of his friends taps his shoulder, and he turns to meet me about the time I get within two arm's length. He rears back to swing, but he's too assured of himself. He's probably never fought anyone who could give him down the road. He meets that person today.

He swings wildly without using the power in his shoulders. I duck and slap his arm away with my left hand, and rather than hit him in the mouth to shut him up— which is what I want to do—I come underneath with my right fist under his rib cage and push up as hard as I can. The blow lifts him a foot and a half off the ground. The wind blasts out of his lungs, and he lands on his back, gasping for air.

"Nothin' else needs sayin'!"

The loudmouth can't speak. His friends make a move towards me, but men from Sikes town step in and beg the opportunity.

The Sergeant steps in. "All right, this fight's over! You men get to them tables, sign up, collect your bounty, and wait around for instructions." The sergeant winks and nods for me to follow. The men from Sikes town gather around me patting me on the back. Some whisper how their fathers having set their slaves free and others wish Winn Parish was a free state still loyal to the Union. I just stay quiet.

I'm not like the other men yelling, "To Hell with the Yanks!" I don't want to join up to be a soldier, knowing I may not make it back to the life I finally have a chance to live. And though I believe I need to do my part so I can get back home, I don't want to go. I just want it to be over. But I also know that if I don't join up, they'll come make me. And that would be worse.

Mr. Gilmore let me use his address for the recruiters like he did in the 1860 Census. It will make a better cover for his slave-freeing activities if he has a man associated with him fighting in the Confederate Army. After I sign the papers, the recruiter tells us the unit commander will be back in a couple months to gather up volunteers and that we should get our affairs in order. I know what that means—in case we don't come back.

Mr. Gilmore leads me behind the wagons. "I'll take care of Susannah. You get your carcass back home quick as you can."

He hands me a package wrapped in oil cloth, something heavy covered with leather. It's a pistol!

Not just any pistol. I mean *the* pistol! The new .44 caliber Colt Dragoon Rainy Mills said would be coming out soon I got chased by the coyotes.

"There's a leather holster with ammunition," he says.

"How'd you know I wanted this? When did you see Rainy?"

"Rainy sent it mail order saying he's sorry he never got back this way. His business has kept him tied up, but he wanted to keep his promise to you. Wouldn't even let me pay for it. Said he'd come see me about it after this fool war."

Mr. Gilmore kicks the dirt. "Anyway, I'm too old to join up unless they start conscriptin' men over fifty years. You'll need it, son, when the fighting gets too close. I've been in enough gamblin' scrapes to know you'll have a few hand to hand conflicts before you're through. Anyway, get on back here when this damn thing's over, Lummy Tullos, 'cause you got someone waitin' on you. And she's a helluva lot prettier'n me!" He chuckles. "Go practice and get real good with her."

"I don't rightly know what to say, Mistuh Gilmore. This here's too much. I know the price. These here go for at least a Double Eagle, and you're gonna need that twenty dollars. Besides, the stuff to go with it has got to be five dollars or more. I can never repay you."

"You're exactly right, son, you can't, and that's my blessin' to you. Susannah is so excited about your new life together but in pain at the same time about you joinin'. She'll survive and do well. I'll see to that, my son." He pops me on the shoulder. "And it ain't never been about repayin', boy. It's about an old man helpin' this ole world become a better place. I got it figured you and Miss Sweetie Pie over there'll pay me back just fine when I have a sack full of grandchildren crawlin' all over me!" He scratches his beard, straightens his ponytail, and wipes his eyes with his handkerchief.

"Never thought I'd live to be a grandpappy. Just wish my Nancy could be here to enjoy it." He pulls himself together and in typical Mr. Gilmore fashion, throws out his arms looking into the heavens and declares in perfect Shakespearean form. "I simply cannot wait to become a grandfather!"

He let his arms down slowly swooning like a man who just lost all of his energy, then peeks up from under his hat and grins, "So get your ass back here quick, Columbus Nathan Tullos, you hear?"

We laugh.

"Yassuh. I'm givin' Susannah my sign-up bounty. Please help her manage it, Mistuh Gilmore. She'll use it to help keep up your place too. I'll get thirteen dollars Confederate a month, so I'll send half to Susannah, keep a bit for my necessaries, and the rest to my mother."

"Sounds like a fine plan, son, but make sure you keep enough for your soldierin'. Sock your savin' money away somewhere safe so nobody steals it. These are hard times that can make the best of men lose their religion. A hungry man can lose his mind. A hungry wife can resort to things that later never need to be spoken of. I'm glad you're a savin' man. You did convert that paper money into gold and silver a while back like I advised you?"

I nod.

"Then let's you and me pick a place to bury what money we can, and it'll be our treasure for when you get back, what you say?"

We take our time traveling home. We stop at Shiloh Church.

"Now you and I both know that prayin' can be done anywhere, anytime we're willin', but we ought to bend our knees in the church house. That be all right?"

I nod.

After praying for bit, we ride away quietly. We find a suitable place for our treasure cache near the cold spring away from the house in the woods. We dig it three feet deep.

"That should do, Lummy, unless you got something else in mind." I do. I pick a very small arrow point out of the dirt pile. I wipe it off and hold it up for Mr. Gilmore to see. It's about a half inch long, red and brown in color.

Mr. Gilmore admires the workmanship. "Bird point, and a fine one. Amazing, the skill those people had."

"Mistuh Gilmore, I always felt that if you take a gift then you ought to give one back."

"Good, that's what the ancients did." I pull an Indian head cent from my pocket that I've saved because it's dated 1859. Call it my good luck penny or a reminder of the year this entire adventure began. Doesn't matter. I want it be a prayer of blessing that the Lord will return me to this place so we all can all dig up this treasure together.

I throw the penny into the pit.

"Buryin' good things hopin' for better times ahead."

We slowly lower the box we built from bald cypress lined with several layers of oil cloth to keep the moisture out. It fits nicely into the hole. We cover our secret with cypress boards and pine straw, then dirt. I wander down a deer path and sit on an oak stump to gather my resolve before I tell Susannah I signed up today. Susannah cries, but I tell her that this far into the war, it will go better if I enlist than be forced to join up.

"Word is, President Davis will issue a Conscription Act sometime in April to draft men ages eighteen to thirty-five. No sign up bounty is paid if a man is conscripted, and we need the money." She shakes her head, not wanting to hear it. I tell her about burying the money.

"We ain't got no need for no money if you're dead, Lummy! I don't want you to go. I won't make it without you!" I just hold her.

Susannah begs and pleads, but when she understands my decision is final, she stays away until dark. I give her time. Heck, I don't understand all this myself, how could she? By supper time, she realizes the longer she avoids me the less time we'll have together before I leave. She finally says she understands and will pray to Jesus every day that He brings her man back home.

Susannah puts her arms around me and kisses me on the back of the neck. "It'll be all right, my darlin'. Please write your Ma before you leave." I kiss her soft lips. I thank the Lord for a woman as sweet and thoughtful as Ma. But Susannah will be the best mother ever lived.

I pray, "Lord, give us that chance, please."

Winnfield Looseana New Years Day, 1862

Dearest Ma, thank you for the letter you sent awhile back. I'm glad you're doin well. I miss my brothers. I pray for my brother George and the 15th Missip. I hope Amariah, Jasper, and James are all right. I have some good news Ma and something for you to pray about. I married the sweetist girl in Winn Parish. You'll love her just like you do Jasper's wife Isabella. I hope they're doing well and Amariah and Amanda too. How does it feel Ma to have so many grown boys with wives? I know you're just itching for grandchildren! They'll come in time. I also need to tell you that I joined the army and will soon go to training camp. Say extra prayers for me Ma. I need them with leaving my new bride. Ben and Dorcas and the kids are all doin fine. Ben still ain't right about Pa passing. Like Granny used to say, some things don't get fixed this side of heaven. Tell all I miss and love them. I love you Ma, and Susannah says she looks forward to seeing you one day.

You're affectionate son, Lummy Tullos

CHAPTER 24

OLD BATTLES
NEVER END

FEBRUARY 16, 1862

The richest man ain't the one who has the most
but the one who needs the least.

I'M RECRUITED. YEP, I signed up to do my part to end this endless war. Susannah cried and cried, but I told her it couldn't go on forever. But I don't believe my own words. Since I answered the call back New Year's Day, the war has sucked the life out of everyone's ability to do business. There's hardly two bits to be earned in Winn Parish these days. Fortunately, for people who can live off the land, we get by, and trade for what we need. But my decision to join up ain't just about money. And even though it ain't just about money, there's little to be had. Money is just a necessary evil if you ask me.

Mr. Gilmore has been kind to let Susannah and me stay on, even though his gambling funds and farm income dried up. He secretly set his slaves free one night, telling everyone they escaped.

"Must've headed east to find the Union Army," he lies.

Rather, a righteous deception.

Actually, they went north to Kansas by way of the Indian Territory. Mr. Gilmore has his own battles to fight, not only the possibility of losing his farm, but also the skepticism surrounding the mysterious escape of his slaves. Old Bart and a few of the older freedmen stay behind.

Old Bart and I take a wagon into town for the last time to get supplies before I leave for the Army. I'm assigned to the newly formed Winn Rebels. Some of those boys have visited the store, and I've helped out on their farms during harvest. Everybody helps everybody get crops in. It doesn't take so long when we work together and much less is wasted. I like farm folk—salt of the earth people willing to give the shirts off their backs without question to anyone in need. Now the best of them are willing to give more than that. I'm glad I come from the same good stock.

After Bart and I finish loading the wagon, we put the mule team away and leave the wagon alongside Mr. Wiley's place. Bart offers to take care of the mules so I can visit Mr. Wiley. I bound up onto his porch and bang on the door like I'm the sheriff. The door squeaks ever so slowly, and a small voice crackles.

"Get on in here, Lummy, ain't seen you in a coon's age. Glad to see you, son. I ain't feelin' too spry right now, like I been jerked through a knothole backwards." It's chilly with a good breeze kicking up. I get in fast and stoke up the fire.

"What's wrong, Mistuh Wiley? You ain't hurt yourself, have you?"

"I gots the pneumonia. Hurts bad deep in my chest. I'm havin' a tough time breathin.' Better tell Ole Bart to get on in here, or he'll catch it, too. A cold man is a cold man no matter what his skin color, I say." I appreciate that about Mr. Wiley. I slip out the door, and Old Bart grins, stomping his feet to stay warm.

"We're stayin' over night, ain't we, Massuh Lummy?"

"Yep, if that's all right with you. A cloud's comin' up, and we don't want to get caught sideways in no swole up creek with sleet peckin' on us. Come on in, you know you're welcome under this man's roof."

"Surely is the truth! Thank kind Massuh Wiley for the invitation, but I gots family stayin' not too far from here. They ain't blood, but I call 'em kin. I'd like to stay with them if you don't mind. Don't get to see 'em very often."

I half-yell over the growing wind, "You don't need my permission, Bart, you know that. Have a good time but don't eat too much corn pone and taters. We'll leave out early mornin'."

"Yassuh! I'll be ready."

"Let's get that wagon tarp strapped down!"

Bart pulls close his coat and pulls down his hat. "I gots it, you go on in inside. Massuh Wiley don't sound so good. See you in the mawnin'!"

I scoop up an armload of firewood and get inside before the heat escapes. Mr. Wiley lays on his bed muttering something about the Mexican War. I stoke the flames higher and look for something to eat. The cupboards are as scarce as hen's teeth.

"When's the last time you ate good, Mistuh Wiley?"

"Couple of days ago."

I poke around, but there's nothing but a few dried out cornbread crusts. "You lay right here. I'll be back faster'n an owl on a mouse."

I make Mr. Davis's store just before closing. "Mistuh Wiley ain't doin' so good. Believes he's got pneumonia. You got anythin' for that?"

"I told that danged old coot to see the doctor when he came through last week, but he said all doctors are ignert asses, good only for pokin', proddin', and cuttin' off things. Guess he saw too much of that in the war. I couldn't convince him. I know you love that old man, but you want the truth?"

I'm sure I don't.

"He's just tired. Tired of the endless aches from his head wound, tired of living off the dust of other people's boots they call a pension, and he's just tired of this ole world. He loves the Lord and believes in heaven. Take him this elixir. It's the one he likes. Mostly alcohol I'm guessin', but it'll make 'em sleep. Take this ham, these taters and beans, this sack of cornmeal and fix him a fine meal, Lummy."

I start to pull out my money.

"Nawsuh, Lummy, this one's on me. The least I can do to help an old soldier fight old battles that never end." I turn to leave. "Hold up, take this sack a lemon drops. Put about half of them in a jar with the moonshine I know he's got layin' around somewhere. Crush 'em up, and they'll melt about the time he starts the coughs tonight."

My eyes tear up. "And the rest of them lemon drops?"

"Just let him eat them. They're his favorite. Come back if you need more."

I sit down at the end of the porch and cry. There's still kindness in this world. I hurry over to Mr. Wiley's, get inside, and stoke up the fire again. I start supper, and Mr. Wiley stirs a bit. He'd fallen asleep while I was at the store.

"What's that smellin' so good, Momma?" He shakes his head and laughs, "Damn, Lummy, now I'm callin' out for my Momma. Dreamin' I guess. What's on the stove, son?"

"We got us a skillet of fried taters, good brown beans with a big ole chunk of ham, and hot water corn pone golden brown. Compliments of Mistuh Davis."

"Well I be a suck-egg mule! I never knowed you to be a cook. Hell you never done it whilst you lived here. Where'd you learn all that?"

"Well, Mistuh Wiley, it's like this. First, you always did the cookin' when I stayed here. So why mess up a good thing? Heck, you wouldn't let me try it no ways, bein' ornery as a boar coon knocked out of a tree havin' to be in charge all the time."

Mr. Wiley slaps the air with his hand. "Ain't so, but if I could reach you, I'd pop you a good'n, you know that!"

We laugh. Mr. Wiley drops his head. "He's a good ole soul, that Mistuh Davis. Never treated me no ways but fair. God bless his work to make an old man happy."

After supper, I give Mr. Wiley a couple spoonfuls of elixir and some lemon drops. His eyes light up when they touch his tongue,

"Ummm, makes me all warm inside."

He drifts off to sleep.

I sit in his rocking chair watching the fire. He coughs lightly, which reminds me to find his moonshine and make cough medicine with the lemon drops. I crush them into a fine powder so they melt faster and settle back down in the rocking chair with a blanket around me. I shake the jar from time to time when the yellow flakes settle at the bottom.

"Off to war. Me, Lummy Tullos—who hates fightin', hates anger, hates greed, and hates humans treatin' other humans poorly. I wish Susannah and me could find a place where they would accept her and me bein' married. Maybe out west somewhere." I'm talking out loud again. I catch the whites of Mr. Wiley's eyes out of the corner of mine. I don't want to look.

"It's all right, son, I ain't God, and I sure as hell ain't your judge and jury. I guessed it right you was sweet on that Susannah girl not long after you got here, singin' that *Oh! Susanna* song all the time. I saw her when Gilmore brought her through town the first time. Wasn't long before you showed up lookin' like you been rode hard and put up wet. She's a pretty thing, that's for dang sure. I'm glad I got to see you marry her and pray over you. Don't worry about nothin'. I figure we're all kin goin' back to Moses, I mean Noah, but for sure Adam and Eve in the Garden." He coughs. I give him a couple spoonfuls of the lemon drop cough medicine. It helps.

"Naw, can't say a blamed thing about that myself. I never told you I was in love there for a bit, did I? Yep, a sweet little Mexically gal I met down around Mattymoros across the river in Mexico. Dang, she was a pretty thing too. I wanted to marry her, but it didn't work out." A tear rolls down his cheek.

"Her folks weren't too happy about us Americans killin' their people, so she was forbidden to see me. She sneaked out one night to wade the river near Fort Texas when her brother started draggin' her back. Shots rang out from our side, two sentries thinkin' it was trouble. She caught one in the back. She didn't know what hit her." We sit in silence.

"We was goin' to the priest the next mawnin' to get hitched. My commander gave me three days leave to consepshumate the union. That the right word? Hell, don't matter, you know what I mean. And the dang misery of it all? I was up for a discharge on account of my head wound. I wanted to bring her back here and have a sackful of little ones on a farm." He tries to hide the tears.

"I never wanted much. I figured it out early that the richest man ain't the one who gots the most but the one who needs the least. What a damn shame." I give him another lemon drop.

"So I ain't got nary an issue with your marryin' a black woman. Doin' such might just get us all back together like we started and stop the hatin' and killin' in this ole world." I nod. "Never told you about my long walk down south, did I?"

"No, but I want you to."

He straightens up on his bed, and I position his pillow so he can sit up. He breathes hard with a rattle. I heard that sound just before my Granny died.

"Ole President Polk had his eye on the disputed area down south long before he took the oath March of '45. Claimed it was God's will that these

United States expand, something about manifest destiny or some kind of horse shit like that, sayin' God ordered him to take the Mex's land. Anyway, he sent General Zach Taylor south to Corpus Christi. I went along for the adventure of it all. I had nothin' else goin' on. Regular pay with a pension later on sounded pretty good." He hacks a short cough. I give him another spoon of the cough medicine.

"After about six or seven months, we marched south to the Rio Grande, that's Big River in Spanish to you Missip' boys." He chokes and coughs. I hand him a wash rag.

"No, no, I'm all right. Where was I? Oh, yeah. We got to the river, about three thousand of us. I overheard Lieutenant Grant say, 'We've been sent here to provoke a fight.' Wasn't hard to figure that out. We were a fine-lookin' army ready for a brawl, all dressed in our fancy uniforms. Some men were still pretty mad about losing family at the Alamo and Goliad. We were itchin' for a fight." I pour myself a tin cup of coffee and sprinkle in a little sugar.

"It took us twenty days to get there, trampin' through two hundred miles of hot sandy desert full of thorns and big rattlers, some over six foot long. That cordgrass down there was near tall as us and so tough it poked through our shirts. What's worse, the dang Mex's set the grass on fire to keep us back. Didn't slow us up none though, 'cause Ole Zach Taylor came to fight. We immediately hoisted up the flag lettin' them know we came to take what we believed God had promised us, like Israelites takin' Canaan land.

"The Mex's didn't take to that very well. The Mex General demanded we take down the flag, which we didn't do. He ordered us to leave, which we didn't do. We built a defense called Fort Texas. Then the Mexicans brought up their best, General Arista, who actually spoke pretty good English somebody said. It was on then.

"We skirmished, and a few of our men got killed. Made us all madder'n ole wet hens. It got our dander up, and General Taylor made a plan. Most of us got to stretch our legs marchin' over to the coast to fetch some newly arrived supplies. When we got down the road towards Port Isabel, we heard thunder of big guns. The Mex army attacked Fort Texas. I figured too that ole Zach's plan to march to the coast was to sucker the Mex army out in the open for a tussle.

"We got the supplies and some new recruits and quick stepped it back the twenty-six miles to Fort Texas. General Taylor himself led us, him bein' proud of his two thousand men. Boy, was it hot, even in early May. We came up on the Mex army near a place called Paller Alter—better said Pa-lo Al-to. Heh, never could get them Mex words right. They looked like they was headed to a parade. Prettiest army you ever saw. Made us look like amateurs."

I shift in my chair. "Pretty clothes don't make a man fight better."

"Damn straight, but they blocked the road and wouldn't budge. We all was a bit nervous, never havin' been in a fight like this before. They lined up straight and started playin' music! Ole Zach hollered, 'Y'all invitin' us to a dance?' They looked tough like they'd been in some nasty fights. I prayed I wouldn't run when the chargin' started.

"We was like two fightin' dogs sizin' each other up, held back only by the chains of our Generals. About two o'clock, we started movin' forward. We could hear General Arista callin' out 'liberty or death, long live the republic, long live Mexico.' He was either tryin' to scare or rile up his men for a fight. Probably both.

"We started at them slow but steady, and the Mex cannon opened up on us. Shocked the fire out a some of us. Some of the boys should've gone over the hill for their mornin' constitutional 'cause after that first shot they had to wear shit britches into battle. Good thing was, Mex artillery wasn't no good. Ours was, and that gave us the advantage.

"It had rained earlier that day, so the ground turned slippery as owlshit on smooth floor boards. We returned fire and moved quickly to change positions before the fixed Mex artillery could get a sight on us. Our boys just kept firin' and movin', slippin' and slidin' but blowin' big gaps in their lines with grape-shot from our cannons. It was an ugly sight. I felt sorry for them fellers, but we had our work to do. Our guns outfired their cannon five to one.

"Them damn Mex's made us mad. One of the boys picked up a spent Mex cannon ball, and it was made of copper. Now back in them days, everybody thought copper on the cannonballs was poison, so they was outlawed every-where. Gentleman's agreement I guess. But the Mex's used them, cannonball and grapeshot. So our men poured it on them harder with no mercy."

Mr. Wiley takes a deep breath. "Then sparks from our cannons started a grassfire that got out of control. We tried to put it out but finally just let it burn. For about an hour, thick smoke blocked our view. We fired away, not knowin' if we was hittin' anythin'. Some of the Mex wounded got burnt alive in that fire. No man ought to have to die that way or see a man die that way. The officers ordered us to stay put, so all we could do was watch." He hangs his head.

"I found out later one a them boys was my sweetheart's brother. But it weren't no turkey shoot. We formed a hollow square and held off the Mex cavalry pretty good. I ain't never seen anythin' like it. Heads taken off by cannonballs, horses mangled by muskets and still runnin' with blood spurtin' out everywhere. I hope you never have to witnesss all that.

"That's when I got mine. I was loadin' my musket near where Grant sat on his horse when a solid shot took my friend's head off. The same cannonball tore off part of Captain Page's jaw, and buzzed by my head like a big hornet leavin' this long crease. That's all I remember. I woke up the next day in a doctor's tent. Ole sawbones told me I could return to duty in a few days. I shook my head a few times, drank a cup of coffee, and wandered out to the battlefield." Mr. Wiley stares, as if seeing it all again but like it was the first time.

"There was dead Mexicans everywhere. Horses, too. We killed over two hundred of them. Ugly sight. Heads separated from bodies, bodies with no arms or legs, arms and legs scattered ever which away—o-o-o-ugh, get me that bucket over there, quick."

Mr. Wiley throws up his supper in about three good heaves. "Oh that hurts, Lummy. Hurts my soul more, though. I can still hear them Mex wounded, cryin' out for their *madres* and *esposas*. We felt sorry for them.

"Nobody won that day. Called it a draw. Nothin' was accomplished, except we took what rightfully belonged to the Mex government. And good men died, on both sides." I soak in the story, just letting Mr. Wiley have his thoughts. "I wish that dang ball had got me before I'd killed them Mexican boys. They haunt me nearly every night.

"Folk's around here'd shoot me if they heard what I say next, Lummy.

Truth is, I helped take the Mex's land away from them. Only fair the Yanks come take mine." His voice grows weak.

"Lummy, I know you want to enlist with the other men, and I'm proud you want to defend what's yours. But I want you to live and hope you don't get creased by no cannonball. Fetch my little chest hidden up under the table over there."

I pull out a small, handmade cypress box, dust it off, and hand it to Mr. Wiley. He opens it with the care of handling a newborn baby. He picks out a piece of metal, spits on it, and shines it on his shirt sleeve, then holds it up to the light.

"I want you to have this. It's all I got left from the war. Maybe it'll bring you good luck. The hat's long been done away with by my pet mice, but these crossed cannons went on the front of them muffin-top hats we wore. I've kept it all these years, don't know why, but take it. I don't expect I'll be around when you get back, son."

He places it in my hand and holds it there. "I know you'll probably have family get scattered all over this war, but consider one thing. We ain't got the stuffs to win a war like this, not down here in the South. Them damned ole Yanks got too much on us. I know you don't like how folks treats the darkies, keepin' them slaves and all. You take care of yourself and get on back to your wife, you hear?" I stare at the tarnished brass crossed cannons. Mr. Wiley breathes in deeply trying to get air into his lungs

"Let your true beliefs decide whose side you ought to fight on."

It wasn't the first time that thought had crossed my mind. It's tough to be a wise and young man in such troubled times.

"I know you made a promise." He rolls over and hacks out several coughs. He grabs his chest. "Oh, that hurt. I know you made a promise to the Winn Rebs, but that ain't forever. Just roll it around your gourd for a while."

He lies still, then struggles to lift his head. "Did I do all right, Lummy? Livin' life? I'm not sure. Lonely old grouchy cussin' teller of war stories? Should've had a sweet wife and kids. Fightin' and dyin' for country, is it really that important? What've I got to show for it? Crossed cannons from a hat I don't have no more. And them men who sent us down south and never saw a battle? They lovin' up on grandkids by now. Damn shame. Don't be afraid to ask yourself the tough questions, son.

"I'll pray the Good Lord to keep and guide you. How about another swig of that cough medicine, and maybe I'll rest." He takes a long deep rattling breath. He can't raise himself up on his own now, so I hold his head up to feed him the medicine. I give him as much as he wants.

"You're a good son, faithful as the sun comin' up in the mawnin'. Lummy, love you, boy." He dozes. I poke the fire, return to the rocking chair, and run my fingers over the shiny cannons.

This emblem was once part of the uniform that I'm now willin' to fight against. This world just don't make no sense.

I realize I'm talking out loud again, but Mr. Wiley snores softly. I relax and dream about building a house for Susannah. At least I think I'm dreaming. A big thump like setting a ridge pole for a new barn shocks me out of my doze.

Mr. Wiley coughed so hard, he flipped right off the bed. He's barely breathing when I get him back up on the goose feather mattress. He opens his eyes wide, like everything is all right.

"You're gonna make it, Lummy. Trust the Good Lord and keep your gourd down. Love you like a son." He hacks a couple of deep coughs. I turn to get the cough medicine. I fill the spoon and hear a deep sigh. Mr. Wiley breathes his last. I drop the spoon, and I cry. A long time.

THE SUN SHINES bright this morning, and it's like spring. Old Bart came back a little after dawn, and we get Mr. Wiley's body taken care of. I take anything of value to Mr. Davis to settle any unpaid bills Mr. Wiley might have had. I keep the crossed cannons in my pocket. They'll be with me now wherever I go in this war.

"Lummy, whatever's left, is yours. I got it here in writin' that you are to be the receiver of Mr. Wiley's estate when he passed. I appreciate you settling his affairs. Speaks well of him, and I'd expect no less from you. Far as me and Mistuh Wiley go, we're square. You're right as rain, Lummy Tullos, and that old man sure loved you, boy. Talked about you all the time."

"Yeah," I hang my head and paw the floor with my boot, "I sure thought a lot of that old man. Can we have his service pretty soon, say Sunday after preachin'? The dirt's soft enough to get him in the ground." I try my best not to sob.

"Let's see, it's Monday the sixteenth, so the circuit rider comin' is that young Cajun preacher you like. I'll let him know when he gets to town Saturday. He'll do it, but you'd do a better job. You knew Mistuh Wiley better'n anybody. Be better than a speech poured out of a tin can."

I've never thought about talking at a funeral. "Let me think on it a day before we speak of it?"

"Sure thing. Oh, and by the way, Mistuh Wiley's place is yours, too. What you want to do with it, goin' off to the war?" I've never been a property owner before. Going to war and not getting paid very much, it'll be difficult to keep things up.

"Who handles deeds and such around here?"

"That'd be me, at your service, son."

"Can you draw up some legal papers that'll hold up in court?"

"You got lot's on your mind, so let's just get this one thing off it." Mr. Davis pulls out blank sheets of paper. "How you want this to go, Lummy?"

I scratch my head. "I want the property put in me and Susannah's names, with Ben and Dorcas as beneficiaries. That the right word?" Mr. Davis nods. "I don't want no disputin' ownership about it goin' to Susannah if somethin' happens to me. And the same for Ben. I want you, if you're willin', Mistuh Davis, to rent out the buildin's. Somebody'll want a place in town to live, and you get twenty-five percent of the rent for your trouble."

"Nawsuh, Lummy, these are hard times."

"My mind's made up. You're the most honest man I've ever known."

"Thank you." He puts pen back to paper. "And the rest?"

"Fifty percent of the rent goes to Mr. Gilmore for takin' care of Susannah after taxes taken out first. Don't want no government takin' it away over a few dollars. We'll want it after this commotion is over with."

"It's a good plan, Lummy. You're changin' the world for good, makin' it better. It'll be between us." Mr. Gilmore will make sure the bigger part of the rent gets to Susannah.

"Give what's left to Ben and Dorcas. That's a lot of splittin' of what might not be worth much, but everyone stands to get a little help from this deal."

"You're too kind. I'll have these papers drawn up by Sunday so you can sign them after the funeral." He turns. "Hold it a minute. I got somethin' for you."

Mrs. Davis brings out a box. "This is for you. Ain't much, but we wanted to give you somethin' useful for where you're goin'."

It's a brand new pair of boots, better than I've ever had. I hug them both. I shake Mr. Davis's hand and kiss Mrs. Davis on the cheek. They fit perfectly. I don't know what to say.

As I leave the Feed and Seed with my new boots, I find the crossed cannon emblem in my pocket. With my other hand, I touch the alligator tooth hanging around my neck. Three charms to protect me. Three men and a woman I admire much.

I'm happy Mr. Wiley gave me the cannon emblem. I'm happier he called me son, though.

I walk back into the store.

"Mistuh Davis, I'll be doin' that funeral."

CHAPTER 25

AN OLD SOLDIER GONE HOME

FEBRUARY 23, 1862

Don't be so busy doin' everythin' right
that you miss doin' the right things.

SUNDAY COMES TOO soon. I stand before a crowd of two hundred people come to pay their respects to Mr. Wiley. Someone lays an old flag on his box, and the ladies have flowers scattered across it. It's the flag Mr. Wiley served under in Mexico.

The flag of the United States. Not of the divided ones.

All week I struggled what to say. I talked it over with Mr. Gilmore who offered, "You can never go wrong with Psalm number Twenty-Three." I trust the Good Lord to provide words as He has many times before. Today, Sunday, February 23, 1862, a date inscribed on my soul for a long time. Today I help an old soldier go home.

Two sisters sing *Rock of Ages*. A tear drops from my eye, but this is not the time. I ask Mr. Gilmore to read the Twenty-Third Psalm, and Mr. Davis to say a prayer. Mr. Davis put Ben in charge of the pallbearers and makes sure Old Bart is one of the six. I haven't talked to Ben yet and really don't want to right now. Dorcas made a fine soft pillow to put under Mr. Wiley's head. He's dressed in his clean but ragged Mexican War uniform.

The song ends, and the pallbearers lay the top on the casket. I step up in the back of a wagon to speak out over the crowd. People whisper, wondering who I am.

I search the crowd hoping to see Susannah. I find her smiling face in the back where the Negroes stand in the shade of a big oak. I need to see her.

That woman gives me me strength with just a look. I couldn't do this without her. I raise my hand, and the crowd grows silent.

"It is good we gather to honor an old soldier gone home. I'm Lummy Tullos, friend of Mistuh Wiley's. Thank you for comin' today. Let's give a moment of silence for the departed, to say a prayer for him, but also for the livin' here today."

I start with Revelation chapters four and five. I describe the throne scene with all the lights and beautiful colors, the elders bowing, the lightning and rumbles of thunder, the strange creatures, the seven lamps of the spirit of God, and the crystal sea. I tell of the little slaughtered, bloody, crippled, slain lamb, Jesus, standing at the center of the throne, the only one worthy to open the seals to the future. I get caught up in it, as does the crowd, and for just a moment, we're transported into that scene.

"Beautiful, indescribable, amazing, I want to go there now," are the whispers in the crowd that bring me back down out of the clouds to finish the task before me. The comments aren't for me. They come for what people see in their minds and what lies deep within every human soul—the desire for Heaven. I'm sure it looks different for every person. But it gives hope in the midst of uncertainty—hope as more seals of our future are opened.

I don't carry on preaching Mr. Wiley into Heaven like some preachers. I make clear that going to church and presenting a perfect image is not God's only way. I preach on how kindness kills the enemy, not the endless chatter of wagging tongues.

"Always look for the best in people. It's God's way of usin' us to help others become more like Him." I rail on for nearly thirty minutes. I want it all out of my system, and heck, they ain't going nowhere anyway.

"Mistuh Wiley cussed a bit, drank a little shine, and didn't make it to church very often, but he loved people. When I came to Winnfield, led by the Lord I believe, the first person I met was Mistuh Wiley. That was before I knew my family lived in Winn Parish. When I sat down to supper with him that first night, he set a big bowl of stew before me with a chunk of cornpone, a tall jar of sweet milk, and even a towel to wipe my mouth." I steady myself for the tears try to take over.

"Mistuh Wiley looked me in the eye, grabbed my hands across his little table, and asked, 'You a prayin' man, Lummy Tullos? I figure you're a prayin' man, talkin' about the Lord like he's standin' right here with us. Why don't you thank the Good Lord for the vittles.'

"We bowed our heads but before praying, I asked, 'Mistuh Wiley, you don't know me from nobody. Why are you bein' so kind to me, a stranger?'

"He rarely smiled, except with his eyes. 'I watched you walk into town today. You said you doin' your best to walk with the Lord. I believed you. So you were Jesus, and I invited you in.'"

Mr. Davis yells from the back of the crowd, "And Lummy wasn't the first stranger Mistuh Wiley took in. I seen him do that more times than I can count, includin' me many years ago!" The three little old ladies who'd gossiped about Mr. Wiley start bawling. Guilt does that to a person.

I straighten up my shoulders.

"Folks, somethin' my dear old Granny Thankful back in Choctaw County, Missip, used to say fits right here. 'Don't be so busy doin' everythin' right that you miss doin' the right things.'" I just let that one hang for a moment, until one by one, men and women start saying, "Amen. That's right. Say it straight, Lummy. Don't leave no stone unturned, brother. I needed to hear that!" It's like I'm preaching at a brush arbor meeting.

Funny, I don't feel like no preacher.

"But if Mistuh Wiley was here today, knowin' what he knows right now, seein' what he sees, right now in the unseen world, I believe he'd say, be what Jesus came to show us. Be a good and true human bein'. Treat folks right, like you want be treated. Be kind to everyone. Care for those that ain't got nothin', love your family, help out a stranger, talk to your Creator like He's right here with you, 'cause He is. Spend time alone with Him, the One who knows you the best and loves you the most. I know that's what he'd say 'cause that's what he talked about those many nights I stayed in his home, eatin' his famous Cajun muskrat stew."

I look up at the sky. "Mistuh Wiley, excuse me buttin' in on your praisin' time, but it took this Missip boy some time gettin' used to eatin' muskrat, even if all they eats is grass and bugs!"

The crowd laughs. I wave my hand that I'm done. "Let me leave you with this. The resurrection is true, and where Mistuh Wiley is right now, we all want to be someday. Let the church say...."

The whole crowd says, "Amen." The two sisters start up *Amazing Grace,* and the crowd joins in. I sit down on the wagon, sweating and exhausted. I never knew preaching could be so tiresome. I soak up the words of the song. I soak up the moment as good memories with Mr. Wiley flood my mind. 1st Sergeant George Kelly respectfully asks if he can take the stump before the crowd disperses.

After a word of respect for Mr. Wiley, he raises his voice. "I believe this is an appropriate time to announce this message to the newly-formed Winn Rebels, as we honor of this beloved old soldier."

I'm a little embarrassed at Sergeant Kelly's fine command of the English language. He reads an order from our newly appointed Captain Stovall that all men now recruited for military service with Confederate States of America—notably the Winn Rebels—will march from Winnfield this coming Saturday to catch the train for Desoto on the river across from Vicksburg.

Captain Stovall takes the stand. "Blessin's on the dearly departed and on you his loved ones. My first order to you brave fightin' men is be up and ready to march early mornin' March first. Strap on your walkin' boots, it's over forty miles to catch a rail car at Ruston. But you men all look to be fine young bucks ready to do your duty for God, your loved ones, and the Southern Cause!" A cheer goes up from the crowd.

I stand over Mr. Wiley's casket remembering what he said about the futility of war. But I like Sergeant Kelly, and Captain Stovall, too. Sergeant Kelly will train us and walk every mile with us. His professionalism gives me a sense of security that he might just know what he's doing, even though he's not much older than me. Some of the boys look at each other like they have doubts this educated gentleman can lead them. It gives me relief.

Another cheer goes up for the Confederate States of America, and some-one starts a song I've never heard before called *The Bonnie Blue Flag.* When it comes to the part *We are a band of brothers,* the Winn Rebels gather shoulder to shoulder to sing it proudly. These are the men I'll be with every day, fight alongside, and maybe even die with. They look different now.

"Mind if say a few more things, Preacher?"

I've never been called that before, but I am the preacher for a day. "Sure thing, Sergeant Kelly."

I find Susannah and Mr. Gilmore in the crowd smiling at me. The circuit rider preacher gives me a nod of well done. The men sing loud, and the man on my right gives me a friendly push with his shoulder.

"Hey, Reb. I'm J.A. Killingsworth. Seen you at the Feed 'n Seed a few times. You're Lummy, ain't you? Looks like we're in this thing now for sure. Tell you what, I'm lookin' for probably the same thing as you."

"What's that?"

"Why, good friends who'll watch my back and vicey-versy, right?" J.A. sticks out his hand, and I take it.

"You're right. I'm Lummy Tullos. Glad to know you." He's right, and even though I mostly stay to myself, I know that if anyone is going to get through this thing, it'll only be together. A loner probably won't make it in this war.

Sergeant Kelly waves for us to pipe down. "Take a moment, get to know the men around you."

We shake hands, introduce ourselves, and from what part of the parish we hail.

Sergeant Kelly yells above the chatter. "So just to let you know I'm one of you, this is how it's goin' to be with your newfound fellow soldiers. You gonna eat with them, sleep with them, drill with them, even bathe in the creek with them!"

The crowd roars in laughter and people shout, "He is one of us! Can't lose with a man who knows his letters and knows his musket!"

The Sergeant holds up his hands. "And you gonna kick some blue belly hind end fightin' alongside them." The crowd roars again in laughter but then falls silent. Mothers, fathers, husbands, wives, and children act as if they've been struck by lightning.

The truth is, some of these men won't come home. A hush blankets the crowd like a man just sentenced to hang.

Sergeant Kelly throws up both his arms. "So, let's hear it for the Winn Rebels from Winn Parish *Loooooooseaner!*" The crowd slowly comes back, and someone starts the song again.

J.A. leans over, "Well, them damn Yanks sure gonna get a killin's worth out a me!" He shoves my shoulder again, "Get it? My name is Killingsworth."

I grin. It hits me that none of us, not even the Sergeant, have any notion of what we just signed up for. All the hurrahs and dreams of glory will fade pretty quickly when the shooting starts.

"J.A., what's that song they singin'?"

"And you from Missip? Heck, that song was writ by some feller named McCarthy and sung first in Jackson City right after Missip seceded from the Union. He named the song after the first flag of the Republic of Mississippi, well, an unofficial standard until they decided on somethin' else. They started with a white flag with a palm tree, but they kept a blue patch and that single star in the left hand corner at the top. Read it in the papers. Saw a picture of both of 'em. I wonder what our flag will look like. Anyway, it's a good song and the most popular around. Heck, how is it you ain't never heard of it?"

The crowd of yelling men boast what they will do to the Yankees when we meet them in battle. In the midst of all the shouting and whooping it up, I remember Mr. Wiley's Mexican War stories of killing and death. I retreat into myself, and the sounds about me fade.

The sky turns dark, and the faces of so many young boys, so many older brothers and uncles, so many young fathers and their sons, so many middle-aged men heavy with a sense of duty flood my mind. Men standing right here, right now. Each takes a different shape. No longer are they men yelling and raising their arms, giving hurrahs for the bonnie blue flag.

No, just scores of little slaughtered, bloody, crippled, slain lambs standing on a nameless battlefield far from here. They say nothing, just still with dark hollow eyes staring, wounds gaping, limbs missing, some thin and frail from hunger. They just stand there. No whooping it now. No boasting of glorious deeds. Only soft baa-ing like lost sheep calling for their shepherd.

J.A. punches me lightly. "Boy, where'd you just go? Best come on back, there's food laid out, and we need to eat it!"

I nod for him to go ahead. My mind goes back to what I'm being shown.

Are these men the lambs that will have to be slain? Will they give all so others might be saved? Do they know what they've gotten themselves into? Will they stand in the presence of the Almighty and be worthy in the after-life? Will they receive glory? Their hollow eyes stare at me, wishing to be somewhere else.

Mr. Wiley with blood on his head where the cannonball creased him speaks, and though I can't hear him, his lips keep repeating over and over.

"Don't go, Lummy. Don't go!"

Someone grabs my arm, and the vision disappears. It's Mr. Gilmore. "We best be gettin' on home before they start a battle right here in Winnfield." Susannah waits in the wagon.

Eight days. Not much time with Susannah before heading off to New Orleans to enlist. I look back at all those men as we leave town. Will I be one of those hollow-eyed sacrificial lambs?

CHAPTER 26

OFF TO ENLIST

MARCH 1, 1862

Like little painted toy lead soldiers,
we march into the melting pot, one by one.

SUSANNAH IS BESIDE herself these last few days. She wants to run and scream, but that surely won't do. But talk about something that wouldn't do if people found we are married! There's just too many Reb sympathizers to announce the biggest news in my life. As my Granny Thankful used to say, "Them folks might have themselves a conniption fit!"

I witnessed a couple of those fits and asked Granny Thankful once, "Them folks have fever with them fits or what?" They have some sort of illness to get all torn up about things that ain't any of their business. Granny Thankful would say, "Some folk's business just got to be other people's business 'cause they just got too much time on their hands!"

We Winn Rebel boys will soon be somewhere down close to New Orleans by week's end drilling and marching. I still believe I made the best decision to join up rather than wait to get drafted. The boys who make it home from the battles tell us it's better to enlist. Men made to go to war and don't want to fight don't make the best soldiers. Some of the boys with legs or arms missing spit at the word "conscripted." I put together what gear I can carry in a pack along with the Colt Dragoon Mr. Gilmore gave me and ride to town.

I didn't think Susannah would ever let me leave, clutching and hanging on me like a scared kitten. It hurts like hell to walk away. Susannah knows what it's like to get torn away from family and friends, being a former slave.

But I also know the other side of it, tearing myself away from home troubles and the loss of when Susannah was taken by Mr. Gilmore. That change in life surely proved to be God's doing. I believe firmly that my small part in this big ole damn war will make a difference someway, somehow.

I kiss her long and hard, squeezing her as tight as a man can without breaking something. The Good Book is right. When you find the one called Eve, there ain't two anymore, just one. It's breaking me half in two walking away. I'm tired of walking away. I pry myself from Susannah's arms. Mr. Gilmore holds her from chasing me down the road. Old Bart rides along so he can bring the mules back.

The wagon trail from Mr. Gilmore's seems longer than ever, and my heart takes one heavy step at a time. My mule keeps looking back at me like he knows something is wrong. Old Bart looks straight ahead. This is too hard. My heart is stretched as far as it can without breaking.

Ma told me once, "When a body has to leave, and it hurts the heart somethin' fierce, then you know your time has been good." I never understood that until now. But I don't want a memory, I want to go back. To Susannah.

I have to prepare my soul for this war. There will be jackasses of the two-legged sort and "Lesters" I'll meet. I must prepare my heart for loss of friends and brothers when the fighting starts. I'll have to reach deep down to survive this. I have too much good waiting on me here in Winn Parish not to survive. As long as I have Susannah with me.

Cheering and guns firing grow louder as we cross the Dudgemona River. The small square in Winnfield is bustling with noise and excitement. Flags flap in the breeze as women hug and kiss their husbands and sweethearts. Mothers wipe away tears. A pistol shot goes off, and a chorus of *The Bonnie Blue Flag* starts up as we enter town. A small band with a flute and harmonica, a banjo with a guitar play the music. The music is bad, but nobody cares.

I tie my mule to the hitching post in front of the Feed and Seed and walk over to the men near a wagon where Sarge looks over some papers.

Old Bart tips his hat. "I'll be right here, Massuh Lummy, 'til you have to go."

Winn Rebels is the name our Captain decided for us. It fits—*Winn* for home and family and *Rebels* for refusing the Yankee oppressor. Though we don't have fine uniforms or any soldierly equipment, the scene reminds me of when we all went out to see the 34th and 62nd Regiments of the Mississippi State Militia parade in Greensboro back in '46.

Those men got called up with our own 2nd Regiment to go after Santa Anna down in Mexico soon after. Word came later that many of those boys never made it to Mexico. They died from disease in New Orleans. Those men went off to take the Mexican's land. Now the bluecoat comes for ours. I block that out of my mind for now.

Sarge shouts, *"Fall in!"*

Boy, do we look a sight. I bet we're the raggediest bunch of men ever to sign up to go to war. We poke each other like schoolboys, excited as a bunch of rabbit dogs let out of the pen just before a chase. I love rabbit hunting with dogs, hearing those short legged beagles strike and a big old swamper high-tailing it through the briers and cypress knees. As we wait for Sarge to speak, I think about that to keep my mind off Susannah. It was always so exciting! So is heading to the river landing at Desoto. Only difference is, this ain't no rabbit hunt... unless we're the rabbits, that is.

My pack is filled with all sorts of gifts from the girls in town. They gathered together at a local eatery and made a party out of cooking up foods and sweets. I add that to what Susannah prepared so I should be good on food for a while. I rearrange the stuff in my pack as someone walks up behind me.

"Lummy." Mr. Gilmore straightens my jacket and hat like other fathers do to their sons. He grabs my shoulders and shakes me like he's testing my balance. I stand strong. "You ready, son?"

A tear drips on his jacket.

"As much as a soul can be, suh." I give him a strong handshake and pull him close for a shoulder hug. "You're the best man I know, Mistuh James T. Gilmore. I will be back." I pull the big pistol out of my pack. He hands me sack of extra ammunition. Then we march.

I whisper a short prayer. "Lord, bring me back in one piece, please."

We march and yell about how we're going to save the South from northern aggression.

We're a raggedy bunch made up of timber cutters, cotton pickers, pig farmers, hayseeds, town merchants, a doctor, and even an accountant. I look back just in time to see Susannah poke her pretty head around a tree and wave. She smiles, but her tears overpower her, and she falls to the ground, weeping uncontrollably. Mr. Gilmore lifts her up. And we march around the bend out of sight of the small town I've come to know as home.

We leave Winnfield behind at a good pace. It's a forty mile walk to Ruston where we'll catch the eastbound train to Desoto. Down those same tracks I once outran a pack of coyotes.

There ain't no outrunnin' all this, boy.

"Hey, Lummy? Remember me, J.A. Killingsworth? Met you at Mistuh Wiley's funeral, and a damn good job that you did there, Preacher!" Talking out loud again and paying the price of speaking my private thoughts.

I play it off, "Naw, just hope they gots some smart Generals runnin' this thing!" I lean close, "Don't call me preacher. It's not a nickname I want to carry through this thing, all right?"

A corporal walks alongside us. "Shut up, privates, and you ain't even that yet. Keep your face forward, your feet movin, and forty mile'll go by quick. But not without a blister or two!"

"All right, but you're a sight more inspirin' than that, corporal!"

We make the rail tracks in just under two and a half days. Not bad for a bunch of swamp runners and hill folk who never marched in formation before. The woodcutter at the tracks tells us the train won't come through for another day. It gives us time to tend to our blisters and cook food. Sergeant Kelly is right. There ain't nothing here but a small line man's shack, a water tower, and a wood bin for the locomotive.

We make camp alongside the tracks, finding the flattest places to throw down our bedrolls. We break out sweets, smoked meats, and biscuits our womenfolk packed for us. We put it all together and share the feast, like a "Last Supper" before we sample the wonderful army food everyone talks about. We haven't heard much except that it's bad and never enough.

We build fires and settle in on the south side of the track to stave off the cold north breeze. Morning will come soon enough, and I'll catch my first train ride. My blanket is just warm enough to keep me from shivering. It's been three years since I crossed the Mississippi on the ferry. My shoulder ain't been right since.

The night passes fitfully for most—some afraid, some unsure, and some so ready to fight they start trouble with their comrades. Sarge puts a stop to that.

This morning brings sunny warmth with smells of coffee and food cooked over a campfire. A loud whistle blows long and loud as the train pulls in for water and fuel.

The woodman yells, "Twenty minutes before you board. Get your shit together and go whoop some Yankee ass!"

Sergeant Kelly steps up and clears his throat, "As this good man so eloquently informed you, break camp and be ready to board at my command! And another thing"— he went into his uneducated voice—"From now on, don't call me Mistuh Kelly, Sergeant Kelly, or daddy. You call me Sarge. It's short, it's really sweet, and it's what I want!"

In one voice we yell, *"Yassuh, Sarge!"*

Busy packing my gear, I don't hear Mr. Gilmore come up behind me. He lays his hand on my shoulder and asks the sergeant if he can borrow me for about ten minutes for some unfinished business. Sarge squint his eyes and releases me. Mr. Gilmore promises to have me back in just a few minutes ready to board the boxcar.

"There's somethin' you need to do for me before you leave." We round the line shack into the wood yard when from behind a big pile of logs, out steps Susannah. I can't believe it.

"I'll leave you two alone, but I'll be back to get you in five minutes," Mr. Gilmore smiles. I fall into her arms, and in this instant our souls mix without knowing whose is whose.

Susannah doesn't say much. She trembles and gives me the first of several letters she says I will receive from her. There's money inside.

"No, Susannah, everything is gonna be all right. Mistuh Gilmore and I both saved that money to take care of you and the farm. You do good with it and make it stretch. It'll help get us started when I get back."

"But you gonna need it where your goin', Lummy."

"Nope, the army will clothe and feed me and try to keep me healthy. This is our hope for a future together. It's all there in the box near the spring. Mistuh Gilmore will show you where."

"Just like a man who wants to take care of his sweetheart! But my sweet darlin', the love in our hearts for each other and the Good Lord is our hope for the future."

"You're always right, keepin' my mind on the right things, on the straight and narrow." I wipe her tears. I love that about her. She helps me stay the course. She knows about my anger, especially if anyone disrespects Old Bart or makes a catty remark about her. Good thing about that, Mr. Gilmore will have none of it. He even shoos away good business to stand up for his principles.

He occasionally curses them under his breath. "Bastards don't know a human bein' when they see one! Must be tough to recognize another human if you ain't one your own damn self." He'd shrug his shoulders, ask for forgiveness, and get back to his work.

Mr. Gilmore whispers, "Time to go."

I kiss Susannah one last time, holding her close as if to never let go. I pry myself away with the help of Mr. Gilmore's big but gentle hands. As he shakes my hand, he slips me twenty dollars Confederate.

"Your gonna need this for letters and postage. Take note that when you get a letter from Susannah, it'll be addressed from me. That'll at least keep down suspicion. You don't need that kinda trouble where your goin'. Too many boys goin' with you know who she is."

Like a little boy, I hug the man who has become a father to me. He's taught me a more perfect way of life, one of peace and loving kindness I've not experienced before.

"It'll be all right, son. You'll make it back, and Susannah will be waitin' for you right here. I promise. You do your duty, keep your head down, dodge them bullets, and be constantly in prayer. Remember this, God's got something for you to do. So stay alive. Know that the same sun and moon you look up at is the same Susannah looks up at, too. You pray, I mean it, 'cause the Good Lord listens to a righteous man. Be that righteous man. You can't never go wrong doin' right. Do right by God, 'cause He'll always do right by you."

He walks me to the tracks where J.A. yells, "Come on, Lummy, you're holdin' up the train! You don't want miss this ride! It's a long walk to where we're a'goin'!" They pull me up into the boxcar. I grab the door. Susannah waves from behind a stack of molasses barrels.

As they shut the door, Mr. Gilmore yells out, "Stay strong, my son!"

I'll hold that line in my heart. Mr. Gilmore has been good to me. Better than I deserve.

It's like Pa said once, "You never know what a small gesture of civility will do to change the course of a man's life." Mr. Gilmore changed mine. Now I have to focus on living and thriving, not just surviving. I have hope. I've got too much to get back home to not to take care of myself.

As we sail down the tracks, the rhythm of the clickety-clack lulls me off to another place. I think about that small farm I want one day, my wife Susannah, and the children we'll have together. I whisper, "Will I have it Lord, someday?"

J.A. yells over the sound of the train, "Who you talkin' to, boy? You goin' crazy on us already? We ain't even seen the elephant yet."

"It ain't never crazy to talk to the Lord, J.A."

"Sorry, didn't know you was speakin' to the Good Lord."

"It's hard to leave wonderin' if I'll come back alive from this war. You're right, we got to stick together like biscuits and gravy."

He pops me on the shoulder. "Then we'll just have to whoop them Yanks quick so you can get on with your dreams, my friend." J.A. is becoming a good friend. He loves Louisiana, the Cause, and the good meals his wife cooks for him. He claims his sweet wife can make the best deluxe fried chicken dinner in three parishes. Won't be much of that where we're going. But, he's the man I want next to me when the fighting starts.

It's quiet now in the packed car. Everyone's trying to be considerate of the other's space. We all decide we can take a rest if we all sit down together. It works with everyone leaning on each other. Some of the boys in this very car won't get back home to sweethearts and family. But if we're going to make it, it'll be leaning on each other.

It's like Mr. Wiley said the night he died. "Never was about takin' the

Mex's land. Wasn't about gettin' paid either. It wasn't about glory for the man called a private, and that's what most of you boys will be. Naw, it ain't about none of that. It's about the man next to you. If you're clear about takin' care of him, and him you, then you just might come back like I did. And we had some hellacious fights down south."

I figure we're in for some hellacious fights where we're going, and I want to get back home. Friendships will matter. Putting up with each other will make the difference. Taking up the slack for each other will keep us sane. Having each other's back will save our lives. Showing mercy will see us through.

A warm presence covers me as I sit on the floor of this boxcar. I will make it back. I feel it in my soul. I don't know how. And still do my duty, wherever that leads me.

ANTHONY WOOD grew up in historic Natchez, Mississippi, fueling a life-long love of history. Not long after high school, he lived and worked in Alaska for several years. He returned to the South and ministered for nearly three decades among the poor, homeless, and incarcerated. Leading an effort that planted five urban churches inspired him to co-author *Up Close and Personal: Embracing the Poor* about his work in Memphis, Tennessee. He also authored a number of articles and stories about innercity ministry.

Anthony is a member of Turner's Battery, a Civil War re-enactment group, the Civil War Roundtable of Arkansas, the Oghma Creative Media board, and serves as secretary for White County Creative Writers' group. His short stories and poetry have won awards and have been published in *Saddlebag Dispatches, The Vault of Terror,* and *The Avocet: A Journal of Nature Poetry.*

When not writing, Anthony enjoys roaming and researching historical sites, camping and kayaking on the Mississippi River, and being with family. Anthony and his wife, Lisa, live in North Little Rock, Arkansas.

CPSIA information can be obtained
at www.ICGtesting.com
Printed in the USA
BVHW031412170521
607542BV00007B/990

9 781633 736672